They were some distance away,
but close enough to see Molly in her
state of undress locked in Kane's
arms, dripping wet in the
middle of the creek.

Molly closed her eyes.

Kane swore an oath.

He thought fast. "Listen, Molly. I'll make you a bargain.
I'll help you find your brother and you help me ease my
grandfather's mind. We'll get married—temporarily."

Molly blinked, then her eyes grew wide. "Temporarily?"

"I'll explain later. Right now, your reputation is at stake.
Mrs. Rose won't keep this quiet."

Riding in her buggy, Mrs. Rose approached swiftly with the
Sheriff on horseback alongside of her.

Dumbfounded, Molly asked, "Mrs. Rose won't keep what
quiet?"

Kane shook his head and pointed at her attire, or rather lack
of attire. "This looks bad for you, Molly. We're both nearly
naked. I doubt they're thinking we're out here for
an innocent swim."

* * *

Renegade Wife
Harlequin® Historical #789—February 2006

Renegade Wife

CHARLENE SANDS

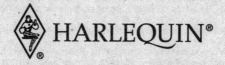

HARLEQUIN®

TORONTO • NEW YORK • LONDON
AMSTERDAM • PARIS • SYDNEY • HAMBURG
STOCKHOLM • ATHENS • TOKYO • MILAN • MADRID
PRAGUE • WARSAW • BUDAPEST • AUCKLAND

ISBN 0-373-29389-5

RENEGADE WIFE

Copyright © 2006 by Charlene Swink

Printed in U.S.A.

Available from Harlequin® Historical and
CHARLENE SANDS

Lily Gets Her Man #554
Chase Wheeler's Woman #610
The Law and Kate Malone #646
Winning Jenna's Heart #662
The Courting of Widow Shaw #710
Renegade Wife #789

Other works include:

Silhouette Desire®

The Heart of a Cowboy #1488
Expecting the Cowboy's Baby #1522
Like Lightning #1668

**DON'T MISS THESE OTHER
NOVELS AVAILABLE NOW:**

#787 THE BRIDE SHIP
Deborah Hale

#788 THE WAGERING WIDOW
Diane Gaston

#790 A VERY UNUSUAL GOVERNESS
Sylvia Andrew

Please address questions and book requests to:
Harlequin Reader Service
U.S.: 3010 Walden Ave., P.O. Box 1325, Buffalo, NY 14269
Canadian: P.O. Box 609, Fort Erie, Ont. L2A 5X3

To my cousin Maria Celeste, whose courage and strong spirit has been a great source of inspiration to me. They don't come any better!

And in loving memory of my wonderful mother, Caroline. You're always with me, Mom.

Special heartfelt thanks to my editor on this project, Melissa Endlich, for helping make this book the best it can be. It's a pleasure working with you!

Chapter One

Bountiful, Texas
1878

Molly McGuire stood at the Bountiful train depot, her Irish ire no longer tempered by womanly grace, then paced the plank sidewalk, waiting. She'd endured the long arduous trip from St. Louis, riding in a crowded, dusty railcar, her hopes for the future mingling with a heavy dose of uncertainty.

She closed her eyes, briefly sending up a silent prayer that she wasn't making a mistake in coming here. Yet, what other option had she? She'd pondered long enough trying to find a way west to keep the promise she'd made on Mama's deathbed. Now, she was here, awaiting a man who hadn't the decency to meet her properly or timely—a man who would claim her as his bride.

A bead of perspiration fell from Molly's unruly auburn hair, the shade from under the depot roof doing little to stifle the sweltering Texas heat. Molly removed her gloves and her emerald-green traveling jacket, and reached up to lift the feathered plume hat from her head. She tossed them onto a nearby bench seat next to her valise and continued her pacing. Shielding her eyes from the bright sun, she squinted southward toward a town seemingly robust with people, who were milling about and conducting business, as well as exchanging pleasantries on the street. That and the heavy summer air were reminiscent of St. Louis yet that's where the similarities seemed to end.

She'd gathered from her correspondence with one Kane Jackson, her betrothed, that Bountiful was a wealthy ranching town—a land rich with prime grazing land and thousands of Longhorn cattle, a special breed that Molly had read about in one of Charlie's dime novels.

She smiled sadly, thinking about her brother and his escapades. Charlie had always been a dreamer, a boy inclined to put his head in the clouds, always thinking lofty thoughts. He'd run away from home to find grand adventure out West, to make his fortune to send back home, but this last escapade had nearly broken Mama's heart.

Molly had come all this way, to marry, yes, but also to find her wayward brother. She'd promised Mama. And herself. No one had heard from Charlie in months. No telling what sort of trouble her sixteen-year-old brother might have found. Molly would do whatever it took to find Charlie. He was the only family Molly had left.

"Miss, would you like me to escort you to the boardinghouse?"

Molly whirled around. The depot operator smiled, an

apologetic expression on his face. She glanced at a tar-
nished wall clock just above the depot's front door.
Heavens, she'd been waiting for more than two hours.
"Oh, um, no, thank you." It wouldn't do to vent her anger at the friendly depot operator. Molly would save that
for the man who'd left her stranded on the outskirts of
town for most of the afternoon.

She grabbed her jacket and gloves, then plunked her
hat atop her head. The feather swooped down to tickle
her nose. With one swift move, she tugged the annoy-
ing feather aside, then lifted her valise and mustered as
much dignity as one could in this situation. "Do you
know where Mr. Kane Jackson lives?"

The depot operator blinked then scrubbed the back
of his neck as if it pained him. "Mr. Kane Jackson,
miss?"

"Yes, he was to meet me here."

"Well, uh, he lives north of here. The Jackson spread
is the biggest in these parts. About ten miles out, I'd say."

Molly realized it was far too late in the afternoon to
hire a driver and a buggy. She heaved a sigh and nodded, "Thank you."

"Wait, uh, miss?"

She peered into the man's light brown eyes. "Yes?"

"Maybe it's a good thing he didn't show. If you
don't mind me saying, Kane Jackson ain't exactly a
friendly sort."

Molly's insides churned. Butterflies gripped tight
and fluttered wildly. She didn't know much about Kane
Jackson, but he'd agreed to her terms and that's all that
had mattered. From her understanding there weren't
too many mail-order brides who could dictate *any*

terms—usually the ladies were the ones making all the compromises. She'd found a man who would help her in her search for her brother. She'd gained passage West. Molly had considered herself fortunate in that regard. But she hadn't gotten the impression from his letters that he wasn't a decent, honorable man. In truth, she'd been looking forward to meeting him, hoping for a future with both a husband and brother by her side.

"I'm not here for friendship—" she said, glancing at the name badge pinned to his chest "—Mr. Whitley. I plan to marry him."

The man's face contorted and his eyebrows shot straight up.

Molly didn't want to think about his reaction. She had a brother to find, with or without Kane Jackson's assistance. And for the moment anyway, it appeared that she was on her own.

She turned toward town and began walking, the butterflies in her belly doing a lively Irish jig.

Kane Jackson reigned in his mare and glanced around the train depot. The place looked deserted, as if no business had been conducted today. If only that were true. But damn it, Kane knew without a doubt that the train had come in early this afternoon, most likely right on schedule. As he'd ridden off the ranch, he'd seen the Southern Pacific head north on its way toward Fort Worth, laying tracks past the Bar J, leaving behind a thick puff of steam.

As well as one young unmarried female.

His mail-order bride.

Kane swore up and down, just thinking about the

trick his grandfather had just pulled. This morning, Bennett Jackson announced that Kane's "bride" would be arriving in Bountiful. Without qualm or warning, the ailing man had just laid that bit of news on Kane as if he'd been speaking about the weather.

His grandfather had sent for a bride from the East without his knowledge. He'd penned a letter in Kane's name and offered her marriage. His grandfather had probably been planning this since the moment Kane stepped foot back onto Jackson land, six months ago. It was clear now in the face of Bennett Jackson's secret maneuver that Kane hadn't yet earned his grandfather's trust. The elder Jackson wanted to see him settled, married with a wagonload of children running about, before he died. "A woman will steady you," he'd said. According to his grandfather this Molly McGuire would make a fine wife and provide an heir for the Bar J Ranch. Beyond just about anything else, Bennett Jackson wanted his legacy to live on.

Hell, Kane wanted a wife like he wanted a Texas-size hole in his boot. He'd had a wife once. And her death had cost him his soul, the ache of her loss gouging out his heart. He'd been left hollow inside, vowing never to marry again.

Nothing was going to change that.

But Bennett Jackson knew a thing or two about sugarcoated blackmail. And he also knew when to play his ace card, leaving Kane no choice but to come into town to retrieve his "betrothed."

"Whitley," Kane called out, peering inside the darkened depot office. He pounded on the glass window. "*Whitley,* you in there?"

Elmer Whitley appeared through the doorway, a startled expression on his face. "I was just closing up." He stepped out and locked the depot door behind him. When he turned, Kane pushed the tintype of the mail-order bride under Whitley's nose.

"Have you seen this woman?"

Whitley straightened abruptly, glanced at the image then frowned with disapproval at Kane. "Yes, I've seen her. Miss Molly McGuire was here all right. Came all the way from St. Louis. She waited the afternoon…for you. She wouldn't accept a thing I offered, except a glass of water."

"Damn it!"

"I know. She weren't at all happy about being left here by herself, a pretty young woman like that."

Kane scowled at Whitley. He was half hoping the woman had changed her mind. He was half hoping she hadn't boarded the train in St. Louis in the first place. But she was here in Bountiful, at his grandfather's bidding. If Bennett Jackson were in better health and not recovering from a bout of pneumonia, Kane would have had his grandfather welcome the young woman to town. He would have let his grandfather explain his deceit and put Miss Molly McGuire right back on that train. But the older man was in no shape to travel and Kane wouldn't put another woman in jeopardy by leaving her stranded in an unfamiliar town. He'd done that once before and that woman, his wife, had met with an untimely death.

Kane had no choice but to find her.

"Did she say where she was going?"

Whitley shook his head. "Nope."

"But she took off toward town, right?"

Whitley shrugged.

"Well, did she or didn't she?"

Again, Whitley shrugged.

Kane took a step toward the man. He had a notion to grab Whitley by the scruff of his neck and shake the answers out of him. Six months ago, he would have done it with no regard or regret, but Kane saw the futility in that now. He knew he had a long road ahead of him, proving his worth to his grandfather.

But marrying Bennett Jackson's handpicked bride wasn't part of the plan. Kane wouldn't submit to his blackmail. Hell, he even felt a bit sorry for Miss McGuire. No doubt his grandfather had painted a rosy picture of the man she was to marry. No doubt, his grandfather had lured her with vivid descriptions of lawn parties, church socials and a home that needed a woman's touch.

No doubt, his grandfather had left out all of the unseemly details of Kane's disreputable past. He was twenty-six years old and had lived more lifetimes than most men he knew.

He wondered what his mail-order bride would think about their wedding nuptials if she knew the absolute truth about him.

I'm a mail-order bride without benefit of a groom, Molly thought grimly, as she marched into town. She'd come all this way to forge a new life for herself. She'd come all this way to meet a decent man, to perhaps find comfort and companionship within his arms. She'd come all this way with the promise of finding her brother. Instead, all she'd found was disappointment.

But Molly had no choice but to continue on with her quest. She strode into the center of town, plaguing her memory for one hint, one clue as to where Charlie might have gone. Those doggone dime novels came to mind. He was forever reading them, curled tight into bed, with the lamplight burning low so that Mama wouldn't catch on and holler for him to turn down the lamp and get to sleep. Those dime novels—outlaws, Indians, saloons and women.

Molly stopped abruptly and peered at the White Horn Saloon. Tinted windows displayed the finest liquor and pictures of bawdy half-dressed women. Oh, heavens.

Charlie would love this place.

Molly mustered her courage and stepped inside.

Her lungs filled instantly, the gasp coming rather unexpectedly as she glanced around. She'd never been so bold as to enter a saloon. The whole place stirred with commotion, a noisy boisterous room filled with smoke and laughter and music. Bright golden-flocked wallpaper decorated the walls along with signs depicting the different beverages served and a moose's head appeared to be coming straight out of the wall. Tiered chandeliers draped from the ceiling. She could only imagine how those dozens of candles illuminated the saloon at night.

No one seemed to notice Molly. Relieved, she approached the bar, hoping the barkeep would recognize Charlie. She set her valise down and dug into her reticule, coming up with a picture of her brother taken when he was twelve. It was the most recent image she had of him. She showed him the picture, explaining a bit about her search.

"No, sorry, miss. I haven't seen him," the barkeep offered, shaking his head.

Molly cast him a polite smile. It was too much to hope yet she'd had to try. "Thank you." She swept her gaze around the room. There must be fifty people crowded within these walls. Surely, someone here might have seen Charlie at one time. "Would you mind terribly if I asked some of your patrons?"

The barkeep pursed his lips and studied Molly. He leaned heavily on the mahogany bar top until his face came within inches from hers. "Wouldn't be wise, miss. Why don't you give over the picture and I'll see what I can do. You can wait outside."

"Oh, um." Molly glanced at Charlie's likeness. To leave the sole picture she had of her brother in the big beefy outstretched hand of the bartender prickled her skin. Why, one spill of whiskey could destroy the image permanently. "That's very kind of you, but I'll just wait by the door and ask as your guests are ready to leave."

The bartender shrugged. "Suit yourself, but you'll have to pay for any damages."

Molly blinked back her surprise. "Damages?"

But the barkeep had already turned his back and moved down to the far side of the bar to serve a handful of cowboys.

Befuddled by the barkeep's comment, Molly lifted her belongings and headed for the saloon door. She hadn't taken but three steps before she felt herself being twirled around. She stared into the chest of a lean, lanky cowboy. His hand, clamped firmly around her waist, tugged her closer. "Howdy, miss."

A smirk emerged through the man's whiskers as he flashed a set of small uneven teeth. Stale whiskey breath rushed out. "I'd be proud to buy you a drink."

Molly swatted at his hand and pulled back until she was free of his grasp. "No, thank you. I'm only here to look for—"

"Looking for a man, are ya? Well, ain't gonna find a better one than's right here in front of ya. How about that drink now?"

"I don't drink." Molly shuddered and turned to leave, heeding the barkeep's words. Perhaps this hadn't been one of her better ideas. But she found herself being drawn back with a sharp tug on her skirt.

"C'mon now, miss."

The persistent man's audacity enraged Molly. She swung around abruptly and cringed when she heard a definite rip in her skirt. She felt the tear go clear down her backside, more than she'd ever exposed to any man in her life. Molly gasped, crying out, "Look what you did!"

The cowboy chuckled. "Sorry." There was no true apology in his words. And now, Molly had caught the attention of many in the saloon. She felt their eyes upon her, heard their lurid whispers.

Her simmering anger boiled over. Molly had had one trying day, this being the last and final straw. She lifted her valise and landed a blow to the cowboy's midsection. Surprise registered on the man's scruffy face. Molly figured she'd stunned, more than hurt him.

"Hey!"

"Stay away from me." She grabbed her valise to her chest and bounded with full force out the saloon doors, ignoring the laughter that followed. Fury mingled with mortification as she forged ahead, right smack into the chest of yet another cowboy. He grabbed her shoulders. Molly shoved at him with all her might, unwilling to have a repeat of the saloon debacle. Were all the men in this town prone to manhandle women? She struggled fiercely. "Let me go," she said, just before she lost her balance as they cascaded down the steps. Both went tumbling to roll ungraciously into the dirt, the valise flying up and over her head.

The cowboy braced her fall and took the brunt of the impact on his back, while cushioning her in his arms. She lied atop him, the strength of his broad body protecting her from injury. For the briefest of moments, Molly relished the feel of him, holding her firm, but oh, so tenderly. She stared into his deep silver-gray eyes, noting the slight hint of concern. His hat had flown off in the fall, revealing raven-black hair, too long and unruly to be considered civilized. Within the seconds that ticked by, Molly took in his high cheekbones, sunbronzed skin and strong powerful jaw. A tingle of awareness, one completely female in nature, coursed through her veins. Molly's heart flipped over itself.

"Miss McGuire?"

Molly blinked at the deep resonating sound of the man's voice, and certain familiar words in the letter she'd kept close at hand fluttered into her mind. *Tall, not too unsightly, with gray eyes and dark hair. I hope you find my appearance adequate.*

Molly swallowed hard, realizing the description more than fit. She quickly hoisted herself off of him. She brushed at her skirt, too humiliated to even think about the gaping hole in her backside at the moment. She glared down at him as he lifted up on his elbows.

His dark gaze raked her over, one sweep like a lightning flash, assessing her unabashedly. Warmth spread throughout her body from that one quick look. She didn't know if she'd measured up or not, his expression giving nothing away. She stared back, out of curiosity now, gaining a full-length view from his position on the ground. He wore buckskin, pants tight enough for Molly to note his muscular legs and a shirt stretched across his chest pulled together by crisscrossing string. But it was the colorful beads circling his neck that told Molly there was something different about Kane Jackson, something that set him apart from other men. It had only taken one look for Molly to recognize that her betrothed wasn't like most men. Yet, Molly couldn't figure the why of it. She only knew it for fact. And to think, she'd been atop him in the middle of the street for all of Bountiful to see. Atop him and enjoying the comfort of his arms.

Molly admonished herself for such a notion, yet she couldn't deny that Kane Jackson was a fine-looking man. Long in body, but broad where a man should be broad. It didn't appear that Mr. Jackson had on ounce of softness anywhere.

She watched as he bounded up with the ease of a graceful animal and she immediately recognized that it was her own clumsiness, as well her state of agitation, that caused the fall moments ago. This was a man who held his ground.

He made his approach, towering over her by at least five inches and as he glimpsed her derriere, his lips twitched.

Molly's fury, the anger she'd saved for this one man, rushed back with full force. She wouldn't be standing on the street, with a torn skirt exposing her derriere, her belongings scattered about and her dignity in question if he'd been on time to greet her.

"Mr. Jackson," she said none too gently. "You're late."

Chapter Two

"Now, that's a real good observation." Kane lifted Molly's silly feathered hat from the ground and handed it to her. She swiped at it, her eyes sharp, filled with fire.

Kane frowned, releasing a heavy sigh. Molly McGuire was a pretty woman, petite and sweet-looking, with just the right amount of vinegar to keep a man's boots shined. She'd make someone a fine wife, to be certain. But she'd traveled all this way only to find great disappointment. Kane would blame his grandfather for that. And the sooner he explained to her that there would be no wedding, the better. "Fact is, ma'am, I didn't know you were coming until late this morning."

Molly's chest rose. Her cheeks grew pink. Kane knew women well and this one was no wilting flower. "I wrote you the date and time I was to arrive."

He shook his head. He had received no such information because it was his grandfather who had corresponded with this young lady, not Kane. "I got no such letter. But we'd best discuss this later, after you've had a meal and cleaned up some."

"I'd prefer to discuss it now."

"No."

"No?" Her green eyes gleamed with indignation. "You're refusing me an explanation?"

"That's right. For now."

Kane removed the bandana from his neck and reached around her backside, fitting the material over the tear in her gown. "Hold still," he said when she jumped back.

"What on earth are you doing?" she asked in a breathless whisper.

Kane had two choices. He could let the young woman walk down the street with her unmentionables showing, certain to entertain the townsfolk, or he could fix the problem. Other than sweeping her up into his arms and carrying her to Mrs. Rose's boardinghouse, he figured this was the next best solution.

"Saving your dignity, Molly," he whispered back. "Now, hold still." He faced her then reached around to fashion the material directly over the tear in her dress. As he came close to lean over her, he caught a whiff of gardenias, the subtle scent wafting up from Molly's throat. He savored the moment, the unmistakable scent reminding him of another time, a happier time, when he was just a boy, helping his mother tend her garden.

Kane splayed the bandana out fully, his hands wrapping around her and his fingers accidentally brushing the soft curve of one delicately rounded cheek. Molly sucked in her breath and Kane swore silently. He hadn't been this close to a woman in a long time, and he cursed himself for wanting to touch more of her. His fingers itched to stroke the other cheek, to feel her firm softness through the material of his solid red bandana.

Kane made quick work of tying her up front, twisting a knot at her waist, tugging a bit harder than he had intended. Her body came up hard against his, the silky material of her traveling suit not barrier enough to conceal the feel of her soft breasts crushing into his chest. Kane wrapped his arms around her—to steady her, he told himself.

Molly McGuire stared up at him, lifting her chin, giving him a full view of her face. Her eyes were large, almost too large for such a small face, and the exact color of a spring meadow as morning dew settles on wild grass. Kane glanced at her pert little nose, then at her cheeks, rosy pink in the fading sunlight, but it was her mouth that had caught his full attention. Soft and full, ripe for kissing, Kane thought grimly. Her lips parted slightly, as a quiet "Oh!" whispered out and Kane's mind wandered down a forbidden path. She felt good against him, damn good, and he thought of all the ways he could pleasure her, of all the ways she might pleasure him.

He bent his head, leaning down, beckoned by a flowery scent and a sweet mouth, but a quick sudden flash pushed through his thoughts. He saw another woman, one who'd been laughing and looking up at him the same way Molly McGuire looked at him now. Little Swan, his wife. He'd almost forgotten. He'd almost forgotten her love, and the trust she'd placed in him.

He'd almost forgotten that he'd been responsible for her death.

"No." Then Kane realized the shout burst forth only in his mind. He pulled away from the woman in his arms, the woman he wouldn't marry.

"There," he said aloud. "That should do it until we get to Mrs. Rose's."

Molly gulped air then repeated, "Mrs. Rose's?"

"The boardinghouse." Kane put his hand on Molly's back urging her forward. He noted all the questions in her eyes. Hell, Kane didn't have the answers she wanted.

All he had was the truth.

Molly sat on the bed in her room at the boarding-house, somewhat puzzled at Kane Jackson's odd behavior. Hours ago, he deposited her on the front steps of the place, introducing her to Mrs. Penelope Rose before taking off as if a pack of wild wolves were after him. Mrs. Rose had shown Molly to her room, giving her some of the history of Bountiful—a condensed version that Mrs. Rose promised to elaborate on later. The landlady left to make the evening meal after spinning Molly's head in ten different directions. Goodness, she hadn't known a woman could talk so much or so fast.

Molly sat on one end of the four-poster bed, wrapping her arms around the base and resting her head against the wood post. Her head ached terribly and if her curiosity hadn't been sparked, she would have given in to her exhaustion. But she'd agreed to see Kane later tonight. He'd said that they needed to talk. Molly assumed he wanted to go over the details of their marriage arrangement. Perhaps then, she could figure out a thing or two about the man she was to marry. He puzzled her. One instant Kane seemed cold and indifferent but then in the very next, why, she would have guessed from the look in his eyes that he'd meant to kiss her. Right there, in the middle of town.

Molly had the feeling that when Kane Jackson wanted something there was no stopping him. And that for one brief moment he'd wanted her.

Heavens, she remembered the way her heart had raced and her blood had warmed. She remembered how it felt to be held in his arms, the heat of his body against hers—comfort mixed with passion. But then, he'd stopped suddenly, denying them their first kiss, leaving Molly to wonder if he'd found her lacking in some way.

Perhaps, in all ways.

Molly sighed. This day had certainly not gone as planned.

She picked up a goose-feather pillow and hugged it to her chest, taking in the small but lovely comforts afforded her. Thankfully, the boardinghouse was civilized enough for an Easterner, with its polished oak and mahogany furniture, Chinese carpets, frilly lace curtains and copper tubs with built-in piping. The bathing room was something Molly thought hadn't quite reached western towns as yet, but she'd been pleasantly surprised. She'd soaked in a tub for the better part of an hour, rinsing her hair with provided lilac-scented soap and scrubbing daylong railroad grime from her body.

Feeling quite refreshed and invigorated, Molly had dressed in a cream blouse, a pale peach skirt and combed through her unruly mass of coppery hair, leaving it down to dry in curls.

Her thoughts turned to her brother. He'd left St. Louis to find his fortune out West, eager to pursue grand dreams of wealth and adventure. He'd promised to contact Mama once he got settled, but they'd never heard back from Charlie. He'd only written once from a small .

town in west Texas and after Mama died, Molly had nothing left for her in St. Louis. Her only family, her younger brother, had apparently moved to Texas. She intended to find him, with the help of her new husband.

"Miss McGuire. Miss McGuire." The loud knocking startled Molly from her musings. "Are you in there?"

"Yes, Mrs. Rose," she offered in a polite voice. Molly decided not to open the door for fear of Mrs. Rose talking her ear off. She wasn't up for the woman's eternal rambling. "Am I late for dinner?"

"Heavens, no, dear. You have a caller. Mr. Jackson is here to see you. I insisted that he stay downstairs. Now, if you don't want to see him, I'll just shoo him away. You know, you really shouldn't mix with the likes of him, if you don't mind me saying. He's not fit for a good decent woman. I don't care how much money his grandfather has, that man is nearly a savage. Why, he was abducted as a child and raised by Indians. Cheyenne. He even married a Cheyenne maiden."

Molly whipped the door open. She stared into Mrs. Rose's vibrant light brown eyes. "Married? Did you say he's married?"

Penelope Rose crossed her arms over her middle as if to settle into a long-winded discussion. "Yes, he *was* married. Lived with the Cheyenne all that time and married one of them."

"Where is she now?" Molly asked, quite perplexed. Of all the things she might have expected from Kane Jackson, his being already married certainly hadn't entered her mind.

"Dead. Some say Kane Jackson wouldn't rest until he caught and killed the man responsible. Took him five years, but he finally found the man. Shot him and nearly hung—"

"Molly, you almost ready?"

Kane appeared in the doorway, his presence looming over the slender Mrs. Rose. The older woman swiveled her head to peer up at Kane, then cringed with awareness that he'd heard every word. Mrs. Rose folded closed like a shrinking flower once the sunlight faded. Molly glanced from Mrs. Rose's tightly pinched face into Kane's cold, unyielding eyes.

"You don't have to go with him," Mrs. Rose whispered, giving Molly's hand a quick squeeze.

"Yes, yes I do. Mr. Jackson and I have things to discuss."

"But you haven't eaten, child." The woman's voice had come back full force.

"Dinner's waiting for us at the Bounty Café." Kane's sharp gaze fastened to hers, holding her mesmerized for a moment. "I'd like you to join me, Miss McGuire."

Molly started at those last words, spoken so softly that she had to blink back her surprise—her pleasant surprise.

"I'd love to," she blurted without hesitation. Kane's polite request had her forgetting about Mrs. Rose's warning. Good judgment should have had her fearing the man, but Molly didn't fear Kane Jackson. Secretly, she admitted that Kane's appearance here had helped her make that decision.

He had cleaned himself up. He wore a newer black hat, which he'd yanked from his head the moment his eyes had met hers, a fresh white shirt, string tie and dark trousers. He appeared a far cry from the rough and ready buckskin-clad Texan she'd met earlier in the day. The one she'd knocked to the ground.

"I'll be right down."

Kane gave a quick nod. "I'll wait outside."

Once Kane's footsteps died away, Mrs. Rose continued on, as if she just hadn't witnessed their encounter.

"I told him you were probably too tired, having come such a long way and all, but some men just won't take no for an answer. Some men are not considerate. Why, my first husband, dear Wally, he was as stubborn as a mule and twice as—"

"Excuse me, Mrs. Rose, but my mama always said it's not polite to keep a body waiting."

"Yes, but—"

"Thank you for your hospitality and good evening." Molly smiled and closed the door, shutting out Mrs. Rose's next bout of incessant babbling. She breathed a quiet sigh of relief when she heard Mrs. Rose finally relent and descend the stairs.

Molly glanced in the cheval mirror, giving her hair a bit of primping, before she straightened the creases from her skirt. She picked up her shawl and headed down the stairs. Dashing past the dining room in a flurry, she avoided Mrs. Rose and the other guests. Once she reached the front veranda, she found Mr. Jackson leaning against a post smoking a cheroot. He took one last long puff, then tossed it down and stomped it out with his boot heel. When he looked up, she caught a quick but brief grin. "Happy to get away from Mrs. Rose, I suppose."

"Why, Mr. Jackson, isn't that why you're out here as well?"

His lips twitched and that single gesture released a swarm of butterflies in her stomach. He put a hand to her back and guided her down the street. Molly remained silent until they reached the restaurant. At least Kane Jackson had some manners. He'd escorted her inside with all the attention one would bestow royalty. He urged her forward, past the other diners to a small private room at the back of the restaurant. The room wasn't lavishly decorated, but some effort had been made to make the room appealing. Bluebonnets filled a glass vase in the center of a table set for two. A lovely beige Irish-linen tablecloth added to the warmth in the room and matching lace curtains, parted slightly, covered the only window in the small area.

Just as he'd promised, a lavish meal awaited them when they arrived. Succulent roast steamed on the plate, enticing Molly with its flavorful aroma. Small potatoes crusted to a golden brown and an assortment of colorful vegetables completed the dish. Molly also noted a half-dozen honey biscuits sitting in a bowl and the mingling of all the luscious smells made her mouth water.

Kane pulled out her chair and she took a seat. "Hungry?"

It wasn't at all ladylike to admit such a thing. "Famished."

Kane took a seat across from her and smiled. The full-out flash of white perfect teeth lit his face and transformed the "savage" Mrs. Rose claimed him to be into a dashing rogue.

Molly wasn't sure which manner of man would prove more dangerous.

"You're honest," he said.

"I always try to be. And I want you to know I don't hold much to gossip. What Mrs. Rose said about you…" Molly hesitated when Kane arched one dark brow. She cleared her throat. "Until I hear directly from you, I won't put much stock into what was said."

Kane studied her, his smile gone. "That's what I want to talk to you about, Molly. After the meal. Eat up. I thought you said you were hungry."

Kane dove into his meal then, and Molly couldn't put off the delicious aromas any longer. She ate with as much gusto as the man sitting across the table from her, holding nothing back. Truly famished, Molly gobbled up every morsel, even the split peas, which Molly had vowed never to eat again. She'd eaten enough split pea soup to last a lifetime back in St. Louis, when Mama didn't have much else to put on the table.

For dessert, Molly ate warm pecan pie and she and Kane sipped coffee from lovely painted mugs. As the meal wound down, Molly wondered about Kane and all the warnings she'd heard. Mrs. Rose hadn't been the only one to discredit the man. She recalled that earlier today the depot operator hadn't had kind words for her betrothed as well.

Kane set his empty coffee mug down, braced his elbows on the table and leaned close. He spoke with slow clarity. "Everything Mrs. Rose said is true, Molly. I was raised by the Cheyenne. I spent most of my life with them."

Molly gazed into his telling eyes, his admission something Molly had already surmised. "You never mentioned that in your letters."

Kane rubbed his forehead. "And how many letters might that be?"

Molly hesitated, wondering about the man's memory. It wasn't all that long ago that they'd corresponded several times. "Over a period of five months you wrote me three times, then wired me once."

Kane stroked his jaw tentatively then shook his head. "Molly, I never sent you any letters. I'm afraid you entered into this bargain with my matchmaking grandfather. He saw fit to go behind my back to send away for a bride for me. I only found out this morning. I suppose he would have told me sooner, but my grandfather took ill a week ago. The pneumonia has kept him down for most of that time."

Molly gasped, her heart racing with dread. "Oh, dear."

"I have no intention of marrying you."

Shocked, Molly took a moment to gather her thoughts before responding. "But, I was under the impression you sent for a wife. I—I came all this way. I need a husband, Mr. Jackson. I, uh, I…have a contract."

"I didn't sign it. My grandfather did."

His *grandfather* had signed her contract? Molly's head pounded. His grandfather had duped both of them. She thought of all that she'd just lost in one quick fathomless second. She'd come to Bountiful to marry, to start a new life, perhaps to have a family of her own soon. She'd come with thoughts of having a mate, someone she could learn to love, someone that might just find a way to her heart. She'd come with thoughts of returning the kindness. And heaven knew that without a husband, she'd have no hope of finding Charlie. And she'd promised Mama she would. She'd vowed to find her brother at all costs.

She was nearly penniless. She'd traveled to west

Texas, a land so different than what she'd known and had no prospects now, no future.

Molly stared at the linen tablecloth, her mind muddled with confused thoughts. Simmering anger churned in her belly. Seems Kane Jackson did that so well—angered her. She hadn't a clue as to what to do. She hadn't a plan in mind. Nothing about this day had turned out as she'd hoped. "Why would he *do* that?"

"My grandfather usually gets what he wants. And he wants to see me married. He wants grandchildren. Plenty of them."

Kane stopped and his gaze raked her over, another quick, almost shocking perusal of her body. Heat rose up her neck from his blatant scrutiny. The thought of having Kane Jackson's babies, of lying with him in their marriage bed, of sharing tenderness and passion lodged a lump in her throat.

"He wants an heir for the Bar J and I'm his only hope."

Molly might have blushed full out but for the severity of the situation. She'd have to deal with her own delicate sensibilities later on. Right now, she had to know the truth. "It seems to me you might want the same, Mr. Jackson."

Kane shook his head. "I don't. It's hard for the old man to understand that."

Molly had a hard time understanding that as well. One day Kane would inherit the ranch. Wouldn't he want to pass down the legacy to his own children? "But why?"

Kane inhaled sharply, then leaned in so close that Molly could see the fan of long lashes shielding his dark eyes. "I'm not the marrying kind, Molly."

"But Mrs. Rose said that you had a wife once."

Kane's mouth tightened. His face turned hard like an immovable stone. He nodded and leaned back some, looking away. A moment passed, then he directed his gaze back to her, captivating her eyes with a dark solemn stare. "I lived on the Bar J with my parents as a young child. I have certain vague memories of my mother and father, but when I was five years old, I was abducted and held for ransom."

"How awful," Molly said, her voice an indelicate squeak.

Kane nodded, glancing away, clearly uncomfortable with the conversation.

"Kane?"

"It's not something I speak about, Molly."

"I have a right to know. I haven't heard much of the truth since your grandfather sent for me."

Kane studied her for a moment then let go a long, labored sigh. He began quietly, his voice distant, his eyes dark. "I'd been playing out by the creek and two men swooped me up. I recall crying and trying to run away. They tied me up, bound my mouth. I don't remember much after that. Just this year, when I returned to the Bar J, I learned that my father had agreed to meet the kidnappers with the cash, a large sum he carried in his saddlebags. But my father never made the destination. Some say he ran off with the money. Others say he'd planned the whole thing. And then there's the notion that he'd been ambushed, shot and killed while trying to get to me. No one really knows what happened. The kidnappers left me in the hills far north from here, up on a ridge that nearly reached the sky. At least that's what my childish mind recalled. I was left for dead."

Molly gasped in horror. "Oh, that's terrible."

"By the time the Cheyenne found me I had nearly frozen to death. I was so sick and starving that my bones nearly poked through my skin. They took me in, brought me to their camp and nursed me back to health. Once I had regained my strength, most of my memories had faded. I remember haunting dreams where my white mother would tuck me in at night, but in the morning, I couldn't see her face. Eventually, I forgot I ever lived in the white world. I became a true Cheyenne."

Kane took a breath, settling back in his chair as if he'd revealed enough to discourage her from marrying him. But he hadn't said anything shocking enough to do that. What he'd gone through hadn't been his fault. He'd been a child, a victim, stripped of his true identity, taken from his family and the only home he'd known. Her heart bled for that little boy, for the fear and uncertainty he must have experienced. Molly wanted to know more. She had every right to know the whole story. "And your wife," she ventured, "how did she die?"

Kane glared at her with fierceness in his eyes. "There was a small trading post near our encampment run by a local merchant named Samuel who had no problem dealing with Indians. Little Swan had rabbit pelts and beaded necklaces she couldn't wait to trade. She was excited and happy that day, wanting to make her trades early and come home. Usually we'd travel together to the trading post, but this day, she went alone." Kane tightened his lips, remembering the joy in her eyes, pleading with him to let her venture out alone. She promised to return early and with many surprises. Kane hadn't the wisdom to refuse her. He'd been negligent, too wrapped up in her joy to realize the danger. "She never made it to the trading post. She met up with a drifter who decided her life wasn't worth more than what he could steal from her. He robbed her, then…beat her."

Kane slammed his eyes shut for a moment. When he peered at Molly once again, he spoke with quiet deadly calm. "I left the tribe then and hunted the man down. It took years to find him. I'd searched the entire territory, hiring on at ranches along the way to earn my keep, until the day came when I would finally seek my revenge. Killing him filled my head and it's what drove me from day to day. It's all that I cared about. I'd made it my mission in life. I finally caught up with the murderer in a saloon in a dirt hole of a town about thirty miles east of here. I called him out. Of course, he denied everything, but I knew I had the right man. He wore one of Little Swan's beaded necklaces, the one she'd meant to trade that day. He pulled a gun, ready to shoot, but I was faster. I shot him right through the heart."

Molly took in a deep breath, visualizing Kane Jackson as a killer, but all she saw was a man who had sought justice for a terrible crime. As awful as the events were, Molly couldn't fault Kane for what he'd done.

"Barrel Flat's sheriff saw fit to arrest me for shooting one of their own. The trial was a joke and I was set to hang. Pretty much had the noose around my neck, when Bennett Jackson came to town. He'd heard about me, a white man who'd been raised by the Southern Cheyenne. He'd been searching for me, never gave up and it's a good thing he had solid hunches. He saved my life that day, paying off the crooked sheriff. We rode off together, back to the Bar J." Kane leaned back, as if a weight had been lifted from his shoulders. "I'm more Indian than white man, Molly. I'm a killer. I have no regrets. I'd do it all again if I had to. There isn't a decent female in the territory who would have me. I'm hardly the kind of man a woman like you would care to marry."

Molly stared into Kane's stony silver eyes, the rims outlined in black, as unusual a color as the man himself. She supposed any other woman would take off running in the opposite direction. She supposed she should be appalled at the man he'd become. She supposed no woman in her right mind would want to marry such a man.

Molly pursed her lips and smiled. "On the contrary, Mr. Jackson. You're absolutely perfect."

Chapter Three

"*Absolutely perfect*," Kane muttered, repeating Molly McGuire's declaration from earlier this evening. Kane slugged back a double shot of bourbon, the liquor sliding smoothly down his throat. He poured himself another from the polished walnut cabinet in the parlor at the Bar J, but then thought better of gulping down any more whiskey. He had to keep his head clear.

"*A bargain was made, Mr. Jackson.*" Molly's words vibrated in his head like the persistent wild howl of a coyote. "I marry you and you help me find my brother," she'd said.

Damn his grandfather for making any kind of bargain on his behalf. And now the stubborn woman was set to head off into the deepest parts of Texas to find her lost brother.

Kane swore silently. He'd offered her a train ride back to St. Louis. He'd offered her money as compensation. He'd offered her free room and board at Mrs. Rose's boardinghouse until she found suitable employment.

But he wouldn't offer her the one thing she wanted. Marriage.

Kane glared at the glass in his hand, tempted by all things unholy to imbibe, to get rip-roaring drunk and forget this day ever happened. He brought the glass to his lips then slammed it down hard on the table. Most of the bourbon sloshed out and a good measure of the amber liquid splashed him in the face.

He cursed again, swiping his cheeks with his shirt-sleeve. The woman was determined to find her brother. She'd come to Bountiful under the assumption that her new husband would help in the search. And if she didn't have help, she'd have to find her brother on her own. All of Kane's efforts to dissuade her went unheeded.

He supposed he admired her gumption. Kane under-stood something about a vow spoken. He understood how the need to honor a pledge could drive a person. Molly had promised her dying mother, as much as her-self. But he also knew that as sure as the sun kissed Molly's pretty coppery hair, she'd find a heap of trouble before she found her beloved brother Charlie.

Hell, on her first day in town, the woman had waltzed into the White Horn Saloon as if she were walking into Sunday services, without a thought to what she might en-counter. Kane couldn't fathom allowing another woman to head straight into danger. He'd allowed Little Swan to go to that trading post without him. He should have accompanied her. He should have protected her. He'd let his guard down, trusting the men at the trading post.

But he'd learned a bitter lesson. No man is to be trusted. He should have known. He'd been a fool. And Little Swan had paid the price.

Even his grandfather had duped him. He'd played his ace card, the old man smart enough to know that Kane wouldn't abandon a female in need.

But hell, he didn't have to marry her.

"Did you meet my new granddaughter?"

Kane turned abruptly to find his grandfather wrapped in a Cheyenne blanket, lowering himself down into the deep blue tufted sofa. The woven blanket had been a gift his grandfather had reluctantly accepted from the woman who had raised Kane as his own, the only mother Kane had really known, Singing Bird.

He watched as Bennett Jackson adjusted two round velvet pillows, making himself comfortable on the wide sofa. He looked frail; his smoky eyes red, his once-vital face pale and ashen. Kane was surprised he was still awake at this late hour.

"She thinks I'm perfect. A savage who knows the land. A ruthless killer who gets what he wants at all costs."

Bennett grunted. "She didn't say that."

"She damn well could have." Kane leaned against the fireplace mantel and faced his grandfather with anger. "You deliberately picked a woman I couldn't send home. You picked a woman who had other motives for marrying. She's determined to find her brother."

Bennett smiled, showing a brief glimpse of the strong imperative man he'd once been. Showing the side of him that brooked no arguments, the side that outmaneuvered his competitors at every turn. "The woman made demands. I liked that about her immediately. She's strong and—a woman who knows her heart. She'll keep you—"

"Steady?" Kane offered. After all, that's what his

grandfather wanted, a guarantee that his only heir wouldn't leave the ranch on a whim. He wanted insurance that his legacy would live on.

"Satisfied." Bennett's eyes gleamed for a moment and a faraway look stole over his face as if he were calling up his own heartfelt memories. He spoke softly, "A good woman can do that for a man. Molly McGuire will make a fine wife for you. She's pretty, too."

Yes, damn it. Molly was pretty—actually prettier than he'd expected with those fiery green eyes and that perfect-for-kissing mouth. Kane had felt a moment of lust earlier tonight, drawn in by soft lips and a curvy little body. "She'll make a fine wife—for some other man."

His grandfather's face set into a frown.

"I didn't send for her," Kane reminded him.

Bennett leaned back, his shoulders slumping against the expertly carved walnut backing of the sofa. So often Kane would glance about the elegantly decorated rooms, and wonder if he really belonged here. So often, he felt like an outsider. He'd lived with the Cheyenne on the plains a long time, then became a drifter, a man bent on revenge. The old man knew that. He knew Kane had a restless spirit.

"What of the brother she's searching for?" Bennett asked.

"She won't back down. She's hell-bent on finding him on her own. Nothing I could say would change her mind."

"Where is she now?"

"Mrs. Rose's boardinghouse."

Bennett's eyes softened. "How is Penelope Rose?"

Kane scoffed. "Same as always. She thinks I'm the devil."

"She's all talk, that woman. Feisty as hell, but a real sweet lady."

"She didn't have a kind word for you, either."

Bennett's smile vanished and he motioned for his walking stick. Kane strode across the room to hand it to him. The old man hoisted himself up and leaned on the cane. "What are you to do with Miss McGuire?"

Kane blinked. "Hell, I'm not doing anything with her. You brought her here. *You* reason with her."

Bennett began coughing violently. The deluge continued, sounding as if his chest were exploding. Kane poured him a glass of water, but he shoved it away, unable to swallow. He continued to cough, hunching over in his fit. The pneumonia seemed to be hanging on. Kane hadn't noted much improvement in these last few days. As crafty as the old man was, Kane had grown fond of him. He was family. He'd been the only one who hadn't given up on him. The only one who'd continually searched for him, the grandson who had been abducted twenty-odd years ago. "Grandfather, what can I do?"

He stopped coughing abruptly and peered deeply into Kane's eyes. Kane noted sharp lines drawing his grandfather's face down, the lifeless expression so unlike the formidable cattle baron Kane had come to know. And his coughing bout seemed to steal all his breath. His voice weak, he responded, "I'm not long for this earth, boy. Marry Molly McGuire, that's what you can do. Honor an old man's dying wish."

"Grandfather, you're not dying." The denial came quick and sure. Kane had just been reunited with his only kin for six short months. He couldn't abide losing him so soon.

Bennett leaned more heavily on his cane. "Doc Beckman seems to disagree. He meant to speak with you today."

"I'll check with him first thing in the morning."

"And Miss McGuire?" he asked.

Kane heaved a sigh. "Her, too."

Bennett exited the room. Kane watched him lumber up the stairs and enter his bedroom.

Kane owed that old man his life.

Maybe, just maybe, he owed him even more than that.

Early the next morning, Kane stood on the steps of the boardinghouse, facing Penelope Rose. With her brown eyebrows pulled together, her mouth pinched and her arms locked across her stomach, he wondered how on earth his grandfather deemed her a sweet lady. "I'm here to see Miss McGuire."

Mrs. Rose tapped her foot several times, eyeing him suspiciously as one would a wolf approaching a chicken coop. "Miss McGuire isn't here."

Kane's brows shot up. "What in hell…" He stopped abruptly, reigning in his temper. He'd never get any information from the woman if he weren't careful. "I mean to say, do you know where she is?"

Penelope Rose launched into a full-out tirade. "She barely ate her breakfast, then took off to search for her brother. I told her she shouldn't ought to go traipsing around town. Why, that pretty young thing doesn't have a notion about the pitfalls a woman might find. There are places a gal shouldn't go unescorted and places she shouldn't go at all. I warned her about the saloons and that randy young livery boy, Burt Baker. But did she listen? Miss McGuire has a spur in her…uh, well, she's set on finding her kin. Can't say as I blame her, but she's…"

Kane tipped his hat and backed down off the porch steps. "I'm obliged to you. Do you have any idea where she was headed?"

Mrs. Rose's face reddened like a ripe cherry pie. "Oh dear. I didn't think to warn her about Miss Tulip's house. You don't suppose she'd have gumption enough to head over there, do you? I mean if anyone's got to know about the comings and goings of young men, it's those…fallen flowers."

Kane held his tongue. Only Penelope Rose would call the town's prostitutes fallen flowers. "I'd best check it out."

The older woman followed him, making her way down the steps. "Maybe I should speak with the sheriff. Wouldn't want one of my boarders to meet with trouble."

Kane stopped her with a glare. "I won't let anything happen to Miss McGuire." The words rushed out of his mouth easily, but with firm resolve. Kane blinked and swore an oath silently. The truth was, he'd protect Molly with his life. He had nothing to do with her coming to Bountiful but now that she was here he held himself responsible for her safety. Foolishly letting his guard down had cost one woman her life. Kane wouldn't allow that to happen again.

Mrs. Rose's eyes went wide. "What are your intentions with that gal?"

"I have no intentions but to see her safe."

"Well then, off you go. Find her."

Kane turned to leave, then a thought struck. He faced Mrs. Rose again. "My grandfather sends his regards. He's taken ill, but I'm sure a visit from you might improve his spirits."

Penelope Rose's mouth dropped open. She stood there, speechless, a truly memorable sight in Kane's estimation. Not too much managed to quiet that woman.

He strode down the street wearing a crooked grin. Sometimes, being "the devil" had its just rewards.

Molly stood at the edge of town, summer heat beating down on her, creating beads of perspiration to pool in places she'd rather not think about. She'd shed her petticoats while dressing this morning, in favor of a lightweight cream skirt and white blouse. Of course, a lady had to wear at least one undergarment for decency's sake, but as her hair stuck to the sides of her neck and those pools of perspiration puddled up even more, Molly wished she hadn't decided to abide by propriety.

Seemed Texas and propriety didn't make a good fit.

She swiped at her brow, determined not to give in to her disappointment. She'd spent the last three hours marching into establishments, showing Charlie's picture in hopes of gathering some information. It would be too much to hope that Charlie actually lived in Bountiful somewhere but she had thought that perhaps someone might have seen him in his travels.

No one had. Not the surly Mr. Gruber, who ran the general store, or Mr. Wilcott the freight operator, who had been quite friendly but of no help. Burt Baker at the livery hadn't seen Charlie, either, although he'd made quick work in offering Molly his aid, in return for her favors. Molly hadn't an ounce of patience left so, unfortunately, the young man had gotten a heavy dose of her ill will along with a slap in the face, for good measure.

After approaching the barber, the café owner, the attorney at law and the newspaper journalist, Molly had almost exhausted all of her options. Almost.

There was still Miss Tulip's house.

She gazed out, sighting the house far off in the distance just beyond a sweeping meadow laden with wildflowers and wild grass alike. The meadow stood between Molly and that dot on the horizon. But though she'd been warned by more than a few townsfolk not to venture there, Molly knew she wouldn't rest until she'd inquired about her brother.

Her feet ached, her head pounded. She'd missed her noon meal and now her stomach grumbled. The dauntless Texas sun seemed to swoop down upon her like a bold eagle to suddenly sap her strength. Yet, she moved forward, spurred on by nothing more than stubborn will, keeping her head up and her eyes focused solely on the house. She found a narrow path that seemed to cut the meadow in half and followed it.

Molly had never met a prostitute before. She'd read about them once in a book not meant for a young girl, and what she'd read hadn't been at all pleasant. The tale was one of debacle, infamy and heartache. It didn't seem possible that anything that distasteful could possibly occur in that pretty house set in the boundaries of such a lovely meadow. Why, Miss Tulip's name alone lent itself to something of fanciful whimsy.

Molly continued on slowly as her legs grew weaker

and weaker. Her mouth parched, she wished she had
stopped at the café for a soda punch. Or better yet, she
wished that she wouldn't have had to search alone. If
things had gone as she'd been promised, as she was
rightfully due, she'd be readying to marry now and
Kane Jackson would be her husband.

Last night, he'd been willful and strong-minded in refusing to marry her. He had offered her every other
compensation for her trouble, except the one she really
wanted. He thought to frighten her with his tales of
hardship, to expose his past in hopes of shocking her
away. And she knew Kane Jackson didn't offer up that
information lightly. He was a man who held his privacy
to heart, certainly not inclined to share his thoughts and
feelings with anyone, much less a stranger, a woman
he'd only just met.

But Molly had known something of hardship herself,
having been abandoned by a selfish father, having lost
her mother at far too young an age and having been left
alone in a world of near poverty. Only her skill with needle and thread kept food on the table as Molly took in
sewing and mending. In those days just after Mama's
death, when loneliness and heartache lulled her into a
restless sleep, she often dreamed of having a family of
her own. Of marrying and having babies. Of having a
good decent man by her side, so that she could provide
a home for her brother as well. But last night, Kane
Jackson had whisked all of her dreams away.

"Keep going," Molly muttered as she placed one foot
in front of the other on the dry, dirt path leading straight
for Miss Tulip's house. The thought of a cool drink and
a spot of shade once she reached her destination gave

her a measure of hope. Certainly Miss Tulip would offer her some hospitality. Molly closed her eyes for a moment relishing that very thought and her lips curved up
in a smile.

But once Molly reopened her eyes, she froze instantly. Panic stopped her cold. And a high-pitched
shriek tumbled from her blistered mouth as she peered
down at a black-and-yellow snake, not three feet away,
making menacing whirring sounds and shaking its black
tail like a baby's rattle.

Oh, dear God.

"Don't move, Molly. Not an inch."

Kane? He spoke from somewhere behind her, his
voice firm and commanding. Molly would take heed.
She wouldn't move an inch.

And then, as quick as lightning the glistening blade
of a knife whizzed by her and sliced through the rattler's
throat. The snake's head flew forward landing on the tip
of her right boot, looking very much like a golden shoe
ornament. Molly gasped in horror. She stared at the
snake's severed head. Her legs buckled, the sun lost its
shine and her very last fleeting thought was that she
never much cared for fancy shoes.

With care, Kane lowered Molly's limp body down
under the shade of a mesquite tree, cushioning her head
with his rolled up buckskin shirt. She'd fainted from the
sight of a snake as any greenhorn would, but he couldn't
rouse her. "Molly, Molly, wake up." He tapped her
cheek gently, but she only stirred slightly.

Her once rosy mouth parched and swollen and her
small body limp, Kane knew she'd been outdoors too

long without benefit of rest or water. Both intense heat and exhaustion had added to her unconscious state now. He bent down and touched her forehead, feeling the burn of her heat on his palm.

Kane walked the distance to a free running creek and dipped his bandana in, soaking it with fresh cold water. As he made his way back to Molly, he wondered what she'd done with his other bandana, the one that had so expertly covered her sweet little behind yesterday.

Molly looked so peaceful lying there under the shade of the tall tree, but Kane wouldn't fool himself. She needed tending. She wasn't used to Texas and the wild nature of the land. Kane bent to dab her face with the moist cloth, pressing it to her mouth, hoping she would part her lips to take some of the water in. When that didn't work, he used his own finger to separate her lips and drizzled a few drops onto her tongue.

Molly was pretty with her perfect mouth, petite body and fiery green eyes—too pretty to become a mail-order bride for a stranger and too pretty to venture out alone in search of her mischievous brother. He closed his eyes, stifling a curse at the stubborn woman. Without his help, surely trouble would find her every step of the way.

Kane sighed as he dabbed a little lower, patting her throat, then lower still as he unbuttoned her dress to the waist, pushing away the material.

"Molly."

She didn't stir at all.

Kane rose then and glanced at her boots. He made quick work of removing them, then the dress. He peeled it off gently, noting the creamy softness of her bare skin. He left on only her undergarment, then once he tossed his own boots aside, he picked Molly up in his arms and walked straight into the rushing creek.

Kane stood there with Molly in his arms, turning about, wondering about the wisdom of what he was about to do. He knew one thing for certain. Molly needed rousing.

This was the only way.

He kept Molly tight in his arms and down they both went, under the flowing current into the chilly waters. Only seconds ticked by and when Kane rose up the female he held sputtered, waving her arms wildly. She gasped for air again and again, until finally her breathing slowed to normal, her body settled against him and she stared straight into his eyes.

"Kane." She sighed his name; the sound so pure, so soft and so darn arousing, Kane's body grew tight.

He set Molly on her feet, making sure she found her footing on the creek bed. Water glistened on her bare skin. White material clung like sheer gauze to her wet body exposing every tempting curve the woman possessed. The cold from the creek pebbled her pink nipples until they seemed to come right through the chemise, reaching up toward the sun.

Foolishly, Kane took his time studying Molly as his manhood grew harder and harder with each breath she took, each movement she made. Bravely, maybe foolishly, Molly stared back at him, her gaze flowing from his damp hair to study his mouth, and finally her eyes lit on his dripping bare chest, taking her sweet time in her perusal. Kane thought to explode. Molly's innocence mingled with her unabashed curiosity was enough to set any man's body on fire.

"You saved me," she said softly.

"You're a fool, Molly McGuire. You shouldn't have gone out without a chaperone. You can't just waltz into an unknown situation, pretty as you please without a thought in your head. The land itself can kill you, if another kind of trouble doesn't get you first. I won't always be there to rescue you."

Molly's face fell. She dipped her head down, her body trembling. Kane had set out deliberately to chastise her, but he hadn't expected to see such hurt in her eyes. He hadn't expected his words to cause such injury. He regretted speaking so harshly to her. She'd been through enough already today.

Molly bent down and Kane thought she was ready to faint again. He reached out, but water splashed his chest and the cold liquid bounced up to hit his face. He sputtered in stunned surprise.

"You're the fool, Kane Jackson."

Molly splashed him again.

"Do you think I have a choice?"

Again, more water landed on his chest.

"I honor my vows," she said decidedly, her chest heaving with indignation. In between splashes, he'd caught quite a tantalizing view. "I promised my mama to find Charlie. And I'll do it, with or without your help."

She bent to splash him again, but Kane caught her wrist. He tugged her forward, water dripping between them. Her breasts pressed tight against his skin, the lush feel of her creating a terrible ache in his groin. He gazed down into the green fire of her eyes.

"With." He pulled Molly's arms around him, placing them at his waist. Then he took her face in his hands, bent his head, giving her no time to deny this pleasure and he pressed his lips to hers, unwilling and unable to stop.

"With," he said again, kissing her full out this time, wrapping his arms fully around her petite waist and drawing her up against his tormented body giving her full knowledge of his arousal. She responded with a tiny moan, affirmation that he'd hadn't forced her. Affirmation that she enjoyed the kiss as much as he had.

Their lips touched gently at first with slow building heat, then more fervently. Kane tasted the sweetness of her mouth, carefully caressing the lips that had been scorched by an unmerciful sun. He kissed her again and again, his hands roaming over her moist skin, weaving through her tangled red curls. She returned his kisses with a steady stream of passion that surprised him. Molly responded to him without fear, which might be a foolish thing on her part. Kane hadn't known such desire in years. It pulled at him, tugging at his barren heart in ways that could only lead to disaster.

He broke off the kiss and stared into the soft glow of Molly's eyes. Instinctively, Kane knew he'd unfairly put that look there.

"You'll help me find my brother, Kane?" she breathed out. "You'll marry me?"

Kane drew in a deep breath, partly to regain his composure and partly to figure a way out of this. He hadn't planned on marrying Molly. He'd vowed never to marry again. But he'd also found out from Doctor Beckman this morning that his grandfather wasn't expected to make a full recovery. The good doctor seemed to think Bennett Jackson's days were numbered. More than anything Bennett wanted Kane to marry—and he'd handpicked Molly McGuire, a woman who'd place herself in danger in order to honor her pledge to her mother.

"Molly, I'll help you find your brother."

"But—"

"There they are, Sheriff! They're in the creek over…oh, my!" Mrs. Rose's shrill voice barreled across the meadow. They were some distance away, but close enough to see Molly in her state of undress locked in Kane's arms, dripping wet in the middle of the creek.

Molly closed her eyes.

Kane swore an oath.

He thought fast. "Listen, Molly. I'll make you a bargain. I'll help you find your brother and you help me ease my grandfather's mind. We'll get married…temporarily."

Molly blinked then her eyes grew wide. "Temporarily?"

"I'll explain later. Right now, your reputation is at stake. Mrs. Rose won't keep this quiet."

Riding in her buggy, Mrs. Rose approached swiftly with the sheriff on horseback alongside of her.

Dumbfounded, Molly asked, "Mrs. Rose won't keep what quiet?"

Kane shook his head and pointed at her attire, or rather lack of attire. "This looks bad for you, Molly. We're both nearly naked. I doubt they're thinking we're out here for an innocent swim." He waited until she frowned, fully comprehending. "Say you'll marry me until we find your brother and my grandfather passes. Do we have a deal?"

"Oh, dear God!" Mrs. Rose's shriek vibrated through the thick humid air. "Miss McGuire, has he harmed you?"

Kane stood in front of Molly covering her body with

his, protecting her from curious eyes as the waters flowed against their legs.

"Molly?" Kane asked again. Seconds ticked by as Mrs. Rose's buggy drew closer.

More impatiently, Kane asked, "Molly, make your decision. Do we have a deal?"

"We have a deal, Kane," Molly whispered from behind.

Kane peered at the sheriff and Mrs. Rose in turn as they stopped along the edge of the creek. The sheriff appeared slightly amused, but the scowl on the older woman's face could bring down the devil himself. "She's fine, Mrs. Rose. No need to worry."

Mrs. Rose nearly toppled off her buggy seat, pointing her accusation. "You've ruined her!"

"That's probably true," Kane responded, feeling the same sentiment, but for an entirely different reason. "Molly has just agreed to become my wife."

Chapter Four

Fighting rushing waters that slapped at her thighs, Molly made her way to the bank of the creek, fighting another battle in her head. She didn't think anything could have equaled her eventful day yesterday, learning about her fate at the hands of a sly old man, but today's events had far outweighed her first day in Bountiful. Today, she'd nearly been nearly bitten by a venomous snake before fainting dead away, only to find herself unclothed then dunked into the creek like yesterday's wash. And then to her mortification, Mrs. Rose and the sheriff had been privy to the lusty encounter she'd had with Kane Jackson.

Her betrothed.

The man she would marry.

Temporarily.

Molly shook her head, clearing water out of her ears and attempting to free her thoughts enough to make some sense out of all this.

Molly was engaged to marry just as she'd hoped. But the proposal had been less than inspiring, coming from a man who had moments ago kissed the stuffing out of her. A man who would rather send her back home than make her his wife.

Kane had been trapped by his own sense of nobility. He'd offered her marriage to protect her reputation and perhaps ease a dying man's last days. He'd agreed to help her find Charlie, and Molly believed Kane would honor that promise. At least, Molly had that. At the very least, she would have aid in locating her wayward brother and then, perhaps she and Charlie could start life all over again here in west Texas.

Molly crossed her arms over her chest, mindful that Kane watched her from behind. He'd already seen what there was to see, but the keen sense of propriety her mama had instilled in her while Molly was growing up had her covering up the best she could, betrothed or not.

When she reached her clothes, she bent and donned her gown quickly, but her rapid movements couldn't shut out the notion of Kane unclothing her, one button at a time, until the garment fell away exposing her skin. She couldn't vanquish the thought of Kane slipping his hands inside, removing the gown entirely. Had his eyes lingered on her? When he picked her up to carry her to the creek, had he been tender with her body?

"Don't dally, Molly. We have to get back to the Bar J."

Molly whirled around. Kane stood beside her, holding his buckskin shirt as sunlight beamed down on bronzed skin, wet, raven-black hair and a strong powerful body. Molly's breath caught in her throat, gazing at the man she would marry, a man who very much appeared a savage right now. Lord have mercy, she'd been held and kissed and viewed by this man and soon he would become her husband.

A shiver coursed through her body, not from damp clothes or a sudden breeze, but from the very thought of bedding Kane Jackson. "You plan to take me to your ranch?"

Kane nodded, lifting his shirt over his head, giving Molly one last view of his muscled chest. She looked away when Kane caught her stare, his lips quirking up. "My grandfather is anxious to meet you."

"All of my things are at Mrs. Rose's."

"I left the wagon in town. We'll get your things and then head out." Kane lowered himself to the ground and yanked on his boots.

"But…but I look wretched. I'll need a bath to tidy up."

He glanced up, trying to hide a smile. "You just had your bath."

Molly stood her ground, running a hand through her hair trying to smooth her unruly damp locks. She didn't know how women behaved in the West, but Molly had been schooled differently. Even in poverty, she always held her head up high. "I can't meet your grandfather looking like this."

Kane stared at her, his penetrating gaze traveling from her hair, to her mouth and down her throat, lingering on her chest in a complete sweeping perusal of her body. "You're pretty enough."

She ignored the slight compliment, whatever *pretty enough,* meant. "But…"

"Listen," Kane said, coming to stand in front of her. He took both of her hands in his. "My grandfather duped both of us. He'll be more than happy to meet you, no matter that you look like you've just been…"

Molly's eyes grew wide. "I look like I've just been

what?" Nearly bitten by a snake, dunked in the creek, embarrassed in front of townsfolk?

"Dallied with," he said with no hesitation.

Molly's hand flew to her mouth. She gasped then whispered, "Is that how I look?"

Kane glanced at her swollen lips and lifted a brow. Even now, she felt the heat of his passion and the gentle bruising on her lips when his mouth had claimed hers.

"We made a bargain, Molly. I'll help you find your brother and we'll play out the ruse of marriage to satisfy a dying man. Grandfather will be overjoyed meeting you today. Trust me."

"I'm not certain whom to trust anymore," Molly said in earnest, releasing her hands from his.

But his dark solemn eyes held her attention. "I'll never break my word to you, Molly."

"You're marrying me, Kane. But it rings false. We both will be breaking those vows." Marriage was sacred, whether entered into by love or by way of a contract. Molly had never conceived on entering into matrimony with anything but a true commitment.

"Think of it as a marriage deal, a bargain to satisfy our needs. Once we meet those needs, the deal will be over."

How lovely, Molly thought wryly, trying to see the good in all this. Soon, she'll have Charlie by her side. Right now, that's all that she would have to hold on to.

"Can you walk the distance to town?" he asked, looking doubtful.

"I think so."

"You're light as a blue jay."

The last thing Molly wanted was to be carried into town by Kane Jackson. She didn't trust herself in his arms. Whenever Kane touched her, her body warmed, her heart raced and she quivered like a frightened little rabbit.

Besides, she would die of mortification if anyone in town caught a glimpse of her that way. Even though they were to be married, Molly had more pride than that. "The last time you carried me somewhere, I ended up soaking wet."

"You're forgetting I took that dunking, too."

Molly hadn't forgotten. She'd never get the image of Kane, dripping wet, looking like a mythical god coming up from the water, out of her mind. But she had forgotten one other more important detail. And again, propriety wouldn't allow her to ignore giving Kane his due. "I didn't forget." Then Molly tilted her head and said sweetly, "But I did forget to thank you for saving my life today."

But Kane ignored her thanks, walking on ahead in silence.

"Welcome to the Bar J, Molly." Bennett Jackson smiled and his aging eyes beamed with joy. Molly had a hard time disliking the sickly man who had graciously welcomed her into his home and his family. "Please take a seat."

She smiled and sat down on a beautifully upholstered crimson chair in the main room. "Thank you."

"I've been looking forward to meeting you." The older man grunted as he lowered himself down into a matching chair.

Molly waited until he made himself comfortable, noting the look of pain on his face he had tried to conceal. "I have, too, but I must say that you did use a bit of deception to get me here."

The old man chuckled. "I like you, Molly. You speak your mind."

"Sometimes, too much," Molly agreed.

"Never. You'll be a good match for my grandson. He'll not bully you into anything."

"Hmmmph."

Molly glanced up at a grumbling Kane, who stood by the fireplace, resting an arm on the mantle, drinking bourbon. He wasn't too happy with her right now. She'd cajoled and needled him all the way into town, until he'd finally agreed to allow her time to wash up, redo her hair and change into something more suitable. She wore a gown of soft pink taffeta, one of her mother's few remaining garments that hadn't been ruined by age. Molly had taken time to alter several old gowns, making them more stylish for a young lady. And though Molly had been grateful to Kane for his patience, he hadn't remarked one way or the other regarding her appearance.

Bennett continued, "You will find a home here at the Bar J. You will wed my grandson and I think you will both find happiness."

"Yes," Molly said, guilty about lying to the older man. She would wed his grandson, but there would be no happiness. There would be no future for her here at the Bar J. Molly understood Bennett's motives better now. The Jackson ranch was prosperous, thriving under Bennett's guidance, but he must fear that once he's no longer capable of running the ranch, his legacy, all of his hard work and sweat and sacrifice, would go to ruin. No wonder he wanted to secure Kane's future here. No wonder he hoped to settle his grandson and make him a true part of his heritage.

"But part of our, uh, after we marry, Kane has agreed to help me locate my brother. He's been missing for quite some time."

Bennett nodded. "I have some experience in searching for a missing boy. I will do what I can as well."

"I do appreciate that. As you know from my letters," Molly added, certain now that it had been Bennett and not Kane who had read her letters, "my brother took off for west Texas nearly one year ago. Mama and I only received one letter from him, and though he promised to write often, that's all we've heard from him. I promised Mama right before she passed that I would find Charlie and one day we'd be reunited. He's all the family I have left."

Bennett bent close and reached for her hand. Molly leaned over far enough to take the offered hand. "You have my word that we will find him. But you're wrong about Charlie being your only family. You have Kane now. And me. You'll be a Jackson."

Touched by his sincere gesture of welcome, Molly's heart lurched a bit. Maybe Bennett wanted her in the family, but Kane surely did not. "Thank you."

"Hmmmph," Kane grumbled again, gulping down the amber liquid until he emptied his glass, a true testimony to his sentiments.

Guilt assailed her again, lying outright to Kane's grandfather. Of course, Kane wouldn't see it that way. He'd already commented how his grandfather had duped them both. But sitting here in this lovely parlor, in a ranch house that was more refined than most Eastern homes Molly had ever visited, she truly didn't fault the old man. Well, not overly much.

She hadn't bargained on any of this, but as her gaze lifted to Kane standing by the mantel, tall, well-muscled and more of a man than any of the Eastern boys Molly had envisioned marrying one day, bittersweet feelings emerged. She'd come here to marry him, and she had received her wish. For the time being, Molly would become a Jackson. Molly had wanted more—she'd wanted a true marriage with the hope of children one day.

But ironically, though Kane made her crazy at times with his surly attitude and demanding nature, she found she *wanted* to marry him. Silly of her, she knew. But she looked forward to becoming his wife and belonging to, if only for a short time, part of the Jackson family.

"The nuptials are scheduled for tomorrow afternoon. I took the liberty of inviting a few guests," Bennett announced.

Molly blinked, surprise registering before reality set in. She was to be married tomorrow. To Kane. She would become a Jackson sooner than anticipated.

Kane's face paled and there was no doubt in Molly's mind that he would escape this situation if he could. He strode from the fireplace to face his grandfather and boomed, "What?"

A coughing tirade set in, Bennett hunching over in a fit. Molly rose immediately to help him, coming to kneel before him. "Mr. Jackson," she called urgently. "Kane, get some water, quickly!"

Seconds later, Kane handed her a glass. When the old man's coughing subsided somewhat, Molly offered the water. "Here, drink slowly."

He sipped from the glass, until he caught his breath. "Better now." He smiled warmly at Molly then reached out to touch her cheek. "I'm sorry you had to see that, but these fits come more and more lately."

Bennett held his chest, hunched over, his face white as a sheet. She saw so much in his deep gray eyes and understood why he'd set the wedding date so soon. The poor man didn't think he would be of this earth much longer.

Bennett peered up at Kane, and to his credit, he appeared as shaken as Molly, seeing his grandfather in such a state. "Kane, she's a sweet one. You'll be happy, you'll see. Tomorrow?"

Kane placed a reassuring hand on his grandfather's shoulder, but his gaze fastened to Molly and he nodded. "Tomorrow."

"This will be your room, Senorita Molly. It is nice, no? But tomorrow, you will move to Mr. Kane's room." Lupe Perez said with a wide grin, setting down her valise. "You will need a big bed to share with such a man."

Molly's face heated. She'd only just met the Jackson cook and housekeeper a few minutes ago, and already the woman had reminded her of her upcoming wedding night. "This is lovely, Lupe. Thank you," Molly managed, glancing around the finely furnished room with bright yellow curtains and sunlight cascading in. This was a room in which she could find comfort and solace. But no room would hold her for long. She had to find Charlie.

Lupe walked behind a light oak partition with decorative carvings of long stemmed flowers and polished to a shine, the workmanship both delicate and precise. "You will wear this *mañana*," she said, coming out from behind the partition with a gorgeous white lace gown. "It is *muy bonita*, no?"

Lupe held up the gown with pride.

Stunned, Molly walked over to touch the dress. Soft as spun cotton and so fine, she marveled at her wedding gown.

"Mr. Bennett, he told me to make a beautiful dress."

Molly's head shot up. "You made this?"

"*Sí.*" She nodded and smiled. "It will fit you, I think."

Molly perused the gown entirely, deciding that Lupe had remarkable talent. "*Sí*, yes. I think it will fit me."

Lupe nodded again, satisfied.

Overwhelmed, Molly had trouble with words. She'd come all this way, with more than a few bumps in the road, but finally, reality hit her. She would wed tomorrow. She would become Kane's wife. And she would step up to the altar in the most luxurious gown she'd ever seen. "This is so…thank you, Lupe. Thank you for making me a magnificent wedding gown. Thank you."

"You will be a beautiful bride, Miss Molly. You make Mr. Kane happy."

Molly only smiled briefly, the mention of happiness and Kane in the same sentence created queasiness in her belly. Again, the falsity of their marriage struck her. It went against everything Molly believed in, everything she'd been brought up to uphold. She turned away from Lupe's joyful face to retrieve her valise.

"I will do." Lupe took the valise out of her hand and

opened it, taking out each garment with care. "You take a bath now. In the room at the end of the hall." She gestured in the direction. "Lupe has the water all ready for you."

A *bath?* Molly had had a dunking earlier today and Kane had only allowed her time to wash up a bit before changing her clothes, but a real bath? It sounded heavenly. She wouldn't argue with Lupe. A bath is just what she needed. "Thank you, Lupe. I would love to take a bath." With pleasure.

Ten minutes later, Molly soaked in a rose-scented bath, the steamy water easing tension and relaxing her tired bones. She washed and rinsed her hair, then lavished leisurely for as long as she possibly could, before stepping out of the porcelain tub. She dried off slowly, taking her time, running a towel through her unruly auburn locks. She wrapped herself up in a huge bundle of towels, making sure she covered herself adequately, then peered out the door, and once satisfied that no one would see her in that state, she raced out of the bathing room and down the hall to her room.

Closing the door behind her, Molly removed the towels, and sank onto her bed. Her hands skimmed over the soft quilt as she tested the mattress only to find it quite comfortable. Without hesitation she climbed in, far too tempted by the warmth and softness offered not to close her eyes for a bit.

Before she knew it, she'd drifted off into an exhausted sleep.

Kane stood outside Molly's door and knocked softly. "Molly, it's Kane."

When she didn't answer, Kane elbowed the door

open and entered, holding a dinner tray. "Damn," he muttered quietly.

Molly slept peacefully in her bed, her auburn locks still moist in a curly tangle around the pillow. Her face sweet with sleep, her shoulders bared and the very peak of one rosy tipped breast peeking out from under the coverlet, Kane swallowed hard, both tempted and disgusted with himself for enjoying the view before him.

His body grew tight and Kane cursed silently, realizing that not once, but twice today, the woman who would become his wife had affected him this way. Kane watched her sleep momentarily, noting her attributes and condemning himself for lingering, and more so for lusting after Molly McGuire.

Had he not learned his lesson with Little Swan? Had he not contributed to her demise in such a way that left his heart cold and barren? The lust he felt for Miss McGuire was nothing but one man's physical desire for an appealing, quite lovely young woman, but nothing else remained within Kane. He'd been emptied, hollowed out inside, and no good would come of his body's traitorous yearnings, no good would come of claiming his soon-to-be new bride. She would remain pure, and he would end their marriage as soon as both had met the conditions of their bargain.

Kane's word was solid and true. He would help Molly find her brother and in turn, she would enter into this ruse of a marriage for as long as his grandfather was of this earth.

He set the dinner tray down atop the armoire, leaving Molly's evening meal within reach. She might wake late at night famished, since Kane knew she had precious little to eat today. She'd been through quite an ordeal and would need her nourishment.

He turned and headed toward the door, taking one last glance at Molly's restful form. Just then, she sat up hastily, quite surprised at finding him in her room. The coverlet fell away, leaving her bared to her waist for the briefest of seconds, before Molly pulled it up to her chin. He kept his face expressionless for her sake, but the mental image of Molly's porcelain-smooth skin and ripe young breasts had already penetrated his head, leaving an everlasting mark, he feared.

"Kane?" she questioned him with dewy-eyed innocence.

"You missed supper. Lupe didn't want to disturb your sleep. She sent up a tray."

Molly clung tight to the coverlet. "Oh, dear. I'm sorry. Your grandfather invited me to dine with him and—"

"You're forgiven. Nobody knows better how a body becomes taxed from an eventful day than Grandfather. He's already asleep. I sent Lupe off, too."

Molly glanced at the tray upon the armoire. "I'm starving."

"Then eat up." Kane reached for the doorknob.

"You'd have me eat alone on my first night at the Bar J?"

Kane turned to stare at her and while he fully expected to see a haughty expression on her face, all he witnessed was genuine loneliness. "You're hardly dressed for company, Molly," he whispered, recalling glimpsing her bare body just moments ago. "You can't ask that of any man."

Molly blushed crimson. "I don't usually sleep…this way."

God Almighty, he hoped not. He hadn't slept with a woman for a long time, and he certainly hadn't married any of them. But Molly would be his wife. He knew the consequences of bedding her and had vowed not to touch her. But he had needs like any man and sleeping beside a woman clothed up to her chin and down to her toes was one thing—sleeping with a naked beauty with soft curves and silken skin was another entirely.

Kane needed no further temptations. Wedding Molly would test his integrity and willpower to the limit.

"If I dress quickly, will you keep me company?" Molly asked politely. The coverlet slipped down past her shoulders, and she grabbed it fast with a hand to her chest before exposing more of her creamy skin.

Kane turned from her and nodded. He couldn't fault her desire for companionship in a strange house, under even stranger circumstances. Kane remembered a time in his life when everything had been abruptly taken from him as well. As a small boy, he recalled waking up in an unfamiliar place, a home unlike any he had ever known. Faintly, he recalled the fear, trepidation and isolation of those days and was indeed grateful those memories had all but faded now. No, he couldn't fault Molly her loneliness. "I'll take the tray down and meet you in the dining room."

"Thank you, Kane," she said quietly.

Kane exited the room, realizing that Molly's dreams of a future had been crushed, too. Neither of them would enter into this marriage with any expectations other than fulfilling their bargain to one another.

For Kane, it would be enough.

He only hoped that Molly would come to see it that way as well.

Molly finished her meal in unladylike fashion and sighed with delight, her appetite satisfied. She'd never had this spicy type of stew before, but she'd enjoyed every last bite. "Lupe is a wonderful cook. I must be sure to thank her."

Kane sat facing her in a dining area with room enough for a large family. Eight high-back chairs surrounded a great oak table and lovely draperies of gold velvet parted in the center overlooked the small garden area of the ranch. Hibiscus and gardenia bushes grew in abundance amid smaller flowering plants. And sandwiched in between this lush garden sat a bench seat made for two.

From what Molly could ascertain, the Bar J, for its rich and stately interior, had only this one comfortable area outside in which one could relax. The rest of the property was strictly designed for animals and their caretakers, bunkhouses, barns and a pasture that went on for acres and acres. Molly didn't know how she would ever become accustomed to the smell of horse dung, a herd of grazing cattle, dust and earth all mingled into one Texas-sized scent.

Kane glanced at her empty plate. "Still hungry?"

She sat back in her chair and smiled. "Oh, no. I'm so full I don't think I could eat another bite for days."

"Mmmm. Too bad. Lupe left you half a blueberry pie."

Molly loved blueberries. And she'd never had them baked up in a pie before. "Half? She must think I'm too skinny for my bones."

Kane swept his dark gaze over her body again, in that way he had of making her nerves tingle and her body heat up. "Lupe likes to keep everyone happy."

"Well, then," she said with a tilt of her head and a little smile, "maybe I'll have a piece of pie."

Kane's lips twitched. "Sure you can fit it in?"

Again, his gaze moved over her body. "I wouldn't want to disappoint Lupe," she said, with a lift of her chin.

Kane stood. "I'll be back."

Molly rose from the table and followed Kane to the kitchen, eager to explore more of the house and to show her betrothed that she wasn't some Eastern ninny who needed waiting on. Molly had always done her fair share of chores and wasn't accustomed to having anyone serve her. "This feels more like home," Molly said aloud, then caught herself when Kane turned abruptly.

"What does?"

"This kitchen, though it's practically the size of the house I grew up in, I like it in here." Molly glanced around to find this room less ostentatious than any of the rooms she'd seen so far at the Bar J. There were all sorts of kitchen utensils hanging up, copper pots and pans, and the cookstove looked similar to her mama's although much larger. Flour and sugar containers along with other staples lined one long table and the worktable in the center of the room appeared worn from decades of meals having been prepared there. "It's warm and cozy."

Kane took the tin out of the pie safe and set it on the table. "Then have a seat."

Molly glanced around, found two plates on the shelf, grabbed knives and forks from an opened drawer and

brought them over. Without asking, she cut two slices
of pie and served one to Kane. Then she sat down on a
long wooden bench at the table.

Kane stared at her.

She stared back.

"You surprise me," he said finally.

"Why?" she asked, wondering what she had done to
bring about that reaction.

Kane shook his head. "Never mind."

He dug into his pie and ate briskly whereas Molly
took her time, enjoying every last bite. She found his
gaze on her more times than not, watching her devour
the pie, licking the utensil clean and cooing with delight.
He inhaled sharply and shifted in his seat never saying
a word. She supposed she'd have to get used to his
ways, whether she thought him rude or not.

"It's late. You'd best get back to bed," he said, standing up ready to clear the table. But Molly beat him to
it. She took hold of the dishes and utensils and walked
them to the sink area. She tried to pump water into the
basin, but couldn't get a drop to flow.

"How does this work?" she asked, fidgeting with a
pumplike device she'd not seen before.

He stood close behind her, his breath caressing her
ear. "My grandfather employs people to do this."

"I prefer to clean up after myself."

Kane didn't argue. He wrapped his arms around her,
showing her how to hold the pump correctly. "It's
touchy. Pump it slow, Molly. Three times and then wait."

Molly concentrated on the task at hand, trying to ignore Kane's presence, trying to block out his warm
breath, his body pressed to hers from behind and his

arms securely wrapped around her. He held firm on to the pump, his hand next to hers and together they pumped slow, up and down, three times.

Water spurted out, a little at a time, until finally the liquid flowed out evenly. "There," she said, feeling a sense of accomplishment. She turned around and smiled. "I did it."

Molly found herself pressed against the sink and encased in Kane's arms. When he didn't back away, her heart fluttered and she glanced up at his lips. He had a beautiful mouth, she noticed with wide full lips that were at the moment, parting slightly.

"You have blueberry on your…" Molly began, reaching up toward his face. Her finger stopped at the corner of his mouth, hesitantly, watching Kane's brow lift in curiosity. She remembered those lips on her and shamefully, she hoped he would kiss her again. Right now. Here in the kitchen. She wanted Kane's kiss.

She moved her finger to the edge of his mouth and wiped clean the stain. "There," she said softly, but couldn't quite manage removing her fingers from his face. She caressed his cheek tenderly and stared into the eyes of the man she would marry tomorrow. He may not want this marriage but Molly would do her best to be a good wife to him.

Kane grasped her hand and brought it to his mouth. She watched in awe as he kissed her palm then wound his tongue around the finger with the blueberry stain, licking it clean. Molly's insides turned to warm jelly and her breath hitched in her throat. "Oh, my," she breathed out.

Kane's dark eyes gleamed and he stepped far away

from her. "You're too innocent to know what a temptation you are. Go to bed, Molly. Now. And don't argue with me."

"But?"

Kane squeezed his eyes shut. "Now, damn it."

Molly stood her ground and when Kane opened his eyes, she witnessed his surprise and fury when she hadn't obeyed him. "I'm not a child, Kane. I'm a woman, if you hadn't noticed."

Kane spoke through tight lips and suddenly his mouth didn't look beautiful anymore. "I've *noticed*. I've spent half the night *noticing*."

"We're to be married tomorrow. I would expect—"

"Don't expect anything from me, Molly. Not one fool thing. The marriage isn't real. There'll be no happy endings."

Tears stung Molly's eyes though she wouldn't allow them a path down her face. She held back, refusing Kane the satisfaction of tormenting her fully. "I'm aware of that."

"Good."

"Yes, good. Then I think I'll get to bed now."

Kane threw his arms up. "That's all I'm asking."

"Well, good night."

Kane grunted.

Molly walked past him but stopped to turn and gaze directly into his eyes. "And I'm not that innocent. I've been kissed a time or two, back in St. Louis."

Kane's chuckle came from deep in his throat. "Woman, what I was thinking had less to do with kissing and more to do with warm and cozy on top of that table over there."

Molly gasped, not so much from shock, but from the images fluttering around in her head of such a devilish thing. Surely, tomorrow she would find out what it would be like to be wedded and bedded by Kane Jackson.

Contrary to what he might think, Molly looked forward to becoming Mrs. Kane Jackson.

Chapter Five

Kane stared into the curious eyes of Penelope Rose as she made her way into the house, carrying a basket full of baked muffins and pastries, wearing a fancy blue dress and a woeful expression. One would think she was attending a funeral instead of a wedding. Only when his grandfather approached her, did she brighten somewhat. Kane watched their interaction from a corner of the parlor, as he sipped whiskey from a shot glass.

Kane wanted this whole charade over with as soon as possible, hoping to speak his vows before Father Tomas and be done with it. But as usual, Bennett had made other plans. His grandfather had prearranged the entire event, inviting a small gathering of neighbors and friends as well as planning a celebration afterward complete with a mariachi band and food enough to feed the entire county.

His grandfather, appearing less worn out and pale today, approached with Mrs. Rose on his arm. "Kane, Mrs. Rose has come to give your betrothed her good wishes. She's quite smitten with our Molly."

Kane smiled graciously. "And I thought she came here to visit you, Grandfather."

Mrs. Rose gasped and turned to his grandfather. "Well, I— Yes, if you must know, after I spoke with your grandson yesterday about your illness, I thought you might need fortification. I brought over some baked goods and chamomile tea that might give a lift during those long dreary days."

Bennett patted Penelope's hand. "That's very thoughtful. Of course, you'll stay for the nuptials."

"Well, I wouldn't want to impose. I mean to say, I didn't receive a formal invitation."

"There was no time for that or you would certainly have been invited. Molly would have insisted if we'd given her a choice. You see, my health is failing and I want to see my grandson married before my time is up."

Mrs. Rose's eyes softened and that perpetual pinch on her face vanished. She looked into Bennett's eyes and smiled. "Only the Lord knows when, Bennett. You may have more time than you think."

Again, he patted her hand. "I'm glad you came, Penny."

Mrs. Rose chuckled and suddenly she appeared twenty years younger. "Heavens, nobody's called me that, well, since I was a young girl."

"I've always thought of you as Penny."

"Have you?"

Kane excused himself to walk out the front door for a breath of fresh air. Soon, the rest of the guests would arrive, and he'd say the vows that would bind him to Molly and their bargain.

Soon Kane Jackson, known to the Cheyenne as Gray

Wolf, would marry for the second time in his life. But this time, the marriage wouldn't be a union of the heart. He would never betray Little Swan that way. No, this time, the marriage vows would be spoken falsely, with no regard to upholding any of the promises made today. Molly McGuire and Kane Jackson had a prearranged pact.

And his promise to Molly yesterday was the only one he planned to keep.

Molly glanced at her image in the tall oval cheval mirror, hardly believing the sight before her eyes. Dressed in a fitted gown of white lace with a mantilla cascading down past her shoulders, Molly was truly a bride.

Goodness. She blinked at her reflection, wondering if all brides felt this way—womanly, feminine, lovely, that special unique sensation that might only occur once in a young girl's life. Molly felt it all, right down to her frilly, white lace-up boots, provided by Bennett Jackson. She'd never had such finery in her life. Molly couldn't help but smile, turning from side to side to pose before the mirror, taking short then sweeping glances at herself.

"*Muy bonita,* Senorita Molly." Lupe entered the room wearing a big grin, no doubt filled with pride on just how perfectly the gown she'd designed had fit Molly.

"Thank you, Lupe. It's the most wonderful wedding dress I've ever seen."

"My husband, he says that a bride should glow as the sun. He says then your man will always know warmth."

Molly blinked at the brilliance of that statement. Then she chuckled. "I think you have a very smart husband, Lupe."

With arms folded, the heavyset woman nodded. "*Sí.* I will keep him."

Molly smiled sadly as a thought flitted through her mind that she would wed today, but she would not be the warmth in Kane's life. She would not be around for years to come, claiming her husband for keeps. Perhaps Lupe didn't know how fortunate she was to have love and happiness in her life. Or, perhaps she did. Maybe that would explain Lupe's eternal wide smile.

"I've always dreamed of a church wedding," Molly confessed, speaking quietly. As a devout Catholic, she'd envisioned saying her vows in front of an altar.

"*Sí,*" Lupe agreed. "Senor Bennett is not up for such a trip. Father Tomas is here. He will marry you and Senor Kane. Come now, they wait."

Molly glanced one last time in the mirror, pretending for a moment that this marriage was real and that Kane Jackson would take her into his life and heart forever. For one moment, Molly had imagined the possibilities and wished that she didn't have to partake in this sham, deceiving everyone in attendance and making a mockery of what should be a sacred union.

"I'm ready."

Molly strode out the bedroom door with a jittery stomach and a terrible ache in her heart. The only good thing to come of this marriage was that soon she and Kane would set out to find her brother.

Molly stood at the top of the staircase holding a small bouquet of gardenias as soft violin music drifted up. She glanced down to find Bennett Jackson, dressed in dapper silver-gray, the exact color of his eyes and full head of hair, waiting for her at the foot of the stairs. He winked and she smiled, the butterflies in her stomach taking flight.

She moved slowly down the stairs, taking one careful step at a time. The look of pure delight on Mr. Jackson's face and the sweetly melodic refrain lifted her spirits so, that next she found herself flowing gracefully the rest of the way down the staircase. With a wide smile on her face and her anxiety quelled for the time being, Molly met Bennett at the base of the stairs.

"You look beautiful, Molly." He placed her arm in his.

"Thank you, Mr. Jackson," she said softly.

"You would honor me by calling me Grandfather from now on."

"Oh," Molly said with a surprised gasp. "Yes, yes, Grandfather."

Together they moved through the foyer to the parlor, where Kane stood waiting next to the priest in front of the fireplace. Molly's heart tumbled, seeing her betrothed, so handsome in a black suit, boiled white shirt and bola tie, standing stiff and erect, looking fierce and unyielding. A tick worked at his jaw, and his eyes held no warmth. Molly thought back to Lupe's comments about a glowing bride bringing warmth to her groom and a sweeping sadness overwhelmed her. She stumbled and stopped.

"He'll be a fine husband, Molly," Bennett whispered, reassuring her as if reading her thoughts. "Give him time. He's a good man."

Molly gulped and nodded, then continued her walk down the short aisle until she faced Kane and Father Tomas. She'd hardly noticed any of the guests in attendance, a roomful of strangers she did not know, as her main focus had been on Kane and the unnerving look on his face. Bennett placed Molly beside Kane and turned to take his seat.

Molly stared at the priest who was dressed in stately black, too nervous to look upon Kane's solemn face, fearing her knees would buckle any second if she dwelled on his expression too long.

Father Tomas nodded graciously and smiled before beginning the ceremony. To her amazement, Kane reached for Molly, covering his hand over hers and squeezing gently. She dared a glance up at him, noting a softening in his eyes, but along with that soft look came a hint of regret and sadness. Kane didn't want this marriage. Both of them had been forced into the union by circumstances, but she wondered if he was recalling his marriage to his Indian wife. She wondered if this ceremony could possibly remind him of another ceremony, years ago, to a woman he had truly loved.

Before too long, Kane bent down to place a sweet chaste kiss on her lips. Startled, Molly came out of her wanderings to realize that the short ceremony was over. She'd spoken her vows to God above and to Kane, and now she was a married woman.

She turned from Father Tomas to find Bennett smiling, a look of relief and satisfaction on the old man's face. And as Molly gazed around the room, she found more than two dozen other smiling faces peering up at her from their seats. Mrs. Rose was the only person she recognized in the crowd, her face unable to mask her worry and, perhaps, condemnation.

Kane bent his head to whisper in her ear. "The show begins now."

His breath lingered, the warmth and sweet melody of his words belied their meaning. He took her hand and together they made their way outside, where they would meet the guests and have the wedding celebration.

"Your wife has danced with every man here," Bennett said with a frown. "Every man but you."

Kane shook his head. "I don't dance, Grandfather."

Gray brows rose with disapproval. "Not even once, on your wedding day?"

Kane stared at Molly, her face aglow, her bright eyes sparkling, her hair catching sunlight as she moved with the rhythm of the music on the grassy flatland behind the house designed specifically for the festivities. His grandfather, through his illness, sure found time to have the yard decorated with ribbons and flowers for the occasion. "She's having a fine time without me."

"Be careful, Kane. Molly is pretty and smart and our friends are taking notice. Treat her right and she'll give you a house full of children. She'll make you happy."

Kane grimaced. "I was happy enough before you sent for her."

Bennett shrugged his shoulder and shook his head. "Just you wait and see." Then his grandfather took hold of his arm. "I wouldn't want Molly to dance too much longer with our neighbors. She might tire out tonight."

Kane pierced his grandfather with a hard look.

Bennett grinned and winked. "A young girl's wedding night should be something special. You'll see to that, Kane."

Kane's mouth twisted as he stared at Molly again just as she looked up to find his eyes upon her. Their gazes locked for a second and Molly lost her footing. Able-bodied Jess Mathias, her dance partner, grabbed her waist to steady her and Kane's nerves went raw.

In truth, he hadn't enjoyed seeing Molly dancing with other men. He hated to admit it, but watching men hold her and make her smile struck him like a knife to his throat. He hadn't wanted this protective and possessive feeling to take hold of him, but it had. And now he found the need to see to his wife. He found the need to show the guests that Molly belonged to him.

Kane strode over to Jess Mathias. "I'd like a word with my wife, if you don't mind."

The Circle B's ranch foreman nodded sheepishly and excused himself. Kane took Molly's hand and led her away from the mariachi band and loud music, away from the male guests lined up to dance with his new bride.

"What is it, Kane?" Molly asked, removing her hand from his hold.

"My grandfather's getting suspicious. Stay by my side."

Molly's face flamed. "What do you suggest I do when these nice folks ask me to dance? Especially since my husband hasn't spent one second by *my* side."

"I don't dance, Molly."

"Don't or won't?"

Kane frowned and refused her an answer. He'd grown up with the Cheyenne and had spent a great amount of time learning their traditional ritual dances. He'd been a part of their culture for so long that still to this day, Kane resented some of the white man's ways. He wouldn't dance with Molly, but not because he couldn't.

"I like to dance, Kane. Besides, it's giving me a chance to ask about Charlie. These men work on neighboring ranches. Some of them might have seen or met Charlie in their travels."

"Today's not the day for that. We'll head out tomorrow and make all the inquiries you'd like. Today is the day to convince my grandfather that this marriage is real."

"And how do you suppose we do that?" Her voice rose with indignation just as he caught his grandfather's sly eyes watching them.

Kane wrapped his arms around her, bringing her up against him and bent his head. "Like this."

Kane claimed her lips in a sweeping long kiss, tasting her sweetness, the mix of Molly and fruit punch a heady elixir for any man, even more so for him. Molly was his wife now. He had every right to kiss her, but he hadn't expected this surge of hot desire to beseech him.

And Molly. She too seemed affected, leaning into him, their bodies brushing together with legs and chests meshed. After her initial surprise, a little gasp that Kane had come to know as hers alone, Molly participated fully, responding to his kiss passionately. Kane held her tight, his palms stroking her back, caressing the fine lace of her wedding dress as he deepened the kiss, caught up in a slow burn that scorched his body.

His lips were hard and demanding, hers soft and supple and so damn willing that Kane had to back away. He broke off the kiss to stare into Molly's dewy green eyes. She smiled at him with softly bruised lips, her face radiant and glowing.

"Kane," she whispered, looking at him as if she truly belonged to him. Looking at him as if he belonged to her.

The music had stopped and when Kane turned around, all eyes were watching with satisfied expressions, and he realized if any of them had doubts of the validity of this marriage before, those questions had been quelled and banished from their minds now.

He turned back to Molly and took her hand. "I think that convinced them."

Molly put her head down, but not before Kane witnessed the injury he'd caused. It was better this way, he told himself. Better for Molly to understand the reality of their marriage—that there was no reality. Better for her not to get caught up in the fancy wedding gown and lively music and inspired guests. Better for her to remember that they had no future together. Kane would dissolve the marriage as soon as they met the terms of their bargain. But there would be no Omaha Dance, no stick-throwing tribal ceremony to toss a wife away as with the Cheyenne. Kane would have to seek legal means the white man's way to gain his freedom again.

"Molly," he said, relieved that he wasn't in the Cheyenne world now. Tossing a wife away caused great humiliation and somehow Kane couldn't imagine hurting Molly in that way.

When she didn't respond, he lifted her chin with a finger to gaze into her eyes. He'd half expected her to lash out at him with her wild Irish temper, but all he saw in her eyes was regret.

She already regretted marrying him.

The notion stung.

And Kane regarded that sharp jolt in the pit of his stomach as weakness, something he would deal with later on. He should be glad Molly realized the futility of this union. It would be better to remind her of the main reason she had come to Texas.

"Tomorrow, we will set out to find Charlie. It's what you want, isn't it?"

She nodded. "Very much."

"Then let's say good night to our guests. It's time for bed."

Chapter Six

"It's time for bed," Molly repeated Kane's words in her head as she made her way up the stairs behind her new husband. With both fear and great anticipation growing, her belly knotted from all the sensations whirling about.

Kane's kisses nearly destroyed her. She could only imagine how his lovemaking might be. Mama had told her of some things to expect on her wedding night before she passed, her mother practical with her advice, but she hadn't gone into any detail. Oh, how Molly wished she'd asked for details. She wished she knew exactly what to expect.

And as Molly took each step, glancing up at Kane, she noticed his tall frame, broad shoulders and well-muscled body. She noted his strength and power and recalled the sometimes savage look he'd cast her. She wondered if he'd be kind and gentle with her. She wondered if…

"Senorita—oh, *Dios*," Lupe called up from the base of the stairs, "I mean Senora Jackson?"

Molly glanced down to find Lupe's usual smile a bit worried.

"I will help you make ready, *sí?*"

"Oh, um—" Molly hesitated, biting her lip and wondering what she meant by making ready.

Kane took Molly's hand and led her up the last step. "No need for that, Lupe. I'll take care of Molly now."

Kane dismissed Lupe as easy as that and suddenly Molly's heart raced with trepidation. Kane led her into his bedroom and she immediately noted the contrast from her room.

His room held no warmth, no frilly curtains, no niceties to speak of, and his large four-poster bed—well it certainly could intimidate a lesser woman, made of stark dark wood and covered with vivid woven Indian blankets. Molly gulped and told herself she'd be all right. She told herself that she trusted Kane and knew him to be a man of honor. She plied herself with all good notions, hoping her impulsive fears weren't apparent on her face. "It's…it's nice, Kane."

Kane closed the door behind her, which didn't help her jittery nerves. She heard the door lock catch, and she whirled around. Kane leaned heavily on the door, his arms folded. "Nervous, Molly?"

"No!" she fibbed, lifting her chin with bravado.

"There's no need to be."

Molly nodded with her head lifting up and down like a silly girl bobbing for apples. "I know."

Kane's sigh went deep and his breath whooshed out slowly. He moved away from the door and Molly backed up several steps until her legs hit the edge of his bed. "Oh."

Kane stopped his approach and stood rigid, his lips quirking up slightly with just a hint of a smile. "Come here."

Molly had never been one to cower or give in to her fears. Her mama had always said she had more bluster than most men she'd known. But Molly wasn't feeling too daring now. Her heart raced wildly and her very breath stuck in her throat. Yet, she moved forward, meeting Kane's penetrating gaze. When she finally reached him, she managed a small smile.

Kane chuckled aloud and Molly's chest heaved with indignation.

Had he been silently laughing at her all this time? Did he not understand how awkward this was for her? Did he not realize that a young woman looked upon her wedding night with a full measure of uneasy anticipation and perplexed curiosity?

"Well?" she said, refraining from tapping her foot like a belabored schoolmarm.

"Turn around," he commanded.

Molly blinked twice and stared at him, confounded.

"Unless you want to sleep in your wedding gown?"

Kane lifted one dark brow and his silver-gray eyes held firm, the blessed amusement from a moment ago gone now.

Molly whirled around, the swooshing of her dress the only sound in the quiet, dimly lit room.

With her back to him now, she felt Kane come closer, crushing the lace of her gown against his thighs. Then he parted her hair, his fingers nimble and gentle on her neck as he moved the tresses aside. His soft touch created tingles way down to her toes.

"You remind me of a little bird I used to watch as a boy," he whispered. "The small creature had courage, coming right up to us, snatching corn and food scraps from right under our noses."

"Do I?" she asked, finding comfort in the notion. She didn't think Kane meant her injury, but rather paid her a small compliment. All too soon, the ease she experienced disappeared as a button was released, then another and another. Cool air struck her back, and the intimacy of Kane's actions finally dawned on her. Her husband was undressing her.

A tremble skittered through her body.

"Don't be frightened, Molly," Kane said as he finished unbuttoning her gown. His breath warmed her back, bared to him now. And when he touched her skin, his palms stroking her and parting the material, Molly's insides quaked with awareness. She was alert to everything now with vivid clarity, Kane's hands on her shoulders, his breath caressing her throat, his body pressed against hers. She felt every single sensation, apart from each other, singled out and so clear in her mind.

And all of her fear vanished. "I'm not frightened anymore, Kane."

"That's good. You'll find no reason to be."

Kane kissed her throat once, a soft sweet kiss that lingered on her skin. Gently, he turned her around and Molly had a dickens of a time, keeping the dress from falling down around her. With a hand, she held tight the material, keeping some semblance of dignity, though there was no hope for her shoulders. The dress had slipped down enough to expose her entire neckline and then some.

Kane's silver-gray gaze scorched her, taking a sweeping glance of her body, before looking into her eyes. And just when she thought she'd die from wanting his kiss, he took a step back, then another, leaving her there in the middle of the room, nearly unclothed and alone.

"I won't touch you tonight, Molly. Or any other night. You have nothing to fear from me."

Molly stood frozen, too stunned to speak. She repeated his words in her head, trying to fully comprehend.

"I'll leave you now, to change into whatever it is you wear at night."

"Kane?" Molly came out of her stupor long enough to pose a question, but then, words failed her. She couldn't ask, but perhaps her expression had spoken silently to him after all, because he answered her.

"It's for the best, Molly. You'll be pure when we part. You can sleep in peace."

On her wedding night, her husband reminded her of their eventual parting, the fact that they shared no future. The injustice of this whole arrangement struck like a slap to the face. Molly had entered into a false contract first with Bennett and now with Kane. And all she had truly wanted was a real marriage with someone she could hope to love. She wanted a family with her brother by her side. But Molly had been deceived and now, she, too, was a deceiver.

"And what of your peace, Kane?" Molly blurted, her mouth spurting out the exact sentiment she intended with no pretense.

Kane swept another glance over her body, the heat of his gaze enough to singe a block of ice. "I know something of sacrifice, Molly. You can't live as a Cheyenne and not. I will not break my vow."

Molly closed her eyes as anger surged forth. She gripped her bodice tight and headed for the door. "Then there's no call for me to share this room with you. I shall sleep in my own room."

She reached for the door just as Kane's hand came out to stop her. He held her wrist firmly, his face red with tightly controlled anger. "You will sleep in here, with me."

Molly struggled with his hold and only when he decided to let go, did she finally pull free.

"I don't want to."

Kane chuckled, a wry deprecating sound to Molly's ears. "I don't want to, either. We made a bargain, Molly. And that old man out there needs to believe that this marriage is real. We've gone too far to change our minds now. We will act as a married couple and that means sleeping in this room together."

Molly turned to glance at the bed.

"It's a big enough bed," he said. "And don't forget tomorrow we'll be sharing a wagon and days alone together. You might as well get used to it."

Molly put her head down. Quietly, she admitted, "I wanted a husband, a family."

"One day, you'll have the husband you deserve—and a family. But for now, we have our bargain."

Molly nodded, realizing that Kane was right. Maybe someday she would have all that she wanted. But her husband made it painfully clear, he would not be sharing those sentiments. For now, Molly would focus on finding her brother. The idea of being reunited with Charlie renewed her fledging faith. "Yes, we have our bargain," she agreed.

"Then, get to bed, Little Bird," Kane said, soothingly. "We have a big day ahead."

Kane woke before dawn, his eyes opening slowly as a songbird just outside the window chirped a morning greeting. But he was met with another greeting as well, one not so welcome as a melodic bird. No, this Little Bird had nestled up against him during the night, or perhaps he had been the one to seek her out in his sleep. Regardless, Kane found himself caught up in a tangle of sheets with Molly pressed to his side, her soft womanly curves and the sweet scent of female creating havoc with his body. His manhood erect, his body tight, Kane released himself from the sheets and moved aside.

He'd spoken to Molly of sacrifice last night, and his vow to leave her pure and untouched. He fully intended to keep that promise, but he also surmised that waking up next to her pliant, giving body each day would prove a true test to his willpower.

Molly was all woman, young and petite and perhaps naive of the world, but he couldn't deny her femininity. He would be a fool to deny the physical attributes the woman held or the pronounced effect her kisses had on him.

She gave with all she had, and Kane figured that would be the case in everything Molly did. He figured she would never allow only a fraction of herself, so when their lips met, he felt the generous giving she offered and knew instinctively the exact moment when Molly's innocent body would have been his for the taking.

"And what of your peace, Kane?" she had asked last night.

Kane now knew he would find little peace in her bed, waking and sleeping and nestling close with his new bride. Yet what choice did he have? To keep up the ruse of marriage, Kane had to act as a new groom, if only to keep one old man happy until he passed on.

Molly turned in her sleep to face him, a restful expression on her face. And even through her chaste white cotton nightgown, Kane found her womanly form enough to cause more havoc to his body. He ached to touch her and weigh the soft-firm breasts in his hands, to mold and caress them and kiss the tips until they grew pebble hard. The Cheyenne taught him that once a man touches a woman's breasts, he considered her to belong to him. It was not something a woman allowed without the benefit of marriage, for if she did, she would lose her reputation within the tribe.

Kane had already saved Molly's reputation. He'd married her but she would never belong to him. He'd known love once and for him, that was enough.

Molly made a little sound, a sigh of contentment as she sought warmth, wiggling her body closer. Kane backed away from Molly, so much so that he rolled right off the bed.

"Damn," he muttered, angry with himself as he thudded onto the floor. But his anger didn't stem from the clumsy move but rather from the fear he had of his new bride. As an adult, Kane had feared little. Gray Wolf had been a strong warrior and a man revered in the tribe even though he had white man's blood. Surely, one Little Bird could not cause him this much grief.

Kane rose from the floor and cast Molly one last

glance before donning his clothes and heading outside. He had to ready the wagon for their "honeymoon."

Soon they would begin their long journey.

Together.

Alone.

The thought brought him no measure of comfort.

Morning sun warmed Molly's cheeks, and she squinted slightly as she looked upon Bennett Jackson. Standing by the barn beside the wagon loaded down with supplies, she hugged the ailing man goodbye and kissed his cheek. "I hope to return soon and God willing, with my brother."

Even though he'd deceived her, she hadn't a harsh thought for him. Somehow, in just the time she'd known him, Bennett had wedged himself into her heart. Her Irish temper being what it was, Molly didn't quite understand her full acceptance of the man's deeds, except to say that after having a dealing or two with Kane herself, she could understand Bennett undertaking the deception. Her newly acquired groom had a strong will and a stubborn streak. In that, she didn't believe the blood kin differed much. Bennett simply had had more experience in being sly. He was a man who got what he wanted in life.

But it was knowing the ill man now, seeing the light go out of his eyes at times, noting how his skin paled and his body grew weak that caused Molly a moment of hesitation.

What if Bennett needed Kane in the weeks to come? What if his health took a rapid decline? Molly bit down on her lip and fretted.

Bennett glanced at her with a frown. "Molly, did my

grandson do something to upset you again? Did you have a bad night of it?"

Bennett shot a quick look at Kane, who, at the moment, was hitching the horses to the wagon.

Molly gasped, her hand covering her mouth. "Oh, no. Nothing like that, Bennett...I mean, Grandfather." Burning heat rushed to her face. "I mean to say, I wasn't thinking of Kane at all."

Bennett shot Kane another glance, narrowing his eyes this time. Kane continued his task, paying his grandfather no mind. "A new bride doesn't have a thought for her groom? What should I make of that?"

Perhaps Molly would have had Kane in her thoughts this morning, if she'd had a true wedding night. But she couldn't admit to Kane's grandfather that she was untouched and as pure as the day she'd been born. But she could tell Bennett another truth. "I'm worried about you," Molly admitted. "You look pale today and fatigued."

Bennett patted Molly's hand. "I'll be just fine, Molly, dear. You just concentrate on your husband from now on. No need to worry over me."

Kane came around to stand beside her. "We'll be back in a few weeks' time. Toby will oversee the ranch while I'm gone. I trust you'll keep out of trouble, while we're away?" Kane asked pointedly.

"Me?" Bennett appeared surprised. "You have a very colorful imagination, boy."

Kane removed his hat and scratched his head, right behind the ear. "Do I? I guess it wasn't you who sent out letters on my behalf? It wasn't you who contracted me a wife? It wasn't you who—"

"Kane," Molly interjected, placing her hand on his

arm, stopping his quiet tirade. Bennett wasn't up to doing battle today.

Kane glanced down at Molly's hand as anger lit his eyes.

Molly smiled up at him, hoping to ease some of his frustration. "It's done."

Bennett grinned then and suddenly he appeared twenty years younger and healthy again. "She's right, boy. What's done is done. Now, you both have a safe trip and don't go worrying after me. I'll be here when you get back."

Kane stared at his grandfather, but slowly those hard steely eyes softened, and he nodded. "You make sure that you are."

There was no denying the love and admiration Kane had for his grandfather even though there was no overt display.

"And Molly, I'll send someone to post wires with your brother's name and description, just like I promised," Bennett said. "I should have news when you get back home."

"Thank you."

Molly took one last long look at Bennett before Kane helped her up onto the wagon bench. She smiled and waved, just as Lupe had come outside to stand beside Bennett.

"*Vaya con Dios,*" Lupe called out.

"I'll see you soon," she said, waving as the wagon lurched forward, making its way out of the gate and off Jackson property.

Kane tossed a straw hat her way. "Better put that on. We'll be on the road most of the day."

Molly glanced at the weather-beaten hat and smiled, yanking it on her head and tying the string under her chin. Kane, too, wore a hat, the leather nearly matching the color of his buckskin pants. He appeared part Cheyenne and part rancher, and Molly realized that perhaps the man she married belonged in two worlds, yet really didn't quite belong to either. "Where's our first stop?"

Kane slid her a sideways glance. She could barely see his eyes from underneath the hat he wore so low on his forehead. "Somewhere between here and Odessa. One thing you'll find, Texas is bigger than you imagined. Most towns are spread out, separated by ranches or nothing but cactus and dust. We won't make a town today."

"We won't?" Disappointment settled quickly and Molly fought the urge to cry. She'd been so eager to make her inquiries about Charlie, that she hadn't given thought to the route that they would take. She'd left that up to Kane.

"No, but tomorrow we'll hit two or three towns. I plan to make a complete circle around the Bar J. When we return we should have a pretty good idea about your brother. Unless we get lucky and find him straight away."

Molly couldn't help but smile. "I hope we get lucky, Kane."

He shook his head. "Then you married the wrong man. My luck ran out years ago."

Molly sighed silently, not believing Kane for one minute. Whether he knew it or not, Kane had been lucky. An unscrupulous sheriff had almost unjustly hanged him but as *luck* would have it, Bennett had rescued him in time. He'd brought Kane back to his childhood home, shown him love and offered him a legacy that many would envy.

Molly settled her backside onto the seat and decided to make the best of today's journey. Glancing at Kane's stony face, she knew she'd not have much conversation today, so she decided to take in the scenery and lose herself in her own thoughts.

This was just the first of many days to come on the road. With trepidation she surmised that west Texas was as big as it was unsettled. She'd never seen so much flat land in her life. She only hoped that somewhere out there, in a distant town or settlement, she'd find her brother. It was that hope, sent up by way of prayer to the Almighty, that had brought Molly west. She wouldn't think what she would do if Charlie was not to be found.

So she closed her eyes against the vile Texas sun and prayed once again.

Molly stretched, pulling her arms up high, her head falling back and her hair flowing in soft waves down past her shoulders. As she stood by the firelight with dusk settling on the horizon, Kane witnessed a smile of relief cross her features. He figured she'd be sore from a day of travel in the wagon, but if she ached terribly, she hadn't yet complained.

Kane admired her gumption—she was a determined woman who knew something of suffering in her young life. But as she stood before him stretching and sighing, all he could see was the soft feminine woman he married, the small fire-haired woman who had come into his life like a wild wind. Watching her twist and sway reminded him of a young bay mare just coming into her own, fully unaware of her graceful innocent beauty.

Kane glanced at the two blankets he'd laid out, wishing he'd set them farther apart. "Lupe sent along a meal for tonight. Fried chicken and biscuits. And something sweet, too."

Molly's green eyes rounded with delight. She rubbed her stomach and smiled. "I'm just about famished."

"Sit down on the blanket. You'll be filling your belly soon enough."

Molly walked over to him. "Let me help."

Kane shook his head. "Not tonight. If you're not sore now, you will be tomorrow. Get some rest, Molly."

"But shouldn't a wife do the cooking?"

"A wife should obey her husband." Kane said the words without thought, and then realized he'd said those words a hundred times before to his first wife, his *real* wife, Little Swan. She'd been as spirited as Molly and he'd had to remind her over and over that her main duty as a wife was to listen to her husband.

Kane's gut clenched at the reminder, seeing Little Swan in his mind, bending over him, her body brushing his, her dark oval eyes gleaming as they lay by the fire in their tipi. "I will obey my husband tonight," she'd say with a coy smile and Kane's heart would soar. He would gaze at his wife with love and devotion and promise to protect her with his own life.

But Kane had failed her. He hadn't protected her.

And she'd died as a result.

He would never forget, or forgive himself.

"Is that the Cheyenne way?" Molly asked quietly.

"It's the way it must be," he said harshly. "You will obey me, Molly. Or I'll turn the wagon around and head home right now. There are dangers on the road and dangers in the towns and you must listen to me at all times. I need your promise."

Molly stared at him and for one moment, Kane thought that he had rendered her speechless. Her eyes searched his and finally she nodded. "I promise."

He nodded back.

His heart had grown hard and cold over the years. He had no room for Molly and her young innocent ways. Yes, he would protect her with his life, for Kane couldn't have another woman's death on his conscience, but he would not open his heart to her. That part of him had been closed off forever.

He watched as Molly sank down on her blanket. Kane set about heating the meal Lupe had prepared. Tonight they would eat and turn in early.

And Kane prayed he would not relive the nightmare of finding Little Swan's body in his dreams tonight.

Molly tossed her fourth chicken bone on her plate, licking the grease off her fingers. She'd never eaten better chicken. "Lupe sure knows how to fix up a good meal. What did she put on this chicken, anyway?"

Kane shrugged, sitting on the blanket beside her, finishing off his meal. "Don't know exactly. But I'd guess she's got some jalapenos ground in, somewhere. Those chile peppers will cure what ails you."

Molly groaned as a quick jolt buckled in her stomach. "Oh," she said, too embarrassed to admit she'd eaten far too much of the spicy food. Her stomach grumbled and she squirmed on her blanket, clutching the edges with both hands.

Kane grinned, a rare gesture, one that exposed his perfect mouth and strong teeth. "Lupe's food will do that to you." He reached over to pick up her plate. "Give it a minute for your belly to figure it all out."

Molly managed a sickly smile. "Coffee might help."

Kane nodded. "It's heating up."

Molly lied down on the blanket, holding her stomach, mortified that she'd eaten so heartily in front of her husband. What must he think of her? "I never eat like that."

Kane swept a leisurely glance over her body. "I wouldn't think so, Little Bird."

Molly saw no mockery on his face, heard no ridicule in his tone. She assumed he meant if she had taken to eating like that every day, she'd be the size of the Bar J by now. At least his fierce temperament from earlier today, when he'd asked for her promise to obey him, had simmered some. She had so many questions for him, and she'd spent the best part of the day in silence. She didn't think she could possibly remain quiet the rest of the evening.

"Kane?"

"Mmmm?"

"After your grandfather found you and brought you home, what did he tell you of your mother and father."

Kane turned away for a moment, keeping busy with the coffeepot. She watched him pour the hot liquid into two tin mugs. He reached over to hand one to her then sat down on the blanket facing her.

Molly sat up to receive the mug. "Thank you."

Kane sipped his coffee.

Molly sipped hers. The heat and rich flavor helped

ease the grumblings in her stomach as she waited patiently for his answer.

"My father was asked to meet with the kidnappers outside of town, at an old feed shack miles away with a valise full of money. He never returned home and no one really knew what happened to him. They searched for days, but he was never found. My mother pined away for my father for years, hoping that he would return with her son. And after a time, she took ill. Grandfather thinks he was right in never telling her that months after my father left to meet with the kidnappers, his body was found, murdered. He didn't think she could take both losses in her frail state—the loss of her only child and the loss of her husband. Grandfather tends to take matters into his own hands. To the world, it's still a mystery, but Bennett and I know the truth. For years my grandfather sheltered my mother, hoping that one day he would find me and bring some joy back into her life. But my mother had given up on me and had given in to her frailty."

"Seems to me, your mother might have been better off if she'd been told the truth. I think I'd want to know the truth."

"Grandfather does what he sees fit. At the time, he did what he thought best. He protected my mother from the truth."

Molly thought on that for a time, but she didn't agree with what Bennett had done. Kane's mother had had a right to know that her husband hadn't run off with the money as was rumored. She had a right to know that her husband's body had been found, but that her son's hadn't. She might have held on to the hope that somewhere out there her little boy, her son Kane, was still alive. "Sometimes the truth is less painful than the not knowing."

Kane sipped from his cup, eyeing her over the rim of his mug. "I guess one could argue that with my grandfather. But there's no point now. What's done is done."

Molly began, "If Charlie is…I mean to say if we don't find him and later on…oh, dear, I can't even think it, much less speak the words." Molly's heart clenched, her nerves raw with pain. She couldn't think of anything bad happening to Charlie. He was all she had left and she loved him dearly.

"You have my word. I'll tell you the truth."

"Thank you," she managed, her voice tight. She believed him. For all of Kane's unpredictable and mulish ways, Molly held firm that she married an honorable man. He would not lie to her. "But I can't think about that. Charlie's alive, having himself a grand old time somewhere and when I get a hold of him, he's gonna get a big piece of my mind, for worrying me so."

"He's a man now, Molly. He doesn't answer to you."

"He's *family,* Kane. A young boy who doesn't even know that his mama is gone."

Molly finished her coffee then stood abruptly, nearly losing her balance from the stiffness in her legs. "I need to…I need to have some privacy."

Kane glanced around the deserted area surrounding the camp he'd set up. Night had fallen, only the stars above shedding a hint of light outside the fire circle he'd built. He set down his coffee mug and stood. "I'll take you…for your privacy."

Molly shook her head, as her eyes grew wide with

Kane's comment. "I need privacy…from you," she said, more than slightly dismayed.

Kane's face took on a stubborn set, his jaw tightening. "No, you'll not walk away from camp without me."

Molly fumed, her dignity at stake. She didn't understand Kane's behavior. Surely, she couldn't be in any danger, out in the middle of nowhere, with the stars overhead to guide her steps.

"Fine." She began walking quickly away, anger simmering on the edge. She didn't know how on earth she managed to marry such an obstinate mule of a man. And to make matters worse, her body ached as though she'd rolled down a steep cliff. Goodness, every muscle seemed unhappy, crying out with tender pain. But she marched on determined to keep her pride intact.

"Oh!" Her boot tangled with something and she lost her balance. She tumbled head first, her legs too weak to keep her upright. Molly fell right smack onto the unforgiving ground, her cheek grazing something sharp. She rolled to the side and glanced at the large broken wagon wheel she'd tripped on, as warm blood began to seep from her face. She reached up to touch her cheek. Sticky crimson liquid oozed through her fingers, rolling down onto her chin. The potent, pungent smell of her own blood frightened her.

In an instant, Kane was by her side, lifting her up, his touch as gentle as a summer breeze. He held her in his arms carefully, studying her face, then began to carry her back to camp. "I'm bleeding all over you," she said lamely.

"You cut your cheek, but it's just a scrape. You were lucky, Molly McGuire. You might have lost more than a slice of skin off your pretty face."

The thought did not soothe her. She realized he was right. She'd fallen face first onto a splintered wagon wheel, and the gash could very well have taken half her face. She shuddered and Kane brought her closer into his arms, as if he had understood her fear. "It's Molly Jackson," she said softly.

Kane's gaze shifted down to meet her eyes and Molly caught a glimmer of the man beneath the hard exterior. For one instance, she witnessed concern and sympathy and perhaps even compassion in those silver-gray eyes.

"For now."

The moment was lost. Kane had once again reminded her of their temporary marriage. In her heart, she knew he thought her less a wife and more a burden. She would always be *Molly McGuire* to him.

When they reached their camp, Kane set Molly down on the blanket, then walked over to the wagon to retrieve some items. When he returned, he knelt down next to her.

"Does it look terrible?" Molly asked, suddenly fearful that maybe she had done permanent damage to her face.

"It'll heal just fine. But you hit your cheek hard. I expect tomorrow you'll have a dark bruise."

He took out a clean bandana, one she'd worn once already around her ripped skirt the day she'd met him, moistened it with water from his canteen, then cautioned her. "Hold still, this might sting."

Molly braced herself, but Kane's touch was gentle as he cleaned up her bloodied face. He dabbed at her cut, the slash as long as her little finger, she calculated. "You have a soft touch, Kane."

His eyes met with hers again and lingered a moment. Molly's breath caught in her throat having Kane so near.

She noticed the breadth and length of his dark lashes, the vivid silvery hue of his eyes and the deep, dark intensity of his gaze.

And once again, Molly braced herself, but not from the sting of her injury. This time she braced herself against the rapid thudding of her heart, the heat that burned through her body and the warm feelings she was developing for her husband. She'd never had these feelings before, couldn't quite name them. But she knew by sheer womanly instinct, that she'd be more than a fool to succumb to those feelings.

Kane reached for a pouch he'd brought over from the wagon and opened the leather thong. "It's Cheyenne medicine, Molly. It'll help you heal."

Molly didn't flinch when Kane applied the salve to her cut, not even when she took a good strong whiff of the medicine. "What's in it?" she asked.

"Roots, herbs, sumac and…"

When Kane hesitated, Molly's curiosity peaked. "And?"

"It's best you don't know."

"I want to know."

"That's because you're a curious little bird. But you have to sleep with the salve on your face. Are you sure you want to know?"

She nodded.

"Animal scrapings, bear grease and—"

"Thank you," Molly interrupted, deciding she really didn't want to know. "Smells like a pack of wild dogs." Then Molly's eyes widened and she lifted her brows in question.

Kane shook his head.

Relieved, Molly figured she could live with the foul-smelling salve for one night. Besides, it wasn't as though she were on a real honeymoon with a man who might want to kiss her or anything.

"Still in need of…?" Kane asked.

Molly nodded.

Kane stood and offered her his hand.

Without hesitating, Molly accepted his hand and together they walked off, away from the firelight, into the darkness.

Chapter Seven

Molly touched a hand to her cheek, noting how much better her face felt this morning. The salve Kane had administered seemed to have worked wonders. She didn't know if she had developed a dark bruise as he had suggested last night, since they'd woken early and taken to the road nearly before sunup, Molly not having time to dig out her mirror from her valise in the wagon to take a look.

But after a good night's rest, she couldn't complain about Kane's hasty departure, she'd been just as eager to leave the camp behind, in favor of embarking on her search for Charlie.

The wagon moved forward at a comfortable pace, Molly adjusting to the bumps and jiggles that occurred on the rutted road as they made their approach to Camp Stockton. They'd already reached and searched the tiny town of Hermit's Edge, with Kane making inquires to the proprietor of the mercantile. Aside from a few shops, a blacksmith and the smallest saloon Molly had ever seen—a shack really, with a three-foot bar and no tables—there wasn't much else in town. They'd moved on rapidly, Kane warning her not to become discouraged—there were more than a few towns along the way just like that one.

Morning sun grew hot as the hours passed, but she endured the heat with a sense of resignation, gaining a better understanding of this rugged land now. She was becoming accustomed to sweat leaking from her brow, to her dress sticking to her body like morning dew on tall grass and to squinting eyes lowering into thin slits against the powerful light.

Molly endured it all for the sake of finding her brother.

As the sun arched directly overhead, the flat, dry desert land they traveled changed color before Molly's eyes, the earth richer now with trees and shrubs that added soft vibrant hues to the surroundings. From her perch atop the wagon, Molly viewed an overly large spring, the cool waters from the glistening pool beckoning her.

She turned to Kane, tugging on the fringe of his buckskin. "Can we stop, just for a little while?"

Kane glanced ahead. "We're less than a mile outside of Camp Stockton."

"I know, but I'd rather not ride into town feeling like a slimy old prairie dog." She plucked her dress from her sticky body at the shoulders, proving her point.

Kane shot a quick glance at the spring then gazed at Molly's expectant face. She mustered her best smile. "Please."

He closed his eyes and sighed. "I'll water the horses while we're there."

Molly jumped for joy, nearly bouncing out of her seat on the wagon, then hugged Kane around the neck. "Thank you!"

Kane backed away from her embrace, but Molly was too happy at the moment to allow his rebuff to bother her.

They were beside the spring instantly, Kane bounding from the wagon and coming around to help her down. Molly placed her hands on his shoulders as he clasped her waist and eased her to the ground. Molly's arms crept up around his neck and she had a good mind to kiss him. She'd been wanting to ever since last night when he'd picked her up from that clumsy fall and carried her back to their camp. She'd been reckless and foolish, but Kane hadn't admonished her as she'd expected. Instead, he'd taken care with her, cleaning her wound and administering the salve that really seemed to have helped heal the painful gash on her face.

Yes, Molly had wanted to kiss him last night. And she had a dickens of a time keeping from kissing him when she woke this morning. During the night she'd awoken briefly to find Kane right beside her, his body wedged against hers, one hand resting lightly on her shoulder while the other latched onto his rifle.

She'd shuddered at first, seeing the deadly weapon in his hand, but then she realized he'd kept her close in order to protect her.

She gazed into his eyes, longing to feel his lips on hers once again, longing to feel his body pressed to hers, longing for so many things Kane was incapable of giving. Her fingers slightly brushed a soft curl at the back of his neck, before she stepped away. She began to unfasten the very top button of her dress. "I'll need my privacy."

Kane drew in a deep breath and his face set with stony determination. Molly was beginning to learn that particular expression far too well. "Molly, I'm not leaving you alone out here."

"Can't you water the horses later, or all the way at the other end of the spring?"

"No."

"Kane, you can't watch me bathe. You simply can't."

"Better me than a troop of soldiers, Molly. We're close to the camp. No telling how many soldiers might be wandering these parts, keeping a lookout."

Molly made a sweeping glance around. She didn't see anyone. But Kane had a point. The very last thing she wanted was to have strangers watching her bathe. At least Kane was her husband. Yet, the thought of him watching her undress and cleanse herself unnerved her. Propriety told her to step back up into the wagon and be done with this, but layers of dust and sweat on her body from hours on the trail won out.

"Okay, but step far away. You can do that, can't you?"

Kane led the horses up to the bank of the spring to let them have a cool drink, then strode over to a large rock about twenty feet from the water and sat down. "I'll be right here."

Molly groaned. Kane may have an earnest desire to protect her, but deep inside Molly felt that he was enjoying his role as protector far too much. "Turn your back for a minute, please."

To her amazement, he did.

Molly quickly unfastened the rest of the buttons on her gown and stepped out of it. Next came the petticoats. She removed all three and laid them out by her gown on a shrub. Keeping her chemise and bloomers on, she bent to remove her boots and stockings.

She wiggled her toes and smiled at the newfound freedom. Within seconds Molly entered the water, slowly and with caution. She maintained a good footing and braved another few steps until she was waist high in water. She splashed water on her arms and shoulders and delighted at the spring's temperature, not too warm, not too cold. Molly could spend the rest of the day frolicking here, but she was all too aware that Kane wouldn't abide a long respite. Though he didn't speak of it, Molly knew his impatience stemmed from thoughts of his ailing grandfather. The sooner they made the journey he'd planned, the sooner they could return back to the Bar J.

Molly fully understood Kane's reluctance to waste time, so she dipped her hair into the water quickly, wishing she'd had the benefit of a bar of soap, and scrubbed clean the tresses the best she could. Next she lifted her chemise waist high to wash her legs, running her hands up and down scouring each limb, and as she turned her body to face the bank of the spring, she froze, unable to move, as Kane's gaze met hers from the edge of the water.

His buckskin shirt tossed next to her clothing, he stood by the horses, with beads of water glistening on his chest. Bronzed and powerful, standing tall with an unabashed glint in his eyes, he watched her.

Oh, how Molly wished she were his wife in the real sense. How she wished she hadn't made this unholy bargain with Kane Jackson. How she wished this mad attraction she felt for her husband would either die in her heart or come to a more satisfying end.

Always hopeful, and bolder than she'd ever been before, Molly moved through the water, her gaze fastened only to his. Kane's face bore no expression, but his gaze roamed over her body possessively with unguarded appreciation. For one instant, she felt like a wife in the true sense. For one second, Molly knew what it was like to have Kane's full attention, to make him see her as a woman with a heart and soul, a woman who would devote her life to him.

For that one unshielded second, Kane showed Molly all the possibilities. And as she came closer to the bank, water dripping from her body, wearing her cotton chemise like a second skin, she witnessed Kane's full intake of breath.

She came out of the water to stand directly before him. Never releasing his gaze, she lifted her chin. "You promised to turn around."

Kane lost all semblance of rational thought. Molly stood before him, unclothed but for the thin wet material covering her body, yet she knew no shame, no hesitation. She stood so close that the fresh scent of spring water teased his senses, and her womanly form, easily seen through the gossamer chemise, did something more than tease him.

Desire shot through straight through him. He longed to take Molly into his arms and press her against him, to kiss her wet lips dry and stroke her body expertly until she bent to his will. Kane cursed himself for each thought, but couldn't deny them, couldn't quite control the longing he felt or the pain wanting her created both in his body and mind.

He explained quietly, "I did…for about a minute."

Molly's eyes went dewy soft. She placed her hand on his bare chest. "Kane."

Her delicate touch scorched him and Kane felt the heat of his betrayal to Little Swan with powerful force. He had already loved and lost one woman. He could not take Molly McGuire, not in the way he'd envisioned in his head already a hundred times. He would not make a true commitment to her. He had no right to touch her. No matter what she offered by way of standing there with askance in her eyes and a body that beckoned him with even the slightest movement. Kane meant to back away, but she stunned him with her next words.

"Kiss me."

A thousand reasons why he should deny her raced through his head, yet Kane's willpower waned and he wondered if he had strength enough to refuse his wife her one request. He thought back upon the will he'd displayed during the O-kee-pa, a rite of passage for young tribal members as they displayed greats feats of courage, hanging by their skewered flesh. Kane had lasted long, had endured the torturous ritual and had earned the respect of the entire tribe. The events of his childhood had made him tough, hard and unyielding, yet this one fiery-haired woman, with green sparks in her eyes, met him head-on and the battle, he feared, was just beginning.

"No."

Molly didn't seem surprised at his half-hearted refusal. Instead she moved her hand on his chest, her fingertips outlining a slow torturous pattern. "You want to."

A guttural chuckle emerged, surfacing to sound more like an animal's growl. "Don't tempt me, Molly."

"What harm can one kiss do? I'm your wife."

On a quick nod, he agreed. "Temporarily."

But Molly seemed too prideful to back down. She dug her heels in and stood firm. Kane witnessed her determination and actually admired her for it. "I'll ask you only this once. One kiss. And I'll never ask again."

Kane stood silent, contemplating, and only the mare's soft whinny broke the incredible quiet.

Molly's eyes watered and she spun around quickly, ready to make a hasty retreat from his rebuff. He witnessed the injury he'd caused, the rejection that Molly couldn't bare to face, and before Kane thought another moment, he reached out, grabbing her waist and pulling her fully around so their eyes met. "This isn't a good idea."

Then he crushed his mouth to hers.

Molly's whimper of delight tore into his senses, nearly destroying his good intentions. He meant to kiss her once and be done with it, but the taste of her lips was a sweet elixir that demanded he drink more. He drank heartily, consuming his mind and body with the softness of her mouth, her heady fresh scent and her willing touch.

"Kane," she murmured softly, and he took that opportunity to mate his tongue with hers, exploring her mouth and teaching her more than he should about lust and desire. He lowered her down to the lush grass just beyond the bank of the spring and stroked her body with greedy hands.

His manhood pressed the confines of his buckskin pants and he thanked all that was holy for the restriction of tight leather and firm resolve. He would not take Molly.

But kissing her like this was a pleasure he neither expected nor deserved. She'd been an obligation, brought upon by his grandfather. She'd been like a thorn prickling his finger, something he had to endure until he could pluck it free. Kane wanted nothing from Molly but to complete the bargain they'd made. At least that's what he had told himself. He abhorred his weakness in giving in to Molly's plea, but he couldn't deny that kissing her brought him immense pleasure and touching her nearly bare body destroyed all his good sense.

Yet, he brought Molly pleasure as well, if her little throaty moans were any true testimony. She responded to his every caress with little movements that drove Kane's sanity to the edge. He kissed her lips, while running his hand over her legs, as he yearned to touch more of her.

But his mind screamed that he could not touch Molly in her womanly places. Fondling her breasts meant that she belonged to him. The Cheyenne way had been deeply rooted in him since early childhood, but Kane found confusion there, whereas Molly was his wife, and a man had rights in that regard.

The need was great. He ached to caress her breasts, to mold the ripe globes with his hands and kiss the tips until they pebbled with desire. He ached to make her body as lusty as his own, to bring her the pleasure she sought with each little moan and undulation of her body.

A sound alerted him and he sat straight up, listening. And far in the distance he saw something that had him rising and lifting Molly to her feet as well. "Soldiers."

* * *

Camp Stockton was a welcome sight to Molly's eyes as they rode past rows of limestone and adobe buildings. The hustle and bustle of everyday life reminded her of St. Louis and the home she'd left behind, though this town appeared much more orderly in the chaos. Molly smiled at the silly notion, glancing at Kane's somber expression, his eyes wary, his sharp gaze focused. He reined the horses to a halt at the request of one of the dozen soldiers whom had escorted their wagon to the center of the camp.

Still reeling from her encounter with Kane by the spring, Molly wet her lips, seeking moisture and a way to repair the damage done by his lusty assault. She'd barely had time enough to dress properly and tidy up her hair, before the bluecoats showed up, Kane shoving clothes her way and hiding her from curious scouts who had spied their wagon by the spring.

Kane had kissed and caressed her until her body shook violently, yet he hadn't touched her in those secret places she'd craved to be touched. He'd held on to his resolve, and Molly would always wonder what might have occurred had the soldiers not arrived at that moment, ready to guide the wagon to their camp. She'd always wonder if Kane would have succumbed to the desire she witnessed in his eyes, on his face and in the power of his kiss.

"Welcome to Camp Stockton. I'm Captain Campbell."

A tall, well-groomed man strode toward the wagon, dressed in full uniform. He put out his hand to Kane.

Kane ignored the man's gesture of welcome. Stunned, Molly sat atop the wagon in disbelief. Many a man might have taken grave insult, but the captain only pursed his lips and eyed Kane with keen interest. "Your grandfather wired me of your arrival."

Kane turned to stare into the man's eyes. "You know my grandfather?"

"If he's Bennett Jackson, yes and no. He has wired our camp every year since your abduction, searching for his kidnapped grandson and hoping to hear news of you. I never laid eyes on the man before, but he holds my respect."

Kane drew oxygen into his lungs and nodded. "Then you know we came in search of another."

Molly smiled at Captain Campbell, hoping to make up for Kane's lack of grace. "Hello, Captain. I'm Molly Jackson. My husband and I are looking for my brother, Charlie." She reached into her reticule and produced the tintype of her brother, handing the small image to the soldier. "He's four years older now. Goes by the name of Charles McGuire."

"Handsome boy," the captain said, squinting at the image. "But I can't say that I recognize him. Of course, we have two hundred soldiers at the camp and I don't know all their faces."

"Would it be all right if we asked around? My brother is from St. Louis. I think he'd be easy to remember."

"A greenhorn?"

Molly smiled. "I suppose one could call him that. He left home months ago and, well, if it wouldn't be too much of an imposition, I'd like to speak with some of your soldiers and maybe others in camp."

Captain Campbell glanced at Kane. "That'd be all right, as long as you have an escort. Some of my men haven't seen a lady in more time than they'd like to recall. You'll be escorting your wife, I presume?"

Kane nodded and stared straight at Molly. "I won't let her out of my sight."

"Fine, then. And might I ask you both to supper tonight? It would be my pleasure to have you sit at my table." He smiled at Molly with warmth and she felt a genuine fondness for the courteous man.

"Thank you," Molly said instantly, but Kane's forceful voice overrode her usual quiet tone.

"No thanks. We'll be moving on as soon as we're through searching the camp."

The captain hid his disappointment well, and he nodded. "Then, feel free to ask of your brother. I wish you luck in locating him."

"Thank you, Captain."

"And Mr. Jackson?"

Kane looked in the captain's direction.

"Your grandfather said you were raised by the Cheyenne. Keep in mind that there are a number of us who would like to see a peaceful solution to our problems with the Indian nation."

Kane spoke harshly, his face no longer expressionless, but filled with disdain. "Treaties were broken, land was stolen, lies were told, Captain."

The captain retaliated with quiet calm. "Homes have been pillaged, wagon trains raided, many have died at the hands of the very people who saved your life. Perhaps both people are to blame."

Kane shook his head. "The Cheyenne don't see it that way."

Captain Campbell sighed resignedly. "Speak with

my men. You'll find them decent folk, here to protect
the settlers and the Butterfield Overland mail wagons.
We've all seen too much of war, Mr. Jackson."

"Kane," Molly interrupted, before the two men lost
their civility. She better understood why Kane had been
so pensive as they approached the camp. To Molly, the
soldiers represented safety and the camp, a sanctuary.
But to a man who'd been raised by Indians, soldiers
meant something entirely different. There wasn't time
to sort it all out now. They'd come here for a specific
purpose. She pleaded, "I'm really anxious to make my
inquiries."

"Of course," the captain said. "You can hitch your
wagon at the livery."

"Thank you, Captain," Molly said.

He tipped his hat. "Good day."

Kane picked up the reins, and whistled softly. The
wagon lurched forward, startling Molly. She hung on to
the wagon seat as they made their way through the camp.

When they reached the livery Kane jumped from the
wagon and came around to help her down, but she released herself from his hold as soon as her feet hit the
ground. "You were rude to the captain."

"He knows nothing of Indians."

"Maybe not. He hasn't had the benefit of living among
them like you had. But he seemed a fair man, Kane."

Kane grunted, his face hard. "None of the treaties
were fair, Molly. None of the people got what they'd
been promised. I lived with a small tribe who had to flee
from their land, over and over again. We were not free.
We had no rights. And *fair* men, like the captain, were
easily fooled as well. Nothing can make up for the loss,

Molly. Now, let's get going. We're leaving here in two hours, so ask your questions and do *not* leave my side."

Molly bit her lip, angry with Kane for his abrupt behavior. She had a good mind to walk off in the opposite direction, but she didn't have time to waste. Her obstinate husband had given her two hours and she needed every last minute of it.

"No one has seen Charlie," Molly said with disappointment. She'd spoken with everyone she could find on the street and in the shops. She'd even barged into several barracks, approaching the men with a warm greeting much to Kane's disapproval. But he'd stood by her side, cautioning the soldiers with dark, narrowed eyes, warning them not to come too close. Molly wondered if he'd been protective of her, or simply displaying contempt for them. Either way, her efforts had not been successful. "Not one man in the entire camp recognized his photograph."

"It's a big territory, Molly. The chance of you finding someone straight away that's seen or knows your brother isn't likely. It's our first day of searching," Kane said as he helped her up on the wagon, "and we still have another town to reach before sundown. Are you ready?"

Molly nodded. She wouldn't give in to her disappointment. Kane was right. They had miles and miles of territory to search, so she bolstered her hopes as they made their way out of Camp Stockton.

Hours later, they reached the town of Whiskey Flats near the Pecos River as dusk settled on the horizon. After unhitching the horses and renting a stall at the livery, Kane checked them into the Blue River Hotel. The second floor room was small and cramped, but clean. Cheery flowered wallpaper and bright curtains over a window that overlooked the main street in town held certain appeal. Molly figured the room would suffice for the night. As she gazed out the window, enjoying the cool early-evening breeze, she noted the banners and ribbons she'd seen earlier today when they'd made their way into town, claiming Whiskey Flats Founder's Day Celebration.

The festivities were slated for tomorrow.

That was a good thing. Most of the townsfolk, as well as local ranchers, usually attended these celebrations. Molly would have the entire town come to her, so to speak. She'd make good use of her time here.

Kane set her valise down by the one small bed they'd be sharing. "Let's have our meal, before the diner closes."

Molly's stomach grumbled, agreeing with Kane wholeheartedly. She'd never been one to require much food, not that there ever was an abundance or leftovers when she lived in St. Louis, for that matter. Her days on the road, out in the wide-open Texas spaces, spiked her appetite and she found herself hungry more times than not during the day. "That's a good idea," she stated plainly.

Kane chuckled. "At least you agree with me about something."

Molly gasped at his remark until she realized he'd been teasing. His mood from earlier today while at Camp Stockton seemed to have lightened. He might even prove a pleasant dinner companion tonight.

"You'll find that I agree with you about *most* things."

Kane shook his head. "Woman, from the day I set eyes on you, you and I have been on opposite sides of the barnyard, and that doesn't seem likely to change."

Molly raised her chin, ready to disagree, but Kane had removed his buckskin shirt, whipping it off in one efficient movement, then reaching down into his saddlebag for another, more civilized-looking garment.

She'd never get over the sight of him, unclothed, his bare well-muscled chest bronzed from days in the sun. The length and breadth of him, and the way he undressed so indifferently in front of her, stole all her breath. Molly watched the muscles play over his chest as he worked the other shirt on, lifting it over his head and finding a place over his torso.

The room was small. Kane was close. And Molly couldn't quite banish the sense of intimacy she felt, being with Kane, here in their cramped hotel room, watching him dress before her.

He was a complicated man, one she didn't quite fully understand, yet he was her husband and a man she had come to admire.

When she wasn't disagreeing with him.

"Ready to fill our bellies?" Kane turned toward the door.

Molly grinned. "How delicately put."

And they walked down the stairs together, hand in hand, just like a real married couple.

The Blue River Diner served up the best food Molly had ever eaten, including savory chicken and dumplings, vegetables in a buttery sauce and warm pecan pie. She feasted heartily at a square table decorated with a cornflower blue gingham tablecloth and a glass Mason jar filled with wildflowers. Molly had already asked around before taking her seat, showing the one picture she had of her brother to the other patrons in the crowded restaurant, but so far no one had recognized him.

She finished sipping steamy coffee from a dainty cup before gazing up at Kane. He stared at her, his eyes focused as if settling something in his mind. "I have to leave you tonight and I need the tintype of Charlie."

Surprised, Molly clutched the image of her brother. That tintype was never far from her reach. "Why?"

"My grandfather knows someone who's good with reproducing images. He's an artist, of sorts, but not the kind of man a lady ought to meet. I'm commissioning him to draw up sketches of Charlie, to help in the search."

Molly's heart skipped with excitement, thinking of all the possibilities. "That's wonderful. We can distribute them around tomorrow, but why can't I meet him?"

Kane sipped the last of his coffee, his hands appearing overly large holding the delicate rose-painted cup. "I just told you that he's not the sort of man you'd want to meet."

Molly lowered her voice. "Is he an outlaw?"

Kane shook his head. "No. Not exactly."

"Then, there's no reason why I can't join you," Molly said with a nod of her head. She hated the thought of relinquishing the tintype to Kane or anyone, for that matter. It was all she had left of her brother.

Kane sighed as if expecting this argument. Molly couldn't help being curious. So far, she and Kane had been in this together, and now he was to ride off into the night, without her. "Molly, I need your trust."

"I do…trust you," she said, biting her lip.

Kane raised an eyebrow.

"It's just that we're supposed to be doing this together."

"Some things a man's got to do alone."

"Why?" she asked, more suspicious now than curious by Kane's behavior. "Where are you going?"

"Remember your attempt to visit Miss Tulip's back in Bountiful?"

Cautiously, Molly nodded, recalling her trek to the whorehouse, and not quite making it. It was her fainting spell and then the dunking in the creek that eventually got her engaged to Kane in the first place. Still and all, Molly wasn't sure where this was leading.

"Well, Miss Tulip's place looks like a Baptist church compared to where I'm heading tonight."

And then it hit Molly. She covered her gasp with a hand, but the words still flew out nosily. "You're leaving me to spend the night in a whorehouse?"

Kane scratched his nose, seeming to ignore the diners who had turned their heads in his direction the minute she'd opened her mouth, but Molly didn't miss their disgusted stares. She felt equally appalled.

And betrayed.

Suddenly she knew why the thought of Kane spending time with "ladies of the night," bothered her so.

Jealousy. Deep, heart-wrenching, unnerving jealousy surfaced like a claw-like ogre to rip at her insides. Kane wouldn't make her his wife in the real sense, but he would spend the night with loose, immoral women.

"Keep your voice down," he commanded.

"I will not! You can't possibly mean to say—"

Kane reached over and, none too delicately, clamped his hand over her mouth. "Quiet, Little Bird. Let me explain, okay?"

Molly pierced him with a cold look of disdain, but finally she relented, then nodded.

He released his hand. Keeping his voice down, he explained, "I'm not going there for any reason other than to commission the pictures of Charlie. It's what you want, isn't it? A way to better our search? Bennett said that when I was missing, he commissioned this man, but he has since gone into seclusion."

"He lives in a whorehouse?" This time, Molly whispered.

"I don't know for certain. But that's where I'm told I can find him most nights."

"So, you'll be gone all night?"

"If that's what it takes."

"And how will you spend your time, while he's working on the pictures?" Molly couldn't help but ask. Kane's answer became very important to her.

"Sleeping, I suppose."

"Alone?"

Kane rose from his seat, tossed some coins on the table, then helped Molly out of her seat. He escorted her with a firm hand to the base of the hotel stairs and gazed into her eyes. "You have much to learn about the Cheyenne, Molly. We honor our marriage vows."

"But you're no longer among the Cheyenne," Molly pressed the point, unable to control her muddled thoughts. "And you're forever reminding me that our marriage is—" she said, lowering her voice to a mere whisper "—temporary."

"Then you'll have to trust me at my word. You're my wife. I will only sleep with you."

"But," she began, biting her lip again, debating whether she should speak her mind. She decided she just couldn't hold back her uncertain thoughts any longer. "You won't *sleep* with another woman, but will you—"

"No, Molly." Kane shook his head. "I won't touch another woman." And he touched her face, his fingertips gentle on her cheek.

"I won't take her into my arms." And he wrapped his hands tightly around her waist, bringing her close.

"And I won't kiss another woman." And he brought his lips to hers, kissing her softly and more gently than Kane had ever kissed her before.

"I won't bed another woman, Molly." He smiled into her eyes and turned her to face the stairs. "Now, go up to the room. Get some rest. I'll try to be back before sunup."

Molly climbed a stair, then another, feeling weightless as if she were floating on a fluffy cloud. Her mind swam deliciously with thoughts of her husband and her body still hummed from Kane's sweet assault. Once she reached the top stair, she turned and gazed down with a question forming on her lips.

But Kane had already gone.

She wouldn't have the chance to ask her boldest question ever.

Chapter Eight

Molly paced the all-too-quiet, stuffy room. No longer did the flowery décor seem cheery. No longer did she enjoy gazing out the window. Fidgeting with the creases on her dress and shuffling her feet about, she wore the carpet out with her constant movement. Restless from thoughts of Kane and what he was doing right now had her too jumpy to sleep.

Her husband continued to baffle her with his often-distant demeanor. And then, there were times like tonight, when he'd behaved completely and wholly as a true husband should, seizing her into his arms and kissing her with enough tenderness to dizzy her. Her limbs had grown weak and her heart might surely have melted from the sweet way Kane had taken her.

Molly's thoughts turned instead to Kane's mission. He was to seek out a disreputable man to commission his talent as an artist. She prayed for Kane's safety, though in her heart of hearts Molly knew no more formidable man. Her husband wasn't a man to cross or deny. Kane knew how to survive in this untamed land.

He had done so for years prior to their meeting and as Molly learned more of his life, her admiration for him grew each day.

As for his kisses, well…

"Oh, heavens!" Molly admonished herself for wishing her husband here, to shed her loneliness in this confined and airless room. She couldn't think of sharing this tiny bed with him without her mind wandering down a forbidden path.

And the more she stared at those overly large flowers on the wall, the more she wanted to scream.

She glanced out the window and saw people milling about. There was yet much to be done to ready for the festivities tomorrow. Surely, there would be no harm if she wandered downstairs and peeped her nose outside.

Yes, Molly decided she needed the distraction, a way to calm jittery foolish nerves. She needed to stop the all-consuming thoughts of her husband. She needed to remind herself that *her* mission was to find her brother and not lust after the man she had married…temporarily.

Molly exited the room with newfound vigor. She nearly glided down the stairs and stopped immediately when she came upon a group of women, chattering along in the most serious of tones.

And before she knew it, the women were upon her at the base of the staircase, circling her like wild dogs upon their prey.

Molly looked at each one of the dozen faces she encountered, seeing neither joy nor amusement anywhere on their expressions. They stared at her with vigilance, until one woman stepped forth, dressed in the silliest of outfits, a short skirt over bloomers that cuffed her ankles.

Regardless of their intent, Molly saw this as a great opportunity to query them about Charlie. She smiled amicably and addressed them all, ignoring that one woman who seemed to be sizing her up. "Hello, ladies."

Kane cursed under his breath as he made his way up the stairs at the Blue River Hotel, realizing that unless he wanted a torturous night ahead, he would be sleeping on the floor. Not that he minded, he'd grown up of the earth, but he'd miss Molly's softness, the little sounds she made during the night, the feel of her silken hair against his skin when she moved closer to him.

But damn it, Kane had ridden hard to get back early for Molly's sake, tiring out both his horse and himself. He hadn't the willpower to fight off her charms tonight—so the floor would be his bed.

Anticipation grew in his belly as he put the key in the lock, imagining far too clearly the beauty sleeping on that small bed tonight, her face full of peace and serenity.

If he wasn't careful he'd get used to coming home to her at night after a long, hard ride, with the sweet taste of her lips still fresh on his mouth. If he wasn't careful, he'd get used to seeing the bright green alight in her eyes when something amused her, and equally, the liquid fire fuel them when something angered her. Kane shoved those thoughts aside, thinking that, yes, tonight of all nights—he would sleep on the floor.

He opened the door and walked with silence, until he reached the bed...the *empty* bed.

Unnerved, he glanced around the hotel room with dread creeping into his gut. He'd known immediately as he swept the perimeter that Molly was gone. Dire warnings flashed through his mind. And instant recollections of another time, another missing wife, struck him like rapid and repeating gunfire.

Sickened sensations cramped his belly. His heart raced and beads of moisture pooled at his brow. He stood there, frozen in the moment, thinking of Molly and the dangers that might befall her. His renegade wife had either gone out against his wishes, or she'd been taken by force. Neither option painted a rosy picture.

"Molly!" he called out, regardless of what his innate instincts were telling him, hoping that she'd somehow magically appear. Hadn't it been the same with Little Swan? Hadn't he had hope-filled moments, thinking she'd walk right back into their camp, smiling up at him with love in her eyes? Hadn't he wished it so, so many times in his dreams?

Kane wasted no more time on fruitless wishes. He checked the gun he wore around his waist like a second skin, making sure it was fully loaded and ready, something he'd also done earlier this evening as he rode out of town. A man couldn't be too careful in that regard. Then he strode down the stairs. The diner was closed, the room darkened, and no one appeared to be working at the hotel desk.

Tamping down his fear for Molly, Kane moved lithely, striding with purpose, heading down the street toward the Pecos Saloon, noting that all other shops and enterprises had closed for the evening. Once there, he took a deep breath to steady his nerves and entered the crowded room. Cigar smoke billowed up, tainting the air and mixing with the keenly distinct scent of alcohol.

With one sharp sweeping glance Kane found the man

he had hoped to find. He reached him in three long strides, and faced him at the bar. The balding man didn't pay him any mind, staring straight ahead, sipping whiskey from a shot glass. Kane noted the empty bottle of Jack Daniel's sitting on the cherry-wood bar directly in front of him.

Kane laid down a silver coin. "The next one's on me."

That got the man's attention. He turned to face Kane, his eyes glazed, his face ruddy. "Thank you, kindly."

"It'll cost you."

"It always does," the man said without qualm.

"I'm looking for my wife. Mrs. Molly Jackson. You checked us both in at the hotel earlier today."

The man perked up, his eyes widening and this time when he looked at Kane, there was a note of recognition. "I remember your wife. Red hair. Little gal and pretty, if you don't mind me saying."

"Did you see her leave the hotel tonight?"

The man shook his head. "No, sir."

"You're sure?"

"I'm sure. I closed up at sunset then headed over here. But, if your wife's missing, then I got me a good idea where she is. Probably with every other dang woman in town."

Kane held his breath. "Go on."

"Seems there's this here *women's movement* to stop all the drinking in town. There's women out there wanting to close down every last darn saloon in the country. Can you believe that? The more they talk about abstinence, the more we come in here, getting our fill. Hell, I know why they call it temperance. Trying to stop a man from drinking sure does get his *temper* a-rising."

Kane narrowed his eyes, considering if Molly would take up with such women. She'd never mentioned one way or another about her feelings toward liquor, but somehow Kane didn't think his wife would have joined up with such a movement. "Where are these women?"

"Hell, I don't know. They have secret meetings."

"So no one knows?"

Sheepishly, the man admitted, "Well, uh, I ain't suppose to say."

Kane's patience quickly ebbed. At one time in his youth, he would have strung the man up by his collar until he talked, but Kane had learned a thing or two since then, so he held back his irritation and instead tossed down another coin. "Jack Daniel's," he told the barkeep. "Bring a new bottle."

When the bartender complied, Kane laid a hand over the base of the bottle and pushed it toward the hotel clerk. "I need to know where that meeting is."

The man hesitated.

Kane waited while the hotel clerk eyed the bottle.

"Mildred is gonna tan my hide for sure."

"Mildred?"

"My wife. She, uh, sorta runs the meetings."

If Kane were of a mood, he would have laughed at the irony. While the clerk's wife was out running meetings to ban liquor, her husband was imbibing whiskey like water, practically drowning in it. "I need to find my wife. She may not even be there."

"Okay, okay." The clerk grabbed the whiskey bottle and tucked it under his arm, then leaned in to whisper in Kane's ear. "They're meeting at the old abandoned Episcopalian church, just outside of town. Due east."

Kane nodded and turned to leave.

The hotel clerk grabbed his sleeve and Kane stiffened, moving out of the man's reach. "Don't tell Mildred it was me that told you."

"You have my word."

The clerk shuddered. "Appreciate that."

"Abstinence is the only way!"

"Liquor is the devil's brew!"

"We shall prevail. We'll dry up Whiskey Flats."

Kane stood in the back of the church watching the horde of women teetotalers pledge their very lives to the cause. Huddled by the light of one lantern in the abandoned church, the ladies circled the one woman who led the crowd. Kane couldn't see much through their calico-clad backs and Molly, being of short stature, would blend in with the rest of them.

"Whiskey Flats will be no more! We'll change the name of this town!"

For the moment, not a soul knew he'd discovered their secret meeting. Kane narrowed his eyes, his heart pounding. He prayed he'd find Molly here amid these women, hoping his hunch had paid off. He had no other possible leads.

"Tomorrow, we'll speak our mind. We'll get petitions signed, boycott the saloon and Founder's Day will have new meaning in town," the leader announced. The others bobbed their heads and voiced their avid agreement.

Kane had no more time to waste. He couldn't see Molly through the dozens of women present. He stepped up and knew immediately when he'd been noticed. The ranting stopped and a sea of women parted, their horrified gasps enough to bring down the failing decrepit walls. The leader appeared.

Mildred.

Kane pursed his lips, taking in her silly attire. She wore something akin to a sideshow costume, complete with billowing bloomers, and if she demanded attention with her garb she'd certainly attained her goal.

She stepped forward, her face humorless. "You have invaded our meeting, sir. What right have you to—"

"I'm looking for my wife. Her name is Mrs. Molly Jackson," he interrupted and upon his announcement, Molly appeared. Slowly, she stepped out from the crowd, blinking her eyes and wearing a shocked expression.

Relief registered first. Kane had never been so darn happy to see anyone in his life. She looked beautiful to him, more beautiful than he'd thought possible actually, with her hair down in curls around her face and those big green eyes staring back at him, causing him a moment of lost breath.

And then his fury set in—angry, hot wrath that rattled all other emotions to the core.

"Your wife has come here for a purpose," Mildred explained sternly. "And has agreed to listen to our proposals."

Kane took the steps necessary to reach Molly. Without giving her another glance, he lifted her into his arms and held on tight, turning toward the leader. "I think I have a far better proposal for her. You see, we're on our honeymoon."

Surprised gasps and romantic sighs resounded in the room.

"But our cause is just!" Mildred exclaimed.

Molly squirmed in his arms. Kane shot her a quick warning glance, which stifled her movement. "No doubt, but you wouldn't want to keep a man from his new bride. There are still things I must teach my wife about being…married."

Another round of "oohs" and "aahs" were heard.

Molly thumped him in the chest.

"Good night, ladies."

He strode out of the church without turning back.

Once outside, Molly thumped him again on the chest. He barely felt her slight fists, but her voice, well, that shrieking sound grated on him. "Put me down, Kane!"

"No."

He tightened his grip in case the woman thought she could wiggle free of him.

"This is ridiculous," Molly exclaimed, but she settled into his arms, hopefully realizing the futility in fighting him. He marched on, heading for the hotel.

"You've got some explaining to do, Little Bird. So start talking, 'cause I'm about to wring your neck."

Molly ignored his demand. "What are you doing back so early? Didn't you find the mystery man?"

Kane held his temper. "I found him, stone drunk. He made one drawing before he passed out completely. But he's good, the best I've ever seen. I'm going back in the morning for the rest of the drawings."

"You didn't leave the tintype of Charlie with him, did you?"

Kane didn't answer, deciding to let her stew a bit. Hell, she deserved it for all the trouble she'd caused him tonight.

"Kane?"

"What?"

"You didn't leave the only thing I have left of my brother with that man, did you?" she asked, alarmed.

Kane waited a moment longer before answering. "No."

"Then how's he—"

"The drawing he made was so close a likeness, I told him to draw up a dozen more just like it. Paid him a small fortune, too. He'll have them ready in the morning."

"You took a drunk at his word?"

Kane lifted his mouth in a crooked smile. "I trust no one, Molly. I gave the man reason to want to do me this service and that's all I'm saying."

Kane threatened him at gunpoint, offering to shoot off his drawing hand, if the man even thought of running out on him. "He'll have them ready before the celebration tomorrow."

"Thank you," she said sweetly, and he felt her body relax in his arms.

But Kane wasn't through with Molly yet. He entered the hotel, taking the stairs quickly and once they reached their room, he kicked open the door.

He walked into the room with Molly in his arms, and once again the irony struck him like a blow to his gut. He'd announced to the temperance women he was on his honeymoon and now here he was, carrying his new bride over the threshold.

He tossed Molly onto the bed and she landed with a plop onto the quilts. "Now, why'd you go out tonight?"

"I didn't exactly," she began, sitting upright on the bed. "I needed a breath of air, and then I met up with those women in the lobby. Then, well, we sort of made a deal. They agreed to hear about my search for Charlie, if I'd listen to their lecture on temperance. It was a good plan, Kane. Why, almost every woman in town was at that meeting. I figured someone might have seen my brother."

"Damn it, Molly. It was a fool plan. I came back and found you missing."

"I didn't know you'd be back so early."

"And I couldn't figure why my wife wouldn't be in bed when I got back."

"I couldn't sleep."

"Hell, anything could have happened to you."

"But nothing did. And none of the women said they'd seen anyone who looked like my brother even after I described him down to the mole on his left cheek. When you showed up, I'd never been happier to see anyone in my life."

"What?"

"Heavens, the last thing I wanted was to listen to those dreary women go on and on about the sins of liquor." Molly smiled. "I knew you wouldn't be happy, but I'd rather listen to your wrath than theirs."

Kane ran a hand down his face. "You don't fear me?"

Surprised, Molly's eyes rounded. "Should I?"

Hell, Kane was a killer. He'd done enough in his twenty-six years to satisfy Satan. Yet Molly was naive in the ways of the West. She'd never really seen the bad side of life whereas Kane had seen too much. "Probably. Once I found you I really thought to wring your neck."

"You wouldn't," Molly said quietly, but she glanced up at him with doubt in her eyes.

Kane pursed his lips, his anger fading. He was too doggone tired and relieved to hold on to his irritation. "Think you can sleep now?"

Molly looked at the bed and then gazed up at him. Kane knew he'd lay with her tonight, the need to hold her, to know she slept safely by his side, too strong.

Kane bent to remove Molly's boots. "What are you doing?" she asked softly.

"Getting ready for bed. Now slide over."

Kane removed his gun belt, his shirt and then off came his boots. He flung them, not caring where they landed. He came down next to Molly on the bed, and took her into his arms, thinking it was better she slept in her dress. He'd already seen her in sheer cotton once today, and that encounter nearly led to disaster.

"Don't ever go out alone, Molly," he said, much like a father would scold a child. "Don't disobey me. Next time, you might not be so lucky."

Molly gazed deep into his eyes. "You worried over me?"

Kane nodded, then kissed her gently on the lips. "You're my responsibility."

Then he rolled over, holding her to him, and fell asleep.

One week later, Molly stood in Kay's Millinery in a town called Fallen Oak, weary from travel, but more so, heartbroken that none of her efforts to find her brother had succeeded. She'd been so hopeful when Kane arrived with the drawings of Charlie, but Founder's Day in Whiskey Flats proved a flop. Not only hadn't anyone in town recognized his likeness, but Molly nearly got arrested along with the Ladies' Temperance League, who had plagued the saloons, disrupted the festivities and stirred up enough trouble to drive any sane man straight to drink. Luckily, Molly had done some fast-talking to the sheriff, and some of the more romance-minded of the ladies had vouched for her innocence in the whole matter.

From there, they'd made a harrowing trek across the Pecos River, visited Midland and towns with obscure names that Molly couldn't remember now. They'd be sure to leave off a drawing of Charlie in each place, usually with the sheriff, if the town had one. If not, Kane always found a prominent citizen to leave the drawing with, sometimes the telegraph operator, sometimes the town barber and sometimes a wealthy landowner.

With desperation, Molly began to realize that Texas was as big as her chances to find Charlie slim. She couldn't abide never seeing him again. She couldn't abide not having any kin to speak of. She vowed never to give up.

So she stood in the hat shop, all but ignoring the beautiful velvet bonnets with fine ribbons and lace, but instead waiting for the proprietor to finish up with her customer so Molly could ask her questions.

She and Kane had set a pattern of sorts. He'd show a drawing to the saloonkeepers, sheriff, blacksmith, wire operator and such, and she would only speak with the ladies at the millinery, dress shops and mercantile, waiting for Kane at the diner or supper house when she was through. It was a deal she'd struck with him after much discussion, making their time more efficient. They could visit more towns and speak to many more people this way. Molly had been on her best behavior since the incident in Whiskey Flats and Kane, she hoped, was beginning to trust her. Still and all, neither had come up with any real leads on her brother.

"May I help you, miss?"

"Oh, yes," Molly said, coming out of her thoughts. "I'm searching for my brother. He goes by the name Charlie McGuire. Here's what he looked like a few years back." She showed the woman the rectangular frame. "Do you think you might have seen him in town?"

The lady began shaking her head, much like all the others she'd encountered recently. Molly had begun to hate that one wretched gesture. "No, sorry. But I don't get too many men coming in here."

Molly realized that, too. She'd been duped by Kane into thinking she'd actually make progress with her inquiries, but all too soon she'd noted that her particular quest for Charlie in places where only women frequented would do her no good. It had just been another way for Kane to keep control of the situation. "Thank you," she said, "I appreciate your time."

The milliner nodded graciously.

"If you ever do see my brother, would you ask him to please contact his sister, Molly, at the Bar J Ranch in Bountiful?"

"I certainly will, miss. I do hope you find him."

"Thank you," Molly said with a small smile, before exiting the shop.

She stood on the sidewalk looking east, then west, wondering if she would ever see Charlie again, when a young boy approached her, tugging on her dress. The child couldn't have been more than ten years old.

Dressed in pitiful clothes that appeared more like rags and dirt stains on every part of his body, Molly had never seen a more unkempt child in her life.

"Lady, lady. I know where your brother is, lady."

Stunned, Molly blinked several times, allowing the words to sink in. She bent down to gaze into the boy's light brown eyes. "You know where Charlie is?"

"I don't know his name for sure, but my mama told me to come for you." The boy grabbed her hand and yanked. "Come now."

Molly straightened but refused to move. "Wait. I need to find my husband." She darted glances up and down the streets looking for Kane. He was nowhere to be found.

The boy shook his head. "Your brother's hurt, ma'am. Mama said to fetch you in a hurry."

Alarmed, Molly's heart raced furiously. "Charlie's hurt? What happened to him? What happened to my brother?" she asked, her voice nearly a shriek now.

"He was shot. He's bleeding bad."

"Oh!" Tears stung Molly's eyes. She'd prayed for months to find her brother, but she'd never fathomed that they would be reunited in this most troubling way. From the urgency in the boy's voice, she knew she had little time to waste. Kane was nowhere in sight and she couldn't wait any longer. Her brother needed her. "Take me to him."

The boy once again grabbed her hand. They walked briskly down the sidewalk turning down an alley and ventured farther from town almost at a run. They stopped when they reached a broken-down shanty with splintered walls and rotting floor planks. Molly couldn't see into the window for all the dirt.

"He's in there," the boy said, pointing.

"Let your mama know we're here," Molly ordered with impatience, yet she held to propriety.

The boy opened the door slowly. "Mama, we're here."

The boy stepped into the shanty and Molly followed. She held her breath in anticipation, both fearful and hopeful, but that very breath was knocked out of her in one frightful blow as she was shoved forcefully against the wall. A toothy man held his big beefy hand over her mouth, his body pinning her in place. He tossed the boy a coin. "Good job, kid. Now get out."

The boy took off running.

Molly gulped fear and held back nausea, realizing far too late her mistake. Another man reached over to rip the reticule from her arm. From the little light filtering in, Molly saw him dig deep into her purse, coming up with all of the contents. "Ah, Clyde, ain't but a few dollars in here," he complained. "I thought you said she was rich."

"Hell, her man's probably holding all the cash."

"I got me a good look at him. He ain't one to mess with."

"No, but we got us his woman. Bet she can ease my disappointment," Clyde said, sliding his free hand up and down Molly's arm. She tried pulling her arm free but he clamped on tight, holding her firm. Molly squirmed and kicked and struggled until the man had to release his hand over her mouth to hold her still. Panicked, she screamed. "Kane! Help! Help me!"

The slap to her face stung. "Shut up!" Clyde covered her mouth again. "Get the rope, Tooley."

"Rope? I didn't bring no rope."

Clyde turned from Molly to glare at his partner. "I

told you to bring a rope, damn it! Now, how we gonna keep her still enough."

"You hold her down."

Molly took her captive's lack of attention to shove at his chest with balled fists. She spit in his face and kicked hard, right between the legs.

"Ow!" Blood drained from his face and he doubled over.

Molly ran for the door, but the other man grabbed her from behind, lifting her up as she screamed and kicked.

"Ain't nobody gonna hear you way out here!" Then he silenced her with his hand over her mouth, holding her tight, his arm wrapped around her middle. "You okay, Clyde?"

"Hell, no," he muttered. "I ain't okay."

Just then, the door burst open and Kane appeared. Taking a split second to survey the scene, he threw his knife at Clyde, striking him in the shoulder and once again he doubled over, falling to the floor and crying out in agony.

Then, methodically, Kane focused on the man holding Molly.

"Let her go," he demanded, his voice venomous.

The man who held Molly released her instantly, but Kane didn't stop. He approached the man with murder in his eyes. He grabbed him, tossed him against the wall and pounded him with his fists over and over again. The man raised his arms in surrender, unable to put up much of a fight, but Kane continued, bloodying his nose and Molly thought she heard the man's jaw crack. Blood spurted from the man's mouth, his eyes nearly bugging out of his head. With the ruffian slumped against the wall, Kane continued to pummel him until Molly couldn't stand to watch another second. "Kane!"

Her plea went unnoticed.

"Kane!" she repeated, her voice shrill. She tugged on his sleeve and pleaded. "Enough, Kane."

He shook his head. "Not enough. He has to pay." He landed another blow.

Tears filled Molly's eyes. Kane's unleashed rage frightened her. She'd never seen him lose control. She'd never seen this untamed, wild, ferocious side to him. Warrior came to mind and she envisioned him as a true Cheyenne, protecting what was his, seeking vengeance and retribution, perhaps for all that was done to him, for all those whom he'd lost.

His chest heaved with anger, his face was tight and determined—Molly knew she had to stop him. "Let him go. You're killing him!"

"He deserves to die, for what he did to—" And then Kane stopped to look at her, a light dawning in his eyes as she pleaded with him in silence this time. He released the man, who sagged to the floor in a bloody heap.

"He didn't kill your wife, Kane," Molly said softly.

Kane nodded, as if just realizing that himself. Then he lifted a finger to her cheek. The sting had subsided long ago, but Molly knew her face would show the handprint of violence. Kane closed his eyes tight, as if warding off any further fury. "Are you hurt?" he asked.

Molly rubbed her arms up and down, thankful that Kane had arrived in time. She was scared—frightened half to death, if truth be known—but she wasn't hurt. "No. You got here," she said with a shudder, "in time. How did you know?"

"The boy. I saw you walk down an alley with him. Next thing I know, he's running away like a wild rabbit, looking guilty. When I caught up with him, I didn't give him much choice but to tell me where you were."

"I shouldn't have gone with him, Kane. But he told me Charlie was here, and hurt bad."

"You got to stop trusting in people, Molly. Even little boys," Kane offered, too spent to show her any anger, but Molly figured she'd get a good earful soon.

Kane swept a glance at the two men lying near death on the floor. "Let's go."

Kane lifted her up and carried her out of the shanty. Molly didn't protest. Her legs had gone as weak as molasses. "What about them?"

"They're not going anywhere. We'll get the sheriff. He'll deal with them, then we're getting out of this town."

Molly liked the sound of that.

The sooner they departed Fallen Oak, the better.

Chapter Nine

After the Fallen Oak incident, silence filled their days. Molly thought that Kane would surely lecture her on her foolhardy behavior, but nothing was forthcoming. Perhaps both learned a lesson. Perhaps Kane's silence had less to do with Molly's actions that day and more to do with his own.

Molly had stopped him from murdering a man. The experience weighed heavily on her conscience. If she hadn't been so impatient, if she'd recognized the ruse for what it was, that day would have ended differently.

She remembered how they'd left town in haste and made camp when dusk had just settled on the horizon. Kane took her into his arms that night, holding her close, but oh, so carefully, one arm wrapped around her middle, the other, always gripping on to the rifle that lay beside him. Molly had never felt safer. She'd never wanted to be held so much. She'd had disturbing dreams that night, and when she'd roused, Kane had settled her back down, rubbing her arms, kissing her cheek gently, until she once again relaxed.

But that day was in the distant past. Since then, she and Kane had weathered heat that scorched their skin and soaked their clothes, winds that swirled red dust upon their bodies, and unpredictable nights that lent warmth one time and chills the other.

Molly endured it all for the sake of finding her brother. But what she couldn't endure was the day in and day out disappointment she felt every time they left one town to find hopelessness once again in another.

They'd traveled for miles, searched many towns and inquired at ranches and farms along the way, turning up no leads. They'd come full circle and as Molly sat upon the wagon in the late afternoon, seated next to a quiet Kane, she held back tears. They had exhausted their search and were returning to the Bar J.

Molly prayed to the Almighty for guidance. Filled with despair with all hope waning, she asked for a sign, anything that might help to restore her faith. And if the Almighty listened, she had to believe his sign came in the form of quick-moving gray clouds, putting a chill in the air and darkening the once pretty blue sky.

Without warning, a storm raged, the clouds smashing into one another, booming with sound and alighting the sky with friction. Cold rain pelted down, the storm's immediate violence more like the devil's device than anything the Almighty would want to conjure.

Kane halted the wagon under a large oak, the horses too jittery to move forward. He jumped down, and reached for her, grabbing a blanket and shoving it into her arms. "Get under the wagon, quick."

Molly scooted under as she was told, spreading out the blanket, hoping to keep somewhat dry. Through sheets of rain pouring down, she watched Kane make quick work of unhitching the horses, leading them to another nearby tree. After tying the mares securely, he raced back to the wagon and, using two blankets, attached them to the sides of the bed, creating a tent of sorts then rolled his way under. He carried only a saddlebag, one she knew that was filled with provisions and, of course, his rifle.

Molly stared at Kane's soaked clothes. Without benefit of the hat that had flown off his head in the storm, Kane's hair hung in his face and dripped water onto his shoulders. Molly reached up to push his hair back, looking deeply into his eyes. He shivered from the cold, and Molly hadn't realized that she, too, had been shivering all along. "You're drenched."

"So are you."

Molly's clothes hung like wet rags to her body. Her hair was equally as wet, the storm catching them both off guard. "What do we do now?" she asked.

"Get out of our wet clothes and wait."

Thunder boomed directly overhead. Molly jumped from the horrific sound, and the eerie flash of lightning illuminating the ground like a quick burning match brought goose bumps. "Oh!"

Kane moved closer, realizing her fear. As a child, Molly had hated storms, but none she'd encountered had frightened her quite so much. Texas storms, like everything in this wild unruly land seemed angrier and fiercer than the ones she'd recalled from back home. "Come here, Little Bird."

Molly moved into Kane's arms and once again, she felt safe and protected. She trembled from cold, yes, but she also recognized the familiar tremble she sustained each time Kane held her in his arms. He began unbuttoning her dress and Molly allowed it. He'd seen her unclothed before, and funny, but she knew no shame with Kane. He was her husband and a man she had come to trust.

With all buttons unfastened, Kane slid the dress from her shoulders. He helped her pull it down along her legs and remove it completely.

"Your boots, too." And Kane helped her take off her shoes.

Next Kane removed his buckskin shirt, lifting it high overhead and Molly took the shirt from him, marveling at its waterlogged weight. She set it in the same pile with her dress.

Molly shivered again, this time the chill seeping way down to her bones. Thunder rocked the sky with powerful force, making her feel so small at the moment, so insignificant. She rubbed her arms back and forth, the chemise she wore offered little protection from the cold.

"Let my body warm you, Molly," Kane said, dragging her closer to him. "Turn from me."

Molly did as she was told, grateful for any warmth Kane could offer. With her back to him now, pressed beside him, Molly gritted her teeth. "Your pants…they're soaked."

Kane groaned. "I hoped you wouldn't notice." Then he sighed. "For this to work, we need no clothes between us."

"We need to lie naked?" Molly croaked.

"For body warmth, yes. That's how we'll stay warm through the storm."

"There's no other way?"

Again, she heard Kane groan. "There are no more dry blankets, Molly. If you know another way…"

Kane's voice warred with another clash of thunder. Molly jumped at the deafening sound.

Then when all was quiet again, she heard Kane's struggle to remove his wet trousers. "May I help?" she offered, through ingrained politeness.

"Don't turn around, Molly."

And all too soon she understood why he didn't want her help. Kane brought his body to hers and slowly lifted the plastered chemise from her body, thankfully leaving on her drawers, but not before Molly realized Kane's aroused state. "Kane?"

"Shhh!" And it was as if he didn't want to speak of what was happening between them. Instead of answering her, he wrapped his arm around her middle, tucked one leg over hers and pressed her back to his chest. Molly swallowed hard, forgetting about her chilled bones for the moment.

"Can we lie like this all night?" she asked pointedly.

"We can try," was his honest answer. "Are you warming up?"

Oh, yes! Molly couldn't think much beyond Kane's inflamed state, his heat becoming hers within seconds.

"Maybe if we talked. That might ease, uh, that might make time pass more quickly."

Kane didn't seem to agree. He grunted.

"Tell me about the Cheyenne," Molly said, broaching a subject she knew little about. "What was it like living with them?"

Kane seemed to relax a bit, his body's rigid stance becoming much less tense. "You really want to know?"

She bobbed her head. "I do."

Absently, Kane stroked her belly, his hand warming her skin and he said, "In many ways the Cheyenne aren't so different from the white man. The children play silly games, just like white children. They play camp with miniature lodge villages and make-believe families. The boys pretend to go on hunts and use stick horses to hunt buffalo. The little girls have toy tipis and deerskin dolls. Children are revered in the tribe. Boys especially, because their birth means warrior strength."

"Was it frightening for you in the beginning?"

"Not really. I'd been so sick when they found me, that when I finally healed, I'd become accustomed to them, and they had already welcomed me into the tribe. I had only vague, fading memories of my parents by then. Luckily for me, an elder in the tribe had worked as a guide for a wealthy adventurer. He spoke to me in English enough that by the time I'd grown to manhood, I could speak both languages."

"Was it strange, coming back to the white world?"

"After Little Swan was killed, I didn't feel like I belonged anywhere anymore. All I knew was that I couldn't rest until I brought her murderer to justice."

"You must have loved her a great deal."

"Since I was twelve."

"Twelve?" Molly's heart broke for Kane, who had fallen in love with a young Cheyenne maiden, only to have her taken brutally from him a few years later. And her heart broke for herself as well, to have also married Kane, knowing him as a husband and yet not really knowing him at all. "I'm sorry, Kane."

He became silent then, his hand still stroking her

belly, and at times, his fingertips grazing just beneath her breasts. Oh, how she wanted him to caress her there, to make her come alive, to make her feel like a woman, a wife.

The rain stopped for a moment and all was quiet. It was as though she and Kane were the only two people on earth, the silence almost as deafening as the thunder.

"Are you warming up?" he asked.

Molly wanted to smile. How could she not warm to Kane's body huddled around hers, his massive form almost enveloping her? "I'm warmer. Do you think the storm is over?"

"Doubtful. More clouds will move in. These storms usually last all night."

Molly figured what saved them was that Kane had stopped the wagon on higher ground just under a colossal oak, its leaves helping to divert the rain somewhat.

"Close your eyes, Little Bird. Try to sleep."

Molly couldn't sleep, but she did close her eyes, trying to block out the emotions roiling around inside. And she found peace for a moment, a lull in her own storm, as Kane continued to stroke her arms and belly, keeping her warm.

But her peace soon shattered as an earsplitting clap of thunder boomed overhead. Molly jumped and turned into Kane's arms, trembling in fear as lightning struck a tree just ten yards away. She saw the horrible vision through the wheel of the wagon. "Did you see it, Kane?" she cried out. "It's coming closer."

"No, it's moving away. Don't be scared."

Molly gripped Kane's neck and stuck her head under his chin. She clung to him, wishing away her fear.

He held her tight, wrapping his arms around her, and it was only once the rain had subsided again, the thunder a distant sound now, that Molly realized their intimate position.

She felt the crush of Kane's chest to her breasts, the press of his taut belly to hers, but most of all, she felt his rigid desire and knew without a doubt that she wanted him, the way a wife wants a husband.

She kissed his chest, licking at the moist skin, then she lifted her head to plant a kiss to his mouth. Kane responded immediately, a low guttural sound escaping his throat. He took her face in his hands and kissed her back fervently, his lips taking hers like wild whipping wind, until Molly thought she would surely lose all of her breath. Kane moved his hands to her shoulders and then slid them down her arms, stroking her up and down.

Molly broke off the kiss long enough to take his hand. "Touch me, Kane." And she placed his palm on her breast.

A shudder ran through Kane and she witnessed hesitation in his dark, hungry eyes. "If I do, there'll be no going back," he whispered.

His large calloused hand against her soft skin created sharp tingles that reached her toes. Molly didn't want to go back, she wanted to go forward. She wanted to know Kane as a husband. "I know."

Kane swept a slow glance over her naked body, then moved his hand on her, stroking her breast, flicking the tip with his thumb. A cry of pleasure erupted inside her. Molly wiggled under Kane's hand, wanting more.

"You respond to me, Molly."

Molly knew no shame with Kane. She made it clear with her body that she wanted him. "I always have."

Kane kissed her then, a long slow exploring kiss that left her weak. He moved on to kiss her chin, her throat, her shoulders. And when he put his mouth to her breasts, Molly cried aloud this time, the sweet torturous pleasure almost too much to bear.

Kane stroked her with his hand and suckled her with his mouth, the softness of his wet hair tickling her skin. Molly giggled between her soft moans, enjoying every single sensation Kane elicited from her.

"Am I warming you?" Kane asked with smoky eyes.

"I don't think I can get much warmer," she responded, hot all over.

Kane smiled and kissed her once again. "Just wait, Little Bird."

Molly kissed him back and wove her hands in his hair gently, then moved down to touch his shoulders, spanning the wide expanse with her palms and marveling at his perfect body. She kissed his throat, his shoulders, moved down to kiss his chest once again, trailing her fingers down along a torso that narrowed down a dangerous path.

Molly knew the exact moment when Kane's body went rigid. She had yet to glance down past his waist, yet she'd known of his erection, having been pressed against him half the night. She had only imagined...

She dared a quick peek, but one fast look was not enough. Molly stared at his manhood, the length and breadth of it, with wonder. "Oh, my," she breathed.

Kane's well-guarded restraint seemed to vanish then. He cupped her face with both hands and kissed her hard on the mouth, driving his tongue inside in search of hers. They mated in open-mouthed frenzy and when the kiss ended, Kane looked deeply into her eyes. She found desire there, a hungry look that might have frightened her if she had not wanted the same.

He took her hand and placed it on his manhood. "Touch me," he said, repeating her words from before.

Molly gripped him gently and Kane's eyes closed, his face unmasked now. She moved her hand on the velvety silk, learning the texture, absorbing the feel of him.

Kane lay back as Molly explored further, stroking and sliding her hand up and down. An expression of pleasure and peace stole over Kane momentarily, and Molly found comfort and joy knowing that she brought him this satisfaction.

The rain had subsided now, only a drizzle remained, leaving a fresh scent in the air. They had survived the dangerous storm and would continue on to the Bar J in the morning, but tonight they were alone, on this prairie land, sharing their bodies and, for Molly, sharing her heart.

Kane reached up to take her hand away, his face tight, and he rolled her over onto her back now. "It is your turn now," he said, kissing her fully on the mouth.

He cupped her breasts once again, weighing them in his hands, caressing and stroking her over and over, until her body moved rhythmically with each of his movements. Little moans of pleasure escaped and Molly's heart pounded rapidly.

Next Kane stroked her belly, his hand laying flat against her skin, almost fully covering her torso, teasing and tempting as his hand traveled lower and lower. Molly had never known such dire yearning, her body crying out for something she couldn't quite fathom.

Kane smiled down at her. "You're a beautiful little bird," he said, kissing her lips at the same time he found her woman's mound. Molly jolted when he touched her there, the sensation so new, so startling.

"Close your eyes, Molly," he said. "Let me bring you pleasure."

Kane removed her drawers then cupped her, his fingers finding her most sensitive spot. He stroked her slowly, and Molly moved with him, crying out softly from this new and wonderful sensation. "Kane," she called, never expecting an answer.

All tension oozed out of her. She moved more freely now, her body undulating, absorbing, enjoying Kane's ministrations. She glanced up into his eyes, to find his, hot and gleaming with desire. She felt herself lifting up, her muscles contracting, waiting, wanting.

And then Kane rose above her. "I will not hurt you, Little Bird."

Molly knew he wouldn't. And when he pressed into her, all she felt was a sharp painless burst. Elated and filled with joy, Molly looked up at Kane, his powerful body now joined with hers and her heart nearly exploded with love.

Molly had tried not to fall in love. She'd tried not to surrender her feelings. But Kane was a man to admire, a man who would forever be in her heart. She only hoped that he would come to have the same feelings for her one day.

Tonight she would give him the gift of her body while he took her heart. Tonight, she would not think of the future, but live in the present. Tonight she would love Kane with everything she had inside.

* * *

Kane slept well. It had been years since he'd known such peace. Ever since he'd avenged Little Swan's death, Kane had slept with unease, bad dreams troubling him throughout the night. He'd not had undisturbed sleep for a long time, but in the dawn of a new day, Kane knew a sense of peace reminiscent of the serenity he'd experienced in the arms of his first wife.

But when Kane opened his eyes, it was not Little Swan in his arms, but Molly McGuire Jackson, the woman he'd married temporarily. She slept like the dead, her breaths slow and calm. He'd held her through the night, keeping her warm, but what Kane couldn't abide was his lack of restraint when he recalled the way the night had ended.

He'd made love to his virgin wife.

Kane cursed silently at his stupidity. Molly had made it clear what she'd wanted, but Kane should have held back and not have succumbed to her charms. He should have resisted the fire in his groin and urgent need he had had to possess her. Kane had touched her. He'd taken her virginity last night. By all rights, both in the Cheyenne and white world, Molly belonged to him now.

He shuddered at the thought and chastised himself for giving in to his desire. Molly could never truly belong to him. Yet as she lay with him, her hair a blazing sunset of red and gold spread out along his arms, her body warm and creamy soft, Kane had little regret about making love to her. For in truth, Kane had never experienced anything more satisfying than to have Molly come alive, then apart in his arms.

Kane's body reacted just recalling the night of pas-

sion they shared, Molly's instinctive responses spur-
ring his desire even more. Kane closed his eyes once
again, allowing himself this one moment to recapture
the night in his mind because he knew that he could
never make love to Molly again. Not fully, not unguarded. He also knew that once back at the Bar J, he'd
be hard-pressed to sleep in her bed and not want her. But
Kane would not make the sort of love to her that would
bring about a child.

He couldn't. He wouldn't. Kane knew in his heart
that he would let Molly go once they'd both met the
terms of their bargain. He'd already broken one vow last
night. He'd not break another.

With that thought, Kane left the comfort of Molly's
soft body, rolling away from her, leaving their little safe
haven to meet with the cool unforgiving morning. Naked, his first order of business was to retrieve their
clothes, hoping that the small chest he'd stashed under
the wagon seat faired well through the storm. He pulled
it out and though the chest was soaked, when he reached
inside he found the clothes dry enough to wear.

Kane dressed in trousers and a shirt and found something appropriate for Molly to wear. He set her clothes
under the wagon where she slept, then went about
checking on the horses.

Soon, Molly would awaken and if the roads were
ready to travel, they would arrive back at the Bar J by
late afternoon.

Molly dressed quickly, eager to see Kane this morning. She had much to say to him, so much… And her
heart soared just thinking of the night they'd shared.

Molly had never known such ecstasy existed. She had never known such fulfillment. Last night, Kane had heated her body to boiling over. He'd taught her lessons of love. He'd kissed her senseless, caressed her tenderly, and when their bodies joined they climbed together to a glorious peak. She had only to gaze into Kane's half-lidded eyes to see that he had known great pleasure, too, as they came apart in each other's arms. The thought warmed her almost as much as Kane's steamy body next to hers. And afterward, Molly had fallen into a deep dreamless sleep.

Molly fitted her boots on, straightened her dress, smoothed back her hair and came out from under the wagon. She stood upright for the first time since the storm, stretching out with arms overhead. She ignored the stiffness in her limbs and the tenderness she experienced from making love with Kane, too happy to dwell on small things. She searched the area, looking for him.

She found him adding wood to a small fire he'd built a short distance away. Quickly, with eager anticipation and love filling her heart, she walked over to him. "Good morning," she said, cheerful as a morning jay.

She wrapped her arms around his neck and reached up on tiptoes to plant a kiss to his lips. Bold, yes, but after what they'd shared last night, Molly figured she had a right to kiss her husband good morning.

His body rigid, his eyes unreadable, Kane didn't kiss her back. In fact, his mood matched the gloomy gray clouds overhead. "Molly." He acknowledged her then removed her arms from about his neck. Then he glanced at her briefly, his gaze making a quick sweep of her body. "You okay this morning?"

Hot blood rushed to her face and she covered her blush with a big smile. "Just fine. You?"

Kane nodded, looking off in the distance. "Fine. We'll make the Bar J before the sun sets."

"We're going home," Molly stated and realized that she welcomed the thought. She would have to find other ways to locate Charlie, but the thought of the ranch house, with Bennett waiting, and a nice warm bed to sleep in every night with Kane, suddenly held great appeal. "I'm glad."

"Glad?" Kane looked at her now, his face a puzzle.

Molly nodded. "Seems like we've been away from the Bar J a long time. I've been praying for your grandfather's health every night. I'm hoping he's better."

Molly watched as Kane bent to set a coffeepot over the hot embers. "He's been on my mind," Kane admitted.

"Is that all that's been on your mind?" Molly asked, perplexed by his mood. Just hours ago, he'd made her feel special and wanted and loved. Just hours ago, Molly had felt like a wife, in the real sense. And she knew that Kane, too, had felt something strong between them.

Kane stood and inhaled sharply. "Hell, Molly, what do you want me to say exactly?"

Molly didn't hesitate. Kane had asked and she would surely answer. "Well, for one, you haven't mentioned our coupling from last night."

Kane squeezed his eyes shut. "Our coupling?"

"Well, yes." Molly folded her arms over her middle. "Last night, when we stripped off our wet clothes and got cozy under the wagon. You haven't mentioned that yet this morning."

"Hell, I asked how you were feeling."

"I'm feeling fine, gloriously fine, wonderfully fine, splendidly fine and thank you for asking."

"Damn it, Molly. Last night was unfortunate. We needed to stay warm…."

"You made me hot, Kane."

Kane winced and rubbed the back of his neck. "I took your innocence."

Molly reached out to touch his sleeve. "I gave it to you," she said softly. "It's okay, Kane."

He began shaking his head, moving away from her, repeating, "It's not okay. It's not okay. Damn it, Molly. Do you realize that we might have created a child last night? A child," he emphasized by raising his voice. "I can't abide that."

A child? *A child.* Molly hadn't given that any thought last night. She hadn't even considered the possibility, yet the thought settled smoothly, lending her a measure of sweet peace. Nothing would make Molly happier than to have Kane's baby. How often she'd thought about the time when she would conceive a child. Back in St. Louis, Molly had daydreamed of having a family of her own. A husband to love and a child to cherish. She'd worked out in her mind all the vivid details of the kind of life she'd wanted. That, even through bad times, the family would flourish, sustained by surrounding love and devotion.

Her mama had wanted that, too, but her mama had been sorely disappointed by a man who would abandon his young family. Mama had had a hard life. She'd had to work two jobs to support her young children. Often Molly witnessed her mama selling off the family wares and small pieces of furniture. Once Molly was old enough, she too began working—taking in mending after school, helping her mother wherever possible.

Molly's mother had tried her best and loved with all of her heart, but she'd never known true joy. Not the kind that Molly wished for. Not the kind that Molly vowed to have one day.

But gazing into Kane's stormy gray eyes, Molly saw obvious distress brewing there. She noted his concern. How could she not? And all of her joy evaporated. Just like that. In the blink of an eye. In the smallest of moments, she realized that nothing had changed for Kane last night.

He hadn't been swept away as she had. He hadn't succumbed to a heart filled with love, but rather a body filled with lust. She'd given herself fully, and Kane had taken only what he'd needed.

Molly closed her eyes, placing a hand to her belly. "Don't worry, Kane. If I'm anything like my mama, I won't be carrying your child today. It took years for mama to have me. She said it seems to run in the family."

The storm in Kane's eyes subsided a bit. His rigid stance relaxed as he stared at her. He nodded, and the relief she witnessed on his face destroyed all hope of a real marriage with Kane. He didn't want her. He didn't want her child. Again, she had to remind herself of the bargain they'd struck.

She was a temporary wife—a bride without a groom.

The ache went deep this time, cutting into her spirit, hollowing out her heart. There was no use for tears. Molly cried silently inside.

Kane moved quickly about the camp. Wordless, Molly took the cup of coffee he offered. And when he pulled a rawhide case Molly had once heard him refer to as a parfleche from his saddlebag, he handed it to her. "Try it. It's all we have for breakfast," he said.

"What is it?"

"Pemmican."

Her stomach grumbling, she realized that they hadn't eaten an evening meal last night. She'd been too frightened by the storm to worry about eating. And after, she'd been captivated by Kane, fed only by his sweet words and tender caresses.

Molly looked at Kane, then reached into the bag, coming up with a mixture that didn't appear appetizing at all. She brought it to her lips and tasted delicately. "It's good. Do I want to know what's in it?"

Kane's lips quirked, but never quite made a smile. "Winter food for the Cheyenne. Ground jerky and cherries mostly. It's breakfast for today."

Molly ate up, filling her belly and by the time she'd finished her coffee, Kane had the horses hitched and the wagon reloaded. He stood waiting for her by the side of the wagon. Molly readied to climb up, but Kane halted her. He stood there, contemplating, struggling with something he wanted to say. "Molly, if you are with child—"

Molly shook her head, unwilling to hear him out. He was too noble a man to allow a woman bearing his child to go without. He would do the honorable thing and take care of her. But Molly didn't want to hear that. She didn't want any other bargains or agreements with Kane. She didn't want to be his burden, a responsibility he'd rather not have. "We created a memory last night, Kane," she said softly. "Nothing more."

Molly helped herself up onto the wagon without

glancing back at him. She couldn't bear to see his reaction, his sigh of relief again. With steady nerves, she seated herself on the damp wagon seat and made ready for the ride back to the Bar J.

She no longer felt like she was going home.

The Bar J was as temporary a home as Kane was a husband.

Chapter Ten

"I'm sorry for you, Molly. I know the disappointment you must feel right now. But if Charlie is out there, we'll find him." Bennett smiled and pressed his hand to hers.

Molly sat in a tall comfortable chair in the dining room with Kane's grandfather, grateful to see that his health hadn't declined while they'd been gone. Bennett actually looked better and Molly felt hopeful. But she also knew that when one was ill, they had good days and bad days. Today, Bennett was having a good day, most likely because Kane had returned home. Not that Kane had spent much time with Bennett. As soon as they'd returned, he checked on his grandfather, making sure all was well, then rode off. Molly didn't know where Kane had gone, but he sure as heck had taken off like a jackrabbit while Molly had soaked in a tub before joining Bennett for dinner. "I can't thank you enough for all you've already done. It made our days on the trail easier."

Bennett waved a hand in the air. "Ah! I did nothing but send a few wires. There's more to be done. Don't you worry, now."

Molly managed a smile while she picked at her food, a plate filled with spicy meat and potatoes, vegetables and fresh tortillas, cooked up special by Lupe. She should be famished since she hadn't eaten anything since this morning. Her usual healthy appetite had waned since her conversation with Kane earlier. That, and the sad fact that she hadn't found her brother and had nowhere else to turn at the moment definitely stifled her hunger. Yet, she found that she'd missed Bennett's company. The old man had truly wedged a way into her heart.

"Eat up, Molly. You might be eating for two."

Molly gasped, dropping the fork from her hand. "For...two?" she managed, wondering how Bennett found out about her encounter with Kane last night. Had Kane told his grandfather?

But then Molly realized her mistake. Of course Bennett would naturally assume that she and Kane would soon conceive a child. Bennett believed the marriage real. He had no knowledge of the bargain she'd made. And even though he'd been first to dupe her, Molly felt shame and guilt about lying to the old man. Her duplicity weighed on her like a deep sea anchor. More than anything she hated lying.

"You and Kane will give me a great grandson before I die."

Molly couldn't blame the man. He wanted his legacy to be passed on to the next generation of Jacksons. She didn't have the heart to quell Bennett's hopes. "I, uh, maybe someday."

"Soon. I haven't got much longer," he said in a voice booming with life. Molly hadn't realized just how much better Bennett looked today, his appearance surely contradicting his words. Sunshine seemed to have colored his face, bringing on a healthy glow. He sat tall in his chair and he appeared to have put on some weight.

"I certainly hope not. I hope you have a long, long time, Grandfather."

Molly didn't feel she'd earned the right to call Bennett *Grandfather,* but he'd made her promise and had reminded her again when she'd returned this afternoon.

Bennett smiled. "You're good for my grandson. I hope he has come to realize that by now."

Molly sat silent. She wouldn't try to explain her relationship with Kane. She didn't quite understand it herself. She took a bite of food, reminded of Lupe's wonderful cooking abilities. If nothing else, Molly decided that while living on the ranch she would spend time in the kitchen and learn some of Lupe's recipes.

Surprisingly, Molly finished the entire meal. Bennett had smiled at her with approval. And after both enjoyed a dish of cherry cobbler, Bennett rose from the table, reaching for Molly's hand.

"Tomorrow, after you've gotten some rest, we'll talk about finding your brother."

"Thank you. I don't know what else to do. I appreciate any advice you have for me."

"Don't give up, child. I didn't. It may have taken years, but Kane came back to me, just as your Charlie will come back to you. Come, let me walk you upstairs. You need a good night's sleep."

Fatigue finally hit her after the grueling two weeks she had spent searching. She'd been through a great deal, including getting mixed up with a bunch of rebellious ladies, almost having her dignity taken by two ruffians in that shanty and then last night, the most tumultuous of all, giving herself to Kane only to find disappointment and rejection this morning.

Yes, Molly was tired. She took Bennett's hand and he escorted her to her room. Pride wouldn't allow her to ask about Kane's disappearance from the ranch tonight, but Molly wondered where he'd gone. And she wondered if Bennett knew anything about it.

"Good night," Molly said. "And I'm glad you're feeling better."

Bennett's eyes rounded in surprise, then he slumped a little, as if standing tall had taken all of his energy. "I wish I was feeling better," he said. Amazing how that one gesture had changed his appearance suddenly.

"But you look…healthier today."

Bennett made an attempt to smile, but with sadness in his eyes. "Looks deceive, Molly. I've found that in life, often times things are not truly how they appear."

"Oh, well, I'm sorry you're not feeling well. I had hoped…" But Molly couldn't finish her thought.

Things are not truly how they appear. How true a statement. Guilt assailed her again at having to lie to Bennett about her relationship with Kane. The old man deserved more, but she couldn't bring herself to destroy his hope.

Bennett kissed her cheek. "Good night, Molly. I'll see you in the morning."

"Yes, I'll see you in the morning."

Once inside her room, Molly undressed quickly, putting on her nightgown and climbed into the big, cozy, comfortable bed. She relished the feel of clean sheets and a soft mattress and soon she succumbed to much-needed sleep.

Kane entered the bedroom quietly just after midnight and walked in silence toward his bed. Silhouetted by moonlight, Molly slept with the covers tossed off, her hair tangled around her throat, her nightdress hiked up her legs thigh high. Deep in sleep, she appeared peaceful. And beautiful.

Kane walked around to his side of the bed, regretting his decision to leave the ranch once he'd seen his grandfather. Bennett had looked well, which eased Kane's mind a bit, but even though Kane had others to visit today after his long absence, guilt tore at his gut at leaving Molly alone tonight.

True, she probably hadn't been *all* alone. His grandfather had taken a shine to his wife, and he'd bet his last dollar that Bennett more than made up for Kane's absence today.

Kane hated to admit that he'd missed Molly. He'd planned on spending the night out on the range, leaving Molly to sleep in peace, but thoughts of her kept surfacing, entering his mind at steady and unwelcome intervals, until Kane found himself riding hard and fast back to the house.

He unfastened the buttons on his shirt and tossed it down. Next he removed his boots and off came the rest of his clothes. He glanced once again at Molly and almost turned away from the bed, but her peaceful form beckoned him. He'd slept with her for two weeks, and damn if he didn't want her back in his arms again.

He knew they would never make love the way they

had the other night. No, they both had too much to lose. But he wanted to be close to her once again, and know the same sort of peace he'd had last night.

Kane climbed into bed, rolled over quietly until he came up so close that Molly's flowery scent filled his nostrils. He breathed it in and closed his eyes, laying an arm over her middle, protectively.

"Kane?" she whispered so quietly that he barely heard her.

He opened his eyes, sorry that he'd disturbed her. "Shhh, go back to sleep."

Only half awake, Molly scooted closer, her backside dangerously near his groin. She was a petite woman, yet their bodies adjusted accordingly, like two pieces of a puzzle, fitting in all the right places. Soon his desire would become evident, so Kane pulled that part of his body away. He refused to move away entirely though, wanting the peace Molly offered with her soft sounds and welcoming body.

"It's late," she murmured.

He didn't respond.

"Didn't feel right sleeping without you," she said, her voice drifting and Kane wondered if she'd recall her words in the morning.

He'd be a fool to deny her claim. They'd only been together a short time in a marriage that held no meaning to him yet it didn't feel right without her beside him.

He stroked her shoulders, rubbing them gently, soothing her back to sleep. Kane couldn't have her awaken and turn to him with sleep-drugged dewy eyes. He couldn't have her snuggle closer and touch him the way she had last night.

Kane thanked the Almighty that the day's journey had exhausted her. She fell back to sleep instantly.

Kane closed his eyes then, finding the peace he sought. In Molly's arms.

Three days later, Molly sat in the kitchen watching Lupe make bread. Morning rays warmed the room and brought a brightness that Molly didn't feel. There was nothing sunny about Molly's disposition lately. She slumped in the seat making mental notes on a recipe she would surely forget. Despondent from their failure to find her brother, and Kane's complete withdrawal from their marriage, Molly had little else to do and knew a good measure of boredom.

Molly held on to hope, but with each passing day, her faith seemed to be slipping. And as for Kane, well, he'd slept with her every night, holding her protectively as though if he let her go, something vile might happen to her, yet he kept his distance in all other ways. And she wondered where he went at night, when he'd take off after their evening meal, only to return late in the wee hours of the night. If she were a suspicious woman, she might be jealous.

Oh, heck. She was suspicious. And jealous of whomever Kane spent his nights with. Tonight, she vowed to question him, no matter how late he came in.

"Senor Bennett will not come down today," Lupe said, as she added spices and herbs to the dough before kneading it with her fists. "He is not well."

Molly perked up, sitting straight in her seat now. "What's wrong with him?"

Lupe shook her head. "He coughs. He is weak."

"But he seemed better when we arrived home."

"*Sí*. He had good days. But no longer. He does not want his breakfast, but I make it for him. He must eat to be strong."

"Let me bring his breakfast up to him, Lupe. I would like to see him today."

"*Sí*, he would like to see his new granddaughter. For you, he will eat his meal, no?"

"I hope so. I've grown fond of him, Lupe." And Molly realized to her dismay that she'd fallen in love with both Jackson men, one wily, sweet old man who doted on her truly like one of his own, and Kane, the mule-headed man she'd married.

Molly watched Lupe prepare the meal. She helped by cutting up vegetables and frying eggs while the housekeeper fixed up a lovely tray complete with a small bouquet of vibrant bluebonnets.

Lupe placed the tray in her arms. "You make Senor Bennett feel better. Go!"

Molly obeyed Lupe's command, happy for the diversion and concerned for Bennett's health. She took the stairs carefully, holding the tray in both arms, and knocked on his door with the toe of her boot.

At first, there was no answer.

Molly knocked again, this time louder.

And she waited.

"What is it?" Bennett responded, his voice more irritated than weak-sounding, and Molly wondered if she'd caught him at a bad moment.

"Grandfather?" she said, sliding her hand on the knob and using her hip to push the door open while holding the tray steady.

There was a quick motion and when she glanced up, she saw Bennett tucking himself into the covers of his bed. "Good morning," she said, cheerily. "I brought you breakfast."

"Oh, I told Lupe I didn't feel much like eating."

Molly walked into the room, setting the tray down on a table by his bed. "You need your strength."

Molly glanced at the wide-open window. Curtains billowed from a slight breeze as morning sunshine spilled in. Molly crossed the room and glanced out the window. She spied a wooden ladder leaning against the wall leading up to the window and immediate questions came to mind. If she didn't know better…

She glanced at Bennett, who seemed to have slumped down in the bed, the sheets pulled up to his chin and his eyes closing as if he was just too tuckered out to keep them open.

Molly took a last look at the ladder then shook away her silly thoughts.

"How are you feeling this morning?" she asked, concerned by his sudden poor condition.

"Oh, ah…tired. Didn't get much sleep, coughing half the night, you know. I think I'm gonna sleep the morning away. Thank you for breakfast, child."

"I'll stay while you eat." Molly pulled up a chair. "The nourishment will do you good."

Bennett sighed, the breath whooshing out of his chest in stages until Molly noted a resigned expression stealing over his face. "I guess I can't get away from you women, forcing food on me. First Lupe, now you."

"That's right, you can't. So you might as well make us happy and fill your belly."

Bennett nodded. "All right. But I need some rest first. You go on, Molly. There's no need to sit here and spoon-feed me, though I do appreciate your concern. I promise you, this food will get eaten in due time."

Molly pulled her lower lip in, contemplating. Bennett seemed to want privacy and rest. "As long as I have your word?"

With a smile and a nod, he agreed. "You have my word. I'll eat later, once I've rested."

Bennett closed his eyes again, the struggle to keep them open, perhaps too difficult. Molly realized that her silly suspicions earlier had been ill-founded. Bennett was a prideful man and didn't want the family to know of his declining health. He put on a good show for everyone, until the strength simply drained from his body. Today was one of those days where the illness took from him more than he wanted to give.

Molly bent to kiss his forehead, finding his skin quite cool. Relieved by that good sign, she bid him farewell. "I'll check on you this afternoon."

Bennett smiled with relief. "Yes, this afternoon. After I've rested. I'll look forward to it, Molly dear."

"And I'll read to you by the window."

"I'd like that."

Molly exited the room with a knot twisting in her stomach.

Poor Bennett wasn't feeling better at all. In truth, he was doing everything in his power to pretend otherwise for all of their sakes. How sweet and kind of him, she thought, deeply worried. There had been so many keen losses in her life up until now.

Molly couldn't bear to think of one more.

She exited the room, backing out and closing the door quietly. When she turned around, she bumped right smack into Kane. "Oh!"

The collision might have toppled her off balance if he hadn't immediately reached out to catch her. He held her arms steady. "Leaving so soon?" he asked, glancing at Bennett's door. "Lupe said you were up here."

"Yes," she whispered, "I brought up Bennett's breakfast, but he's too tired to eat right now. He's sleeping again."

Kane nodded and muttered, "Damn, I wanted to see him before I rode out."

He was riding out again? Kane never seemed to spend time at the house. She assumed he worked the land and cattle, just like all the other ranch hands, but that didn't explain why he came home so late at night. "Where are you going?"

Kane hesitated and she could see it in his eyes that he debated about his answer. "Into town."

Molly's heart raced and she nearly jumped out of her skin. "You're going into Bountiful!"

Kane grabbed her wrist and pulled her away from his grandfather's door. "Shhh," he commanded in a low voice and Molly admonished herself for forgetting about Bennett for the moment. "We're low on supplies and Rusty isn't about to leave the ranch while we're in the middle of branding. I figured I should volunteer, since I've been away a while."

Kane's touch, even the cautionary hold he had on her wrist was enough to send her nerves to tingling. "Were you going to invite me along?"

Kane's mouth twisted and he let go a long sigh. He

dropped her wrist and took a step back. "No. I came up here to see my grandfather. It's a quick trip, Molly. I'm not fond of Bountiful and the town's not fond of me."

Molly knew better than to argue. She cast him a genuine warm smile. "Thank you, I'd be pleased to join you."

"Molly," Kane began, shaking his head.

"I need to check with the telegraph operator. We haven't heard any word about those wires your grandfather sent out."

"I'd planned on doing that."

"I'll save you the time. Please," Molly begged, "your grandfather is wonderful and Lupe is so kind, but I need to do something to find my brother. I'm going stir-crazy in the house all day."

Kane swept her a doubtful look. "Every time I take you somewhere, there's trouble."

"Not today. I promise, Kane. I'll do just as you say. You won't even know I'm there."

Again Kane swept her a look, this time his gaze devouring her from head to toe. Molly felt naked, bared to him in all ways and that hungry look made her ache in her lower regions, reminding her of the night they'd made love.

Kane grunted his reply. "Little Bird, I always know you're there."

But Molly only smiled and mentally readied for her trip into Bountiful.

The day was looking up.

Later that afternoon, Molly entered Miss Deidre's Dress shop, her heart nearly crushed with disappointment. She'd vowed not to give up, yet tucked away in her reticule were half a dozen returned messages from far and wide, all claiming they had no knowledge of a Charles McGuire. After reading each one with eager anticipation, she'd crumbled the pieces of correspondence in her trembling hand.

Molly had never known such dire frustration. She knew of nowhere else to turn. She could only hold out hope that the detective that Bennett Jackson had summoned to the Bar J would come up with a clue to Charlie's whereabouts, yet Molly's patience seemed at an all-time low. Detective Wheatley wouldn't even arrive until next week, an eternity in Molly's view. His investigation might be her last hope in finding her brother. She was grateful for Bennett's assistance, but time seemed to be slipping away—the longer she went without word of Charlie, the less she believed the search fruitful.

The bell above the door jingled, startling Molly out of her sullen thoughts. She looked up and glanced around the shop, noting all the finery, from bolts of silk and taffeta and lace, to ready-made gowns, detailed to delicate precision. Yards of ribbon in every color of the rainbow brought one wall to life, while the other wall housed beautiful chemises and petticoats and undergarments.

Garments all female in nature decorated the shop, and an array of flowery scents mingled through the air from one corner of the shop designated for sachets and tiny fragrant soaps.

When Molly saw a familiar face, her sour mood changed into something more pleasant. She'd been so lonely and bored, that even this woman's presence was welcomed. "Mrs. Rose?" She walked over to the older woman, who held a lovely dress in her arms. Oh, it wasn't a fancy gown fit for a social affair, but it was certainly a dress that would brighten any woman's wardrobe. "Hello. It's good to see you."

Penelope Rose appeared startled for a moment and she shoved the dress she'd been holding back onto the rack. "M-Molly, dear girl," she said, stumbling with her words. Molly noted an odd expression on her face. "Yes, it's g-good to s-see you as well."

Molly smiled, deciding that catching the woman off guard did have some merit. "It's a beautiful dress. Are you making a purchase?"

Flustered, the woman's gaze darted around the shop before finding Molly again. "Oh, well, I don't know. Where would I have occasion to wear such a nice dress?"

"Well, um. I don't know, but it's certainly a lovely color."

Molly reached in and pulled the soft cream dress off the rack again, giving it a second look. "Yes, it's a perfect color for you. It will show off your pretty brown eyes."

"My eyes?" Penelope Rose seemed to take interest.

"Yes, and the lace is lovely, don't you agree?"

"Yes, yes. I do agree."

The proprietor of the shop walked up. "We have this dress in two other colors as well. But you may not want the pink one. Miss Lacey Shannon purchased it just this morning. Seems she's smitten with a young cowhand. If Lacey has anything to do with it, when he comes back from the trial drive, Roper McCall won't stand much of a chance."

Molly blinked.

She shook out her ears.

And stared at Miss Deidre for all she was worth.

"Excuse me," she began, her mind filling with myriad thoughts. "But did you say, *Roper McCall?*"

"Yes, yes. I'm sure of it. Miss Lacey went on and on about him. She's hoping for a beau and you know how young girls are. Why, I get half my business from gals trying to gain a boy's favor."

Deidre glanced at Penelope Rose. The older woman's face drained, as if she were guilty of some forbidden act. Molly thought it strange, but she couldn't dwell on that. She had to get to the bottom of this Roper McCall person.

"Did she say what he looked like?"

Deidre put a hand to her head in a mock swoon. "Oh, yes. He's the most handsome boy of all," she said with a sigh. Then her voice changed to an even pitch. "Aren't they all at that young age?"

Molly's heart pounded against her chest. All of a sudden she felt light-headed and if the afternoon had been a tad warmer, she might have fainted. But hope settled in her heart. Dear, dear sweet hope.

"Roper McCall," she rushed out, turning to Mrs. Rose, "was one of the dime novel heroes my brother was always reading about. He worshipped him! Could it be?" But Molly knew it *had* to be. It all made sense now. She hadn't been able to find Charlie McGuire anywhere in west Texas because her runaway brother had changed his name.

Beyond excited, Molly asked the proprietor, "Tell me, how can I find Miss Lacey Shannon?"

"Why, her father owns the Lazy S Ranch, but Lacey might still be in town. She left my shop just half an hour ago."

Molly hugged Deidre tight then did the same to Mrs. Rose. "You buy that dress now, Mrs. Rose," she said. "Even if you're not trying to entice a man, you deserve something new and pretty!"

Mrs. Rose nodded, seeming to take her advice and keeping strangely quiet for longer than Molly had ever recalled.

Molly dashed out of the shop, searching for Kane. And if she couldn't find him, then she'd set out to search for Miss Lacey Shannon on her own.

One way or another Molly would have news of her brother today!

Chapter Eleven

"No, I'm not going to take you to Kansas!"

Kane glared across the wagon seat at his wife and shook his head adamantly. With fire in her green eyes, Molly returned the look with a heated one of her own, but he didn't much care. She'd been irrational about this subject since the moment he'd spied her nearly accosting Miss Shannon at the diner.

The young gal was having a meal with her father, and Parker Shannon hadn't much appreciated Molly's interruption. If Kane hadn't intervened on Molly's behalf, the rancher might have lost all patience with her. But darn, if Molly didn't get exactly what she wanted—affirmation that Charlie McGuire had indeed assumed the name of Roper McCall. At least his description fit and Parker pretty much confirmed that the boy he'd hired was as green as they come. He'd labeled him an Easterner, but a hard worker and someone smart enough to do the job.

"But Charlie's headed there," Molly argued, "and if he doesn't return to Bountiful, I'll lose track of him."

"You heard what Parker Shannon said. Roper McCall has a place at his ranch, if he wants it. And judging by the way Lacey's eyes lit just mentioning his name, I'm sure that your brother's returning."

"But why won't you take me to him?"

"He'll be home in two weeks, maybe less."

"An eternity!" Molly folded her arms and pouted, tears stinging her eyes.

The wagon lurched forward and Kane slapped the reins urging the horses to move faster. The sooner he got Molly back to the Bar J, the better. No telling what thoughts swam around in her head at the moment. "You ought to be glad," he said, watching her pretty face change expressions from angry, to sad, to angry again. Kane had never met a more fired-up woman. "At least you know your brother's alive."

"I am glad. But Kane," Molly pleaded, turning to face him again. "What if something happens to him? What if he decides not to come back? What if I never find him again?"

Kane rubbed his nose, hiding a grin. Wouldn't do to let Molly see that she'd humored him. "And what if the sun decides never to shine again?" Kane shook his head and looked directly into her eyes. "Let it be, Molly. He'll come back. He has a job and a woman waiting for him. That's more than most men have."

Molly sank back in the wagon seat, folding her arms and pouting her lips again. Her chest, heavy with anxiety, heaved up and down and Kane took note. His wife had womanly attributes he couldn't ignore. And each night, as he held her close, those female qualities had tempted and teased him. He'd vowed not to make love to her again, but his body seemed to be ignoring that command.

He wanted her.

And that fact irritated him no end. He couldn't stay away, having to hold her close and breathe in her scent, listen to the throaty, sexy sounds she made in those moments before sleep claimed her. And once she slept, then Kane, too, found the solace he needed.

Molly mumbled again, refusing to give up. "You're not holding up your part of the bargain, Kane Jackson. You agreed to help me find my brother, if I pretended to be your wife."

"You *are* my wife," he said, surprising himself. "Right now anyway," he added. "But I can't leave the ranch now. Not with my grandfather's health the way it is."

Kane slanted her a look. He didn't trust Molly to listen to reason. "And you're not going without me, understand?"

"But I could take the stage or maybe the railroad goes—"

"No." He put as much force in that single word as he knew how. "Remember what happened to you in Fallen Oak?"

Molly shivered. Even though he hated the reminder, Molly had to understand the danger of her traveling alone. "You and I both know what would have happened if I hadn't showed up when I did."

Molly closed her eyes. "I know."

Kane had gone a little bit crazy that day, and Molly believed he'd been acting out his revenge against the man who had killed Little Swan. But while those thoughts are always with him, that day and at that time in Fallen Oak, when those men had brutalized Molly, he had been acting on her behalf and her behalf alone. The thought of either of those men touching her, hurting her or worse, had spurred on murderous impulses. Kane had wanted to kill them.

And he might have, if Molly hadn't stopped him.

"Molly, I need your word you won't run off the ranch, searching for your brother."

Molly made no attempt to agree.

"Molly."

She took another deep breath and Kane noted her generous chest again. Half the time he reprimanded her and half the time he lusted after her. No other woman had had this effect on him, leaving Kane befuddled most of the time.

"I'm asking for your word," he pressed.

When she didn't respond, Kane halted the horses abruptly and the wagon jerked to a stop. He turned and looked her squarely in the eyes, waiting. All was silent, except for the whinny of the horses, each at different intervals, perhaps in complaint as the sun beat down with unrelenting force.

Molly held his attention, her lips trembling, her eyes moist with unshed tears. And finally, she confessed, "It's just that I miss him so much."

Kane understood too well the emptiness that consumes a body when their loved one is gone. He knew of Molly's desperate desire to reunite what family she had left. And he also knew, as she did, that soon Bennett Jackson and the Bar J would no longer be her home. "I know, Little Bird."

Kane bent his head and kissed her trembling lips tenderly. Molly responded as he might have predicted, returning his kiss in a fashion that simply asked for more. He cupped her face, his fingers going into her silky sunset tresses. And when she moaned into his mouth, Kane swept his tongue inside, tasting her once again.

Molly threw her arms about his neck, and in rhythm with each other, they moved closer. There were so many things Kane wanted to say to her, so many things he might confess, but he couldn't and wouldn't, for he and Molly had made a pact, as unholy as it might seem. Very soon, Kane would set her free.

But for now, he took pleasure in her, sliding his hands along her slim frame, caressing her breasts, following the hollow of her slight waist and squeezing her womanly hips.

His hands roamed freely, touching her in places that created sighs of delight, and when he cupped her buttocks, bringing her fully up against his swollen manhood, Molly didn't pull away, but rather slid her body to his in invitation.

"Kane," she whispered into his mouth.

"Molly," Kane said, ready to lay her down in the bed of the wagon. Ready to strip off her clothes and bare her skin under the glistening sunlight. Kane was ready to do all that, but, and with every ounce of his willpower, he did not.

Instead, he pulled away, breaking off their intimate connection. He stared into Molly's questioning eyes, knowing full well what she had wanted. What he had wanted.

But Kane had no answers. He had only the truth of their bargain. And making love to Molly again would only give her hope that would be unfounded.

Kane picked up the reins and urged the horses on.

From the corner of his eye, he noted Molly's slump back into the seat, her arms folded, perhaps her heart damaged with disappointment.

Kane knew that same disappointment. And tonight would be a true test of his will. For turning Molly away on an open road during the light of day was one thing.

Turning her away during a moonlit night within the cozy confines of their bed was another thing entirely.

Molly paced the bedroom. She'd been restless and angry the better part of the day. Kane had made a promise to her, and he'd fully backed out. And now, as night fell, with Kane nowhere in sight, Molly had nothing to do but fuel her anger with undisguised fury.

The bargain she'd made with Kane had reared up to kick her in the backside. His refusal to take her to Charlie hurt. His rejection this afternoon killed. She simply couldn't fathom how he could be so tender and giving one moment, then cold and unyielding the next.

Molly couldn't understand how Kane could hold her lovingly, drink from her lips like a man dying of thirst, touch her where no man had ever dared, making her very senses come alive, and then as easy as peach pie, turn away from her.

Did ice run in his veins?

Or was he still mourning Little Swan's death?

Neither alternative could have improved her mood.

Molly strode to the window and, parting the curtain, stared out into the starlit night. It was truly a night to behold, with freshness about the air and thousands of stars shining above.

Molly felt caged, cooped up in a lonely room.

She'd read to Bennett this afternoon, the only bright spot in her day, keeping him abreast of Charlie's whereabouts, his name change and all. Gently, he had agreed with Kane. She would be smart to stay put, and let Charlie come home to her. Molly hadn't agreed with either of the Jackson men, but she'd given her word.

Or had she?

Molly shook off that perplexing thought, trying as well to shake off Kane's rejection of her this afternoon. Too unsettled and fidgety to sleep, Molly grabbed her shawl and dashed out of the room.

She needed a diversion, something to quell her anger.

And ten minutes later, under the protest of Bernardo, a ranch hand she'd nabbed as he walked out of the bunkhouse, Molly sat atop a mare named Sweet Pea. The ranch hand assured her the horse was the gentlest in their remuda.

Molly knew how to ride, although it had been a while. Back in St. Louis, each time her mama took sick, Molly would borrow her neighbor's mare to fetch the doctor. Clumsy at first, soon she'd learned how to stay atop the old mare without too much difficultly. She'd promised Bernardo. She would ride along a well-worn path and return shortly.

Already, Molly's anger eased some. She breathed in crisp evening air and rode quietly, away from the Bar J and all that had upset her today. The horse knew the terrain, which aided Molly greatly, and she granted the mare her trust. They headed north to a part of the Bar J that Molly had never seen—a place with less grassland, less open spaces, where the earth was interrupted by foliage, low-lying scrubs and trees.

Molly rode along a brook, the waters neither calm nor rushing, but somewhere in between, the steady flow lapping over rocks. And as Molly looked ahead, she spied a shadowy figure coming out from behind a tree.

Her heart stopped.

A sense of dread enveloped her.

The eerie shadow became more visible and Molly shrieked her surprise, completely stunned by the sight of the Indian. Molly's disturbance startled the mare. She spooked, twisting her head and rearing up on her front legs.

Molly couldn't hold her balance. The mare jolted her up from the saddle, and Molly flew through the air, landing hard on the solid packed earth. She hit her head on something sharp, and as she struggled to remain conscious, a blurred vision appeared right before her eyes.

She stared into the curious eyes of a young Indian girl.

Then all went black.

Kane cursed and at the same time sent up a prayer for Molly's safety. Bending over her still form, he didn't know what God to summon, having been born into Christianity but raised by the Cheyenne and their beliefs, so Kane sent up the prayer anyway, for anyone willing to listen.

"Molly," he said softly, laying his palm on her cheek. "Molly, can you hear me?"

She moved her head slightly and with eyes still closed, she returned, "Kane?"

He heard a note of pain in her voice and his gut tightened with fear. "Molly, can you open your eyes?"

She tried. He saw movement, squinting and blinking until finally, she opened her eyes. "There's two of you. No, three. No," she said, closing her eyes once again. "Give me a minute."

Kane waited and when Molly reopened her eyes, she looked up at him again. "Now, there's only one of you."

Greatly relieved, Kane tamped down his anger. For now. Seems no matter how hard he tried he couldn't keep Molly from trouble.

"That's good, Little Bird." He pressed his kerchief to the side of her head. "You're bleeding. You must have hit your head on this rock." He lifted the small piece of granite up for her to see. "Lucky for you, the rock is small and your head is hard."

Molly attempted a smile, then her expression changed to concern. "There was a little Indian girl."

Kane nodded.

"I'd never seen an Indian before. Not up close like that. And I was alone and well, seeing that Indian girl surprised me more than anything. I screamed and, well, I guess Sweet Pea isn't used to female screams."

"No, I don't suppose she is. Can you sit up?"

"Yes," she nodded, and made an attempt. Kane held her carefully, lifting her slowly to a sitting position. He waited while she adjusted, focusing her eyes once again. When Kane noted a pained look on her face, he didn't hesitate. He scooped her up gently and carried her to his horse. "I'll see to your bruises once I get you back to the ranch."

Kane managed to hold her and mount his mare. There, he set her across his lap and spurred his horse on.

"What about my horse?" she asked.

"Sweet Pea knows the way back."

Molly bit down on her lip. "You're awfully quiet, Kane."

He made no attempt to answer.

"Are you angry?"

Again, he kept silent. In truth, he was furious with his renegade wife. She knew nothing of the dangers of living out here in the West. She took thoughtless chances with her life, driven strictly by emotion. She was as impetuous as she was foolish.

They rode back to the ranch in silence, Kane holding Molly in his arms, wondering how she would fare in this world once he set her free. But with that, came another thought. Pretty Miss Molly McGuire wouldn't be alone too long. In a land where men outnumbered women by handfuls, she'd be certain to find a beau, perhaps a husband, in a short time.

The thought did not grant him solace.

And he turned that unwelcome thought inward, hiding the sentiment within the layers of his anger and frustration. Once they reached the Bar J, Kane dismounted with Molly in his arms. He set her on the front porch, and once he was assured she could stand without aid, he took his mare's reins. "Get some rest," he ordered, none too gently. "I'll see to the horses first, then I'll be up."

Molly took a big swallow and agreed.

Ten minutes later, Sweet Pea appeared, snorting loudly by the barn, letting her presence be known. Kane took time with both horses, grooming them down, then corralling them. With a deep sigh, Kane stood in front of the large ranch house, staring up at their bedroom window. A dim light glowed and the golden hue beckoned him to his wayward wife.

Kane was a man who'd always been certain of his deeds. He was a man who could always, without doubt, control his needs. Yet, he climbed the stairs with great reluctance, his anger warring with desire.

And for the first time in his life, Kane didn't know which response would win out.

Kane took one look at Molly, laying across his bed, her silken hair flowing over the pillow, fully dressed but for the boots she'd removed, appearing peaceful and serene amid her bruises, and held on to his anger.

With his back against the wall, he shook his head. "You could've been killed, damn it."

Startled, Molly sat up and blinked.

"Even a fool knows not to go riding alone at night. Especially if she's as inexperienced as you."

"But I—"

Kane approached, shaking his head. "No, Molly. No excuses this time. You were damn lucky. If you'd fallen on harder ground, hit your head on a bigger rock, you and I wouldn't be having this conversation."

"You mean argument," she said, the fire in her eyes, lighting.

"Okay, argument."

Kane sat down on the bed and began unbuttoning her dress.

"Wh-what are you doing?" she asked.

"Checking for injuries. Now, lay down and be still."

For once, Molly did as she was told and he slid the dress from her shoulders. "You need a lesson in listening."

"You mean I need a lesson in obeying you."

"Hell, yes. That would be a start."

Kane glanced at her throat and shoulders, then gently turned her over to view her back. He set her back down, outlining one rather large brownish purple bruise, just over her right breast. "You're going to be sore here," he said, his finger retracing the bruise. "And here," he traced along another smaller bruise.

He heard Molly's intake of breath. She responded to his touch the way no other woman ever had. And she gave him full access to her body, conveying her trust in him.

Kane rose from the bed. He wasn't here to seduce his wife. He was here to teach her a lesson, to admonish her for once again, putting herself in danger. He poured water from a pitcher and soaked a cloth, then strode back to sit on the bed and set the cool cloth on her chest. "I need to know why."

"Why?" Molly asked, her fingers brushing his as both held the cloth in place.

"Why do you do the things you do? Why do you get yourself in so much darn trouble?"

"I—I d-don't know. Headstrong, I suppose," Molly said, but with no apology in her voice. She simply stated it as fact.

"And tonight? Why'd you go running off tonight?"

"I wasn't going for Charlie, if that's what you were thinking," she defended.

Kane shook his head. "If you were, then you packed lightly. You wouldn't have gotten too far without provisions. No, I know you weren't running off to your brother."

Molly stared out the window, her lips trembling, her eyes filling with moisture.

"Why?" Kane pressed and, with her eyes diverted, he looked his fill at his wife. Her shoulders glistened in the faint light, a stream touching on the softness of her skin, the frailty of her beauty. She lay there exposed to him, yet not with her body this time, but with her heart. And Kane knew that whatever Molly had to say to him, he would listen intently.

She turned to look at him then, one sole tear escaping down her cheek. "It's just…everything."

Kane pursed his lips and leaned back, perplexed. "Everything?"

She nodded. "It's not being able to go after Charlie," she said slowly. "And this bargain we've made." Another tear escaped. "I hate lying to your grandfather everyday."

Kane listened as she went on. "And you, you're the worst of all."

Stunned, Kane took a moment to let that set in. He'd always prided himself in doing his best, and to hear that he had failed Molly in some way rattled him. "Me?"

She nodded without hesitation. "You're my husband. But, you're not really. You proved that again, just this afternoon. You go off every day and every night. I'm lonely and bored most of the time."

Molly sat up, then rose from the bed to walk to the window. She stared out, holding her dress with one hand to keep it from slipping down her backside.

She made a lovely vision, standing there against the moonlit night. And the gentle sobs she tried to hold back tore into his gut.

Kane's anger vanished in that one second and suddenly he came to see Molly's plight with wide-open

eyes. She saw her life as it truly was—a woman depen-
dent on finding her only kin. A woman, who within a
short time would have no home and no means of employment. She wasn't a deceiver, yet she'd been expected to deceive an old man and live her life as a lie.
Kane saw all those things in Molly and so much more.

He strode the distance to the window and faced her.
There in her eyes, he saw all he needed to see. Willingly,
Kane shed his defenses, breaking the barrier that sepa-
rated him from his wife.

Kane knew what Molly needed. It was the same with
him. It was what he'd fought against for weeks. For the
time they had together, he would be a true husband to
her. And then, perhaps the lie they lived would not be
such a great one.

"Molly," he said, unfolding the fingers that held her
dress in place. It slipped to the floor in a puddle around
her bare feet. She stood before him in a thin chemise and
a layer of petticoats. "I will be the husband you need."

Molly's intake of breath, a bit unsteady because of
her sobs, gladdened his heart. Her lips parted in a slight
smile. "And I'll be the wife you desire."

Those bold words shot straight to his groin. His body
tightened, the shaft of his manhood growing hard as
stone. Kane bent to kiss the bruises on her chest, his
hands palming the soft round mounds of her breasts.
Molly threw her head back, allowing him full contact,
and Kane knew at that moment, that he would never
fight his desire for her again.

Within moments, Molly was bared to him, her beautiful body fully exposed for his viewing. Kane kissed her
lips over and over while his hands roamed freely, once

again absorbing her softness, learning her textures. She wrapped her arms about his neck and drew up closer, her breasts crushing his chest and her woman's mound teasing the tip of his erection.

Kane had never known such desire before. He groaned and reached around her backside to bring her fully against him. Both moaned at the heady pleasure, standing there against the window with moonlight spilling in, oblivious to any world but the one they created with each other.

"I can't breathe," Molly said, kissing him fully on the mouth. "And it feels wonderful."

Kane cupped her derriere and lifted her legs. Automatically they wound around his waist. He walked her over to the bed and even through his buckskin pants her female form tormented him. He laid her down on his big bed and, standing over her, he removed all of his clothes.

Chapter Twelve

Molly held her breath watching Kane undress before her. He kicked off his boots, then with steady hands removed his buckskin shirt, the fringe catching a thin stream of light as he lifted the garment over his head. Bronzed and rippled with muscles, Kane was a man to admire. Molly's heart raced. Her body reacted. The anticipation of having Kane join her on the big, wide bed left her giddy and eager.

And when he removed his pants and she witnessed the full extent of his desire, Molly couldn't help but think him a powerful warrior, a man who belonged in an untamed world—a man she would love with the whole of her heart, regardless of their differences, regardless of the unholy alliance they'd made.

With outstretched arms, she beckoned him and the returning smile he cast her warmed her heart. Kane joined her on the bed and kissed her with hot, hungry lips. Molly lay there, bared to him, giving up her body as well as her heart. Kane stroked her with gentle loving hands, touching her skin and searing her soul. She moved with him, finding the pattern he set, the rhythm. Together, they glided in this world of lusty strokes and emboldened moves. They touched and explored each other, finding ways to pleasure one another, murmuring sweet words until their sounds became more anguished, their touches more demanding.

Kane whispered to her hurriedly, repeating his words from before, "I will be the husband you need." He cupped her between the legs, and with deft fingers found the center of her womanhood. She cried out from the sheer pleasured force of his stroking. But Kane did not stop there, he continued kissing her in places that made her body tense with joy. His lips moved onto her throat, her shoulders, and then he spent time laving each breast, making each peak pebble and come alive from his ministrations. She ached from the tormenting pleasure and moved alone now, setting a pace of her own. Higher. Higher.

Kane whispered, "Let go, Little Bird. Fly."

And Molly did fly, her body and soul reaching up to grasp the highest cloud, her world filling with wonder and grace.

"Kane!" she screamed at that exact exhilarating moment, and his mouth came down to muffle her cries.

She sank slowly to the bed and gazed up at the man she loved. He smiled and kissed her lips and somehow Molly felt as if she'd pleased him, when it seemed obvious to her that he had been the one to do all the pleasing.

"There's more," he said, nibbling on her throat. "If you're willing."

Molly moved her body, spreading her legs, ready for Kane's lovemaking. "I'm willing," she breathed out, and within moments, she and Kane were joined.

She closed her eyes, relishing the feel of being one with her man. She loved the sensation, the tingles that swept through her body, the feeling of being possessed solely by this man. And when Kane moved, his manhood filling her full, her body accepting him in all ways, Molly's heart soared to new heights.

He was her husband. She was his wife. This was real.

Molly had never known such utter joy. She moved with him, trying her best to please him in every way, allowing her instincts to take hold. She kissed him passionately, stroked his shoulders, his back, absorbed his strength, enjoyed his beautiful body until once again they moved in a world of their own, faster and harder. Molly let go all of her inhibitions, until once again she felt herself flying.

Kane kissed her one last time.

And to her surprise, he left the warmth of her body. He flopped onto his back, lying very still.

"Kane?" Stunned, she rose up to look at him.

He shook his head and spoke softly. "We cannot create a child."

Molly's joy evaporated, realizing that her reality and Kane's were so different. Yes, they were married and yes, they would make love. But Kane had never deceived her of his feelings. He didn't love her. He didn't want her child. Molly had to face facts and learn to accept that Kane offered her all that he possibly could.

Was it possible to love someone so very much and experience hatred at the same time? Molly thought so, because deep down inside, Kane had injured her beyond repair. Her heart bled from the loss. But he'd always been honest, giving her no reason for false hope. And for that Molly was truly grateful.

She sat there for a moment, making a decision. She could either keep a fine distance from Kane, making herself miserable or she could accept what he offered and rejoice in the time they had together. Molly chose the latter. She would have time to be miserable later on once they'd met all the terms of their bargain.

For now, Molly decided to hold on to what she could.

"You didn't fly," she whispered, surprising herself at her brazen remark.

"No, and it will be this way," he admitted.

Molly laid a hand on his abdomen. "Show me how to help."

Kane gazed at her, a bit surprised, but also with a hint of appreciation. "You would do that?"

Molly nodded, wondering if what she suggested was somehow forbidden or, worse, abhorred. "Is it all right?"

Kane covered his hand over hers and began her lesson. And soon she learned it was not only all right, but for a man like Kane, perhaps it was a blessing.

Kane woke in the minutes before daybreak, finding himself in a tangle of sheets and Molly's limbs. Decidedly, not a bad place to be. He closed the small gap of their bodies, snuggling up against her, placing an arm around her waist. Her female scent mingled smoothly with the aftermath of their lovemaking, flavoring the air with an alluring mix. He breathed in deeply and silently sighed.

Molly slept nude beside him, a fact Kane had trouble ignoring. Kane leaned in to kiss her cheek before he rose for the day, but Molly made a provocative sound, a little whimper that alerted his body in a very male way.

He marveled at how she responded to his slightest touch, how she gave as much as she received. He still reeled in pleasant shock at Molly's bold behavior last night. She had brought him unforeseen satisfaction so innocently that Kane also marveled at her unselfish nature.

Kane kissed her again, nipping at her earlobe. He sensed her smile, and when she covered her hand over his and guided him to her breast, he knew that this morning would start out far better than the last.

Kane palmed her breast, weighing the size and firmness to Molly's soft moans. Then he brushed his thumb over one rosy tip, flicking it gently between his fingers until it grew firm and hard. He stayed there for a time, satisfying all his playful urges, creating a tempting picture for him to view—Molly's body readying for him.

Kane was beyond ready to take Molly, his shaft growing hard at first contact with his naked wife. But he continued this soft play as the new day approached, touching and molding and caressing her as she pretended to lie lazily in bed, only her soft sounds and sighs of pleasure giving her away.

Kane's shaft nudged her from behind, there was no help for it and he thought of all the different ways he could make love to her. He envisioned new positions for both to try, but there would be time for that. Molly was too new to lovemaking and so Kane shoved those thoughts away, and gently turned her onto her back.

He rose above her and her acknowledging smile was all he needed. He entered her carefully, feeling the tight squeeze of their joining.

"Oh, Kane," she whimpered right before he took her in a long heady kiss.

She felt right and so good, that when he moved inside her welcoming body, a satisfied groan escaped. His need for Molly was great and he showed her in each loving move, each powerful thrust, his yearning and desire. It was then that he realized he would make love to Molly every night they had together. It was as if the choice had been taken from them. Kane knew he could no longer sleep in bed beside her and not make love to her.

"Ah, Little Bird," he called out when the time was right. He knew that his little bird would, once again, fly.

Molly rose with Kane, feeling still quite playful. Kane helped her dress, but in truth he did all he could to keep her from dressing, pulling at her dress to kiss her shoulder, swatting her behind instead of helping with her petticoats and pulling the wrong way on her chemise to expose her breasts.

Finally, after minutes of indulgence, she stood in front of the cheval mirror to find a rosy glow of color on her face, despite the one nasty bruise on her forehead. Kane came up from behind to view her. They gazed at each other in the mirror. "I didn't do such a bad job of dressing you."

"*You* didn't dress me. Undressing is your specialty."

Kane only smiled and she turned to him. "Have breakfast with me."

He nodded. "I think I heard my grandfather come down. We'll have breakfast together."

"It'll be good to see him up and dressed."

And with that, Molly knew she'd have Kane for a few more minutes before he rode off for the day. Already, she missed him. Since they'd returned home from their "honeymoon," they hadn't eaten too many meals together or spent any real time together.

And ten minutes later, they shared the breakfast table with Bennett. He looked much better than he had yesterday and it gladdened Molly's heart.

Bennett spoke to her at first glance. "Good to see you two having breakfast together."

Lupe had put out quite a spread. Thick bacon strips filled one plate, while spicy potatoes filled another and, of course, Lupe's handmade tortillas were stacked a dozen high. Kane grabbed several—Bennett, too—and Molly decided by the grumbling in her stomach that her appetite matched both the Jackson men. She filled her plate as well.

"Yes, and I'm glad you came down for breakfast this morning, Grandfather," Molly said. "Are you feeling better?"

Bennett attempted a small smile. "A bit. What happened to your head, dear girl?"

"Oh?" Molly reached up self-consciously to touch her bruise. "I took a fall."

"Molly went riding," Kane said to his grandfather, "late last night."

Bennett turned to her. "By yourself?"

With reluctance, Molly nodded.

Bennett cast her a look of concern then he focused his attention directly to Kane. "Why'd you let her go out without you, boy?"

"He wasn't home," Molly said too quickly, then realized how that must have sounded. "I got restless and went for a ride. Everything was fine, really…until I saw a little Indian girl."

Bennett glanced at Kane, narrowing his eyes. "She saw an Indian girl."

Molly explained. "She took me by surprise, that's all. I don't think she meant any harm. But Kane, you didn't give me a chance last night," she began, then cleared her throat. Her cheeks burned with embarrassment. "I mean to say, after you took me home, we never discussed her."

Bennett grinned.

Kane smiled.

Molly wanted the earth to swallow her up whole.

"I mean to say that after I fell, and you took care of my injuries, I was too...too—"

"You were too tired to ask," Bennett finished for her.

Relieved, Molly slumped in the chair. "Yes, that's what I meant to say."

Kane bit into a tortilla. "You didn't find time to ask this morning, either."

Bennett coughed, spurting out his coffee, but with a distinct and satisfied twinkle in his eyes.

Molly glared at her husband. "There's time for an explanation now. Do you know anything about her?"

"Yes," Bennett agreed with a bit of glee. "There is time for your explanation, Kane."

Kane finished his coffee and leaned back, taking his sweet time to answer, but Lupe rushed into the room and interrupted. "We have a visitor. Senora Rose is here to see Senora Molly."

Bennett stood. "Penny is here?"

"*Sí,*" Lupe said, nodding her head.

"Well, show her into the parlor."

Lupe dashed off and Molly looked at Kane. He shrugged as if to say he didn't know what was going on.

"Shall we?" Bennett said, appearing more youthful than she'd ever seen him.

Molly took Bennett's arm and they all walked into the parlor. Kane stood by the mantel while Bennett took a place by the door, waiting. When Penelope Rose entered, Molly's mouth nearly dropped open. Mrs. Rose had a new hairstyle and she wore the pretty cream-colored dress they'd seen just yesterday at Miss Deidre's dress shop. And Molly had been right, the color brought out the dark brown hues in the older woman's eyes.

"Good morning," Molly said in greeting.

Mrs. Rose glanced about the parlor, greeting her and Kane, but she didn't give Bennett more than a quick glance. "Good morning, everyone. I brought a basket of warm biscuits and muffins to welcome you both home from your honeymoon. I take it the trip went well?"

Kane nodded and Molly answered, "Very well, thank you. How nice of you to think of us. And don't you look lovely this morning, Mrs. Rose."

"Yes," Bennett agreed. "Very lovely."

Mrs. Rose blushed, the color rising to her cheeks instantly. She straightened her dress, nervously fidgeting, meeting only Molly's eyes. Molly smiled warmly in return. "Please, have a seat." Bennett showed Penelope to a tufted wing chair.

When Mrs. Rose sat down, Kane came forward. "Sorry, but I'm afraid I was on my way out. I have work to do. Thank you for coming," he said politely. Then he turned to Molly. "I'll be home later tonight." He bent to kiss her cheek then made a hasty exit.

Molly frowned and followed him out the door, "But

we haven't discussed—" It was too late. Kane had taken his leave.

She returned to the parlor to find Mrs. Rose in deep conversation with Bennett. Molly sat down on the velvet sofa and listened to the two of them while they reminisced about old times. She figured Mrs. Rose had finally eased into the situation because she hadn't much stopped talking to take a breath. And Bennett seemed to be enjoying every word.

Molly should be rejoicing. She had lively company this morning. Things were certainly improving with Kane. She'd heard news of her brother. Yet, that same sense of restlessness stole over her. She faced another day with nothing of consequence to do. Kane had deserted her once again, and the day would drag on until he returned in the evening. Yes, she should be rejoicing, and that's why she couldn't quite understand why today of all days, she never felt more alone.

Kane strode quickly to the barn, happy to get away from another of Mrs. Rose's longwinded stories. How that woman could talk. Kane had never met such a talker. Molly never spoke out of both sides of her mouth like that, making him wish he were anywhere but with her. No, Molly had a soft soothing voice, and most times, when she wasn't irritated with him, he didn't much mind listening to her.

He saddled his mare and mounted, ready to head off for the day, but Molly's face kept popping into his head. He hadn't missed the unhappy look she cast him when he'd excused himself just minutes ago. Kane had more things in one lifetime to keep him busy, but Molly had nothing. And the more she dwelled on not going after Charlie, the unhappier she would become.

Kane rode north on the same path Molly had followed last night, and he'd made it about half a mile out when her words from yesterday echoed in his head.

I'm lonely and bored most of the time.

Maybe it was because they'd made love last night, this morning, too, or maybe it was because keeping Molly happy meant keeping her out of trouble, but for whatever reason, Kane turned his horse around. "Ah, what the hell," he muttered.

He picked up the pace and rode hard until he returned to the Bar J. He dismounted and strode into the house, his boots clamoring noisily on the floor. Entering the parlor, he immediately sought Molly's attention. She looked up, her expression changing from sheer boredom to one of curious expectancy. Witnessing her bright eyes and a face filled with hope, Kane was glad he'd returned.

"Something wrong, boy?" Bennett asked.

Kane shook his head. "No, nothing's wrong, Grandfather." He kept his eyes trained on Molly. "I forgot something."

"Oh?" Bennett said with a bunching of eyebrows.

"My wife."

Mrs. Rose gasped, as if he'd said he came to strangle every last living person in the house. And if truth be told, he had a feeling she'd come over here today just to make sure he hadn't done some grave injustice to Molly while on their "honeymoon." Darn if that woman didn't get on his bad side.

Kane crossed the room to take both of Molly's hands.

"There's something I want to show you. Something you need to see. Will you come with me today?"

Molly swallowed. For a moment, he'd rendered her speechless. And then she smiled and looked over at her guest. "If you'll excuse me?"

"Why, um, of course, dear," Mrs. Rose said.

Bennett stood. "Take all the time you need." He gave Molly a playful wink as Kane led her out the room.

"Kane?" she asked, once they'd climbed down the front porch steps. "Where are we going?"

"Be patient, Little Bird. Soon, you'll know everything."

It was time Molly learned the whole truth.

Molly rode Sweet Pea, the otherwise sedate horse, carefully making sure she didn't let out a shriek as she had last night. And Kane kept glancing at her, as if making sure she was secure on her horse. Kane, being ever so mysterious, hadn't given her any indication as to where they were going, but they traveled the same path Molly had last night.

"Are we getting close?" she asked for the third time.

Kane shook his head, refusing her an answer. "Just hold your tongue for a few more minutes, and no matter what you see, do not startle your mare again."

Molly's heart pounded. What would give her cause to shriek out again? She couldn't figure out why Kane was being so secretive. All he'd said when they'd first set out was that seeing is believing. And that soon all would become clear. He wouldn't answer any questions, but rather sat on his horse quietly as they rode up to the northernmost edge of Bar J property.

Off in the distance, a thicket appeared, a lush green wall of tall scrubs and trees amid the grazing land. Kane led the horses that way and once they'd reached a cluster of cottonwood trees, he stopped and dismounted, then helped Molly down from her horse.

Kane held her in his arms longer than usual, their eyes meeting for a long moment. Molly smiled, her heart doing a little dance within her chest. Each time he was near, each time he held her, her body unconsciously reacted.

She couldn't help loving him the way that she did.

Kane looked deeply into her eyes, his face no longer masked with indifference, but he held an expression of concern and apprehension. She knew that what he was about to show her was of great importance to him.

"Come," he said and took her hand.

Molly followed Kane into the thicket, Kane parting branches to widen the path. They walked only a short while, and once on the other side, a clearing appeared. Kane stopped and Molly nearly collided into him. But Kane paid her no mind, his eyes were on something in the distance.

Molly followed the direction of his gaze.

And then Molly witnessed something she thought she would never see in her lifetime.

An Indian village.

She swallowed and blinked and looked again. Yes, a whole small village filled with tipis and cooking fires and hides hung up to dry in the sun and a string of horses, corralled in a pen.

And people.

She witnessed what she assumed to be Cheyenne going about a daily routine as if, as if…they belonged there.

She turned to Kane, but his gaze was still fastened to the village, and when Molly glanced back, a small child approached, running headlong and fast right into Kane's legs.

The young Indian girl hugged him tight. Molly knew they were not strangers. There was obvious affection there. Kane bent to her and spoke softly in her ear. That's when the young child glanced up at Molly, giving her a long curious look, before running off.

And Molly recognized the young Indian girl from her escapade with Sweet Pea last night. This sweet-faced child had been the one who had startled her, causing her to fall from her horse.

"She's the one," Molly said in wonder. It was as if they were in another world, this one so different from the world Molly had always known.

Kane nodded. "That's Smiling Eyes."

And he spoke with such pride that a cold chill traveled the length of her body. She all but froze, deep in thought, her mind spinning. She had so many questions for Kane, but this one suddenly became of utmost importance.

She looked up at him, her mind clouding and her heart aching. "Is she yours?"

Kane didn't hesitate. "Yes."

Molly felt such loss, such heartache. A dozen emotions coursed through her body and the impact of his admission buckled her legs. Kane, as if sensing her dismay, gripped her arm and held her upright. Then he announced with that same sense of pride, "They all are. They are my family."

Molly stared at Kane. "What do you mean?"

"These are my people, Molly. They saved me years

ago. I couldn't turn my back on them. At least for this small band of thirty Cheyenne, life is tolerable. I couldn't see them on a reservation. Here, they are learning to work the cattle. Here, they have a chance."

"Does your grandfather know?"

Kane drew in a breath. "He knows. It was a condition I made to stay at the ranch. It's not his choice to have them here."

"But surely if they saved you as a boy, he must be grateful to them. Surely, Bennett—"

"My grandfather wishes them no harm, but you have to understand, there's a long history here between the Indians and the white man. Early in his life, my grandfather lost many friends and follow ranchers in Indian raids. Doesn't matter that they weren't necessarily from this tribe. The white man doesn't see a difference."

Molly shuddered. She had to admit, she, too, had always thought of Indians as only one people. Yet, she knew that some tribes were not hostile to whites, while others held fierce resentment. And as she looked upon this peaceful village, where half a dozen children ran through the grounds, their laughter filling the air, she began to see them in a different light.

"So, Smiling Eyes is—"

"She belongs to Swift Water and Spotted Elk. She has a brother who is older by two years."

"And they all live here?"

"Yes, they are free to roam the land within our boundaries."

"And this is where you go when you leave for the day?"

"Sometimes, Molly. But I help run the Bar J, too. I have duties and obligations to both."

Kane had said seeing is believing. And now, she understood more clearly. She saw Kane's life with much better perspective. Torn between his white lineage and his Indian upbringing, Kane divided his time and his loyalty to both worlds. No wonder Molly had only gotten a tiny piece of him. Kane had little left to give. Sadly, she did understand his plight.

"I'd like you to meet my…my mother. Singing Bird raised me. She's waiting in her lodge."

"Oh, I'd love to," she said in earnest, but she couldn't help her apprehension. Even with Kane by her side, Molly felt like a trespasser, someone who certainly didn't belong here. He took her hand as if understanding her need and led her to the village.

Chapter Thirteen

Molly found herself amid a circle of tipis and a swarm of cautious eyes. She couldn't blame the Cheyenne for their mistrust, yet their stares made her uneasy. Kane had told her that she was the only other white person to enter this village.

A small boy approached and Kane reached out to pat the boy's head with affection. "Hey there, Moksois." He explained, "He is Smiling Eyes's older brother."

Molly leaned down a bit to come closer to the boy. "Hello, Moksois."

The boy stared at Molly with big round dark eyes and Kane chuckled.

"Why are you laughing?"

"Moksois isn't his real name. I think he's surprised you spoke to him that way."

Perplexed, Molly drew her brows together. "In what way?"

"Moksois is an affectionate name for young boys. It means Potbelly."

"Potbelly!" Molly gasped in horror but the boy only

smiled back at her. Then she glanced at Kane and shook her head. "I'll get you for that, Kane Jackson."

"When—tonight?" Kane asked. Then he whispered for her ears only, "When you're in my bed."

And Molly's heart did that little dance again at the reminder of their lovemaking and of what was to come. "Maybe."

Kane took her hand again and as they approached his mother's tipi, he instructed, "I'll enter first, you follow and go the opposite way around. Sit down and I will introduce you."

The flap to the tipi was open and Molly followed Kane inside. Her first impression was how large the inside appeared, having all the necessities of life, without the clutter. Firewood and cooking utensils sat against one part of the lodge while at the far end she noted bedding. Closer to the center was a fire pit, and behind a fire that had long since been extinguished sat a Cheyenne woman.

While Kane went to the right, Molly circled around to the left and sat down by Singing Bird. The woman appeared more youthful than Molly expected. She wore a dress of soft deerskin beaded with delicate intricacy, her dark hair braided down the middle of her head. A soft smile lifted her lips. "Welcome."

Kane sat next to his mother. "This is the woman I have married. Her name is Molly. She is small and delicate, like you. I have named her Little Bird."

With pride in her eyes, Singing Bird listened to Kane and Molly realized how much affection the two held for each other.

"It is a good name," Singing Bird said, nodding. "I

have asked Gray Wolf to bring you here. I am glad he has listened."

Gray Wolf? Molly had forgotten that Kane had told her of his Cheyenne name, weeks ago, when he had attempted to send her back to St. Louis. She'd dismissed the name, dismissing his upbringing as well in her mind. But now, she couldn't dismiss Kane's other life, his Cheyenne life. He, too, had a name, given to him by the Cheyenne when he'd been just a boy.

"Yes," Molly said. "I am glad he has brought me here as well."

"My son makes it possible for us to live."

Molly understood that statement more than she had realized. While she hadn't spent a good deal of time learning current affairs, she knew that many tribes had been sent to reservations. Others, who had refused to lose their homes and their way of life, had fought and still did to regain what they'd lost. Bands of Indians, raiding parties were still feared in this part of the country. "I have just learned of your village today."

And Molly's heart went out to Kane. He'd almost lost one family, Bennett being the only relation left in the white world. He couldn't bear to lose another, this Cheyenne family, the people with whom he obviously felt a keen sense of loyalty and love.

"Gray Wolf hopes our young boys will learn to ranch."

"It is a good thought," Molly said, agreeing with Kane's beliefs.

"They learn fast. A small herd of cattle graze up here and we have rounded them up. They have learned how to brand. In time, I hope that our braves will work on the Bar J," Kane said.

Singing Bird reached behind her and presented Molly with a gift, a beaded dress so lovely in design and workmanship that she was certain she'd never seen anything quite so stunning in her life. "A gift for you," she said as she handed over the dress. "If you married in our village, you would wear this."

"A wedding dress?" Molly looked at Kane with tears in her eyes. "This is so…the most…I don't know what to say. Th-thank you."

Once again, guilt enveloped her. She'd lied to Bennett over and over, but Singing Bird also believed the marriage real. And she'd made Molly a dress that obviously had taken a great deal of time. Molly hated accepting such a beautiful gift, but she knew to refuse the offer would be a great insult to the kind woman. Instead, she hugged the gift to her breast. "Thank you. I shall cherish it."

Singing Bird nodded, apparently satisfied.

"My mother is a member of the Quillers' Society."

Molly glanced at Kane askance. "Quillers' Society?"

"Women with special talent gather to perform the sacred task of decorating using porcupine and bird quills. My mother is one of a selected few who have this honor. When I was young I would watch the women perform the ceremony. Women in the society are highly respected."

Molly fingered the delicate beaded pattern on her dress, the workmanship unequaled. "I can see why."

They spoke for several minutes about the village and Singing Bird explained how Kane had sought the tribe out and urged them to move onto Bennett Jackson's land. She credited Kane with so much of their survival up until this point, and Molly knew all that she said to be true. Kane was, despite his claims otherwise, a very honorable man.

They spoke also of Charlie, and Molly explained that after months of wondering and weeks of searching, her brother had been located. Singing Bird seemed to understand Molly's desperation to find her loved one. Though their conversation at times seemed stilted due to the language barrier, Kane had intervened enough to help explain what each woman meant to say. And Molly felt acceptance from Singing Bird, not so much from her words, but from clear, dark brown eyes that relayed what was in her heart.

Shortly after, all three exited the tipi, Molly stretching out her legs and straightening her wrinkled dress. Smiling Eyes ran up to Molly and without qualm, took her hand. Molly glanced at Kane, who gestured for her to follow the little girl. She handed Kane her new wedding dress before Smiling Eyes led her to a small clearing behind the tipis, a playground of sorts, where close to a dozen children played. The boys, she noted, had a circle of their own where they played with small bows and blunt-ended arrows, and beyond them some older children seemed to be playing camp, boys and girls alike, pretending to live in a make-believe village with make-believe families.

The younger girls had a place set up with dolls made of deerskin, and each doll had its own miniature cradleboard. Smiling Eyes handed Molly a doll and gestured for her to sit down. Molly sat down on the grassy ground and played with Smiling Eyes while Kane and Singing Bird looked on.

* * *

"I don't understand 'temporary' wife," Singing Bird said to Kane. They stood several yards from the play area where Molly seemed to be enjoying the time spent with Smiling Eyes.

Kane shrugged and wished he hadn't told his mother about the arrangement he'd made with Molly. But Kane had never lied or purposely deceived his mother, and he couldn't have her think he'd betrayed Little Swan's memory in any way. He couldn't have her think that Kane had found love again.

"I have explained the bargain I have made with Molly."

"Yet, you give her a Cheyenne name."

"She is small—petite—like you, isn't she?"

"She is a woman who looks at you in a special way."

Kane glanced at Molly, who was obviously enjoying the outing and her time here with the tribe children. He hadn't expected her to react with such calm and acceptance. After her fright last night, startled by Smiling Eyes, Kane had been certain Molly would have reacted differently, perhaps with fear and apprehension at seeing a true tribal village.

Once again, Molly had surprised him. "She will leave when the time comes."

Singing Bird shook her head. "You say the words, yet you do not want it so."

Kane turned sharply to stare at his mother. "You forget about Little Swan? You forget that I had a wife once?"

"And now you have another wife."

"Yes, for now, Molly is my wife."

Singing Bird faced him and looked into his eyes.

"You have touched her the way a husband touches a wife. You have lain with her. I know this. She belongs to you now, son."

Kane closed his eyes. Yes, he had touched his wife. He had tried not to—tried to ignore the desire he felt for her. But Kane had no regrets. Not even now, as his mother made her point with him. He wanted Molly. He couldn't deny it. There would be many nights to come where Kane would be alone, but for now and as long as Molly wanted him, he would make love to her. But he would not create a child. Yet, he couldn't explain those intimate details with Singing Bird. Some things a man had to keep to himself. "It is hard to explain, Mother."

"Not so hard, Gray Wolf. It is clear to me. It is my son who does not see."

Hours later, Kane and Molly rode down the path leading back to the Bar J. In the distance Kane noted Mrs. Penelope Rose's buggy leaving the house. *Just* leaving. Now, four hours after they'd left her with his grandfather.

Bennett stood on the porch waving farewell. Kane glanced at Molly. She, too, had witnessed the exchange.

"I thought Mrs. Rose came to see you this morning," Kane said.

Molly nodded. "And you, too. Remember, she brought us a 'welcome home' basket of treats."

"So what's she still doing here?" Kane asked, as suspicion crept into his gut. Molly only shrugged. He hadn't expected an answer from her.

Kane and Molly approached the house. When Bennett spotted them, he turned around on the porch, heading inside the house.

"Grandfather!"

Bennett stopped and turned around slowly.

Kane dismounted and, after helping Molly down from Sweet Pea both approached the porch.

"Afternoon," Bennett said, his eyes narrowing against the streaming sunlight. Kane couldn't read much more in his expression.

"That's just it, Grandfather. It's afternoon. What was Mrs. Rose still doing here?"

Bennett slumped, his face paled and the coughing began.

Molly rushed to his side, holding onto his arm. "Oh, dear. He's having another attack. Get him some water, Kane."

Kane stood stock-still, watching his grandfather.

"Kane, he needs water," Molly scolded.

Kane wasn't sure what his grandfather needed at the moment, perhaps an alibi, but after several more seconds Kane entered the house and came out quickly with a glass of water. By that time, Molly had seated Bennett onto the porch chair and she continued to hover over him.

Kane handed Bennett the glass of water.

"Thank you, boy. Seems the worst is over now." He sipped the water.

Molly explained. "Your grandfather had an attack this morning and Mrs. Rose wouldn't leave him until Lupe returned to the house."

"Where was Lupe?" Kane asked. These days, Lupe never left the ranch when Kane was off the property. She worried too much over Bennett.

"I sent her over to the Wilkinsons' place. Seems one

of their young'uns took sick and Elena Wilkinson needed help, what with the five other children she's got."

"That's very thoughtful of you, Grandfather," Molly said, glancing up to give Kane a sharp look.

Kane twisted his mouth, ready to comment, but Molly shook her head and he thought better of saying something he might regret. The two had been alone in the ranch house all morning. And in truth, his grandfather's illness seemed awfully convenient at times, but he'd keep that thought to himself for now.

"I think you need to rest." Molly put out her hand.

Bennett rose slowly and took Molly's hand.

"Did you have a nice visit with Mrs. Rose?" Molly asked cheerily.

He shrugged. "She chatters all the time."

"Still, I'm glad she stayed with you. It was nice of her."

"Yes," Bennett agreed, "I didn't say she wasn't nice."

Kane watched as Molly helped his grandfather up the steps. "Kane, are you coming?" she asked, glancing back. "We need to settle him into his room."

Kane scratched his head, then bounded up the porch steps to take hold of his grandfather's arm. "I've got him, Molly," he said as he led him into the house and up the stairs.

He heard her mutter quietly. "Well, it's about time."

Kane entered the house before dusk, yanking off his hat and hanging it up on a hook in the kitchen. He'd been out on the range the entire afternoon, checking fences, watching the herd, and helping their cookie, Sully, make repairs on the chuck wagon. "*Hola,* Lupe."

"Senor Kane. I cook a nice meal for you tonight."

Kane nodded, looking at the spicy meal Lupe had in store for supper. Stomach grumbling, his mouth watered, and he could think of only one thing better than digging into Lupe's fare. "Molly around?"

"No, Senora Molly is up in her room. She has spent time with Senor Bennett, and now she rests."

Kane didn't want to eat alone. Hell, he worked like a demon to get home early tonight.

To see Molly.

She'd been on his mind all day, and in truth he didn't much like the power she had over him. He wanted her. He wanted to take her into his arms, make love to her and witness once again the lusty look of completion on her face when he brought her to pleasure.

"Lupe, do me a favor?"

Lupe nodded. *"Qué?"*

"Make up a tray for Molly and me. I'm going to clean up and then bring the meal up to our room."

Lupe grinned, nodding. *"Sí, sí.* Senora Molly will like, no? And so will you, perhaps even more?"

Kane grinned back. *"Gracias,* Lupe."

With that, Kane exited the hot kitchen, heading for the water barrel and looking forward to sharing a meal with Molly.

And more.

Chapter Fourteen

Kane held the tray in one hand, opened the bedroom door with the other and quietly walked into the room. He set the tray down on the nearby table then stood over Molly's sleeping form. A mass of coppery curls spilled over her pillow, her face soft and serene in the setting light. She'd removed her dress and slept in a tangle of sheets in her thin chemise, the gauzy straps slipping down her shoulders, exposing her translucent skin. The tip of one small perfect breast peeked out, teasing, tempting and tormenting him.

Kane swallowed down, his pulse escalating. He uttered a curse and turned to exit the room, leaving his sleeping wife in peace.

"Kane?"

At the sound of her voice, he pivoted around slowly to find Molly sitting up in bed, her hair loose and wispy around her face as she struggled to lift the straps of her undergarment. But Kane had already seen enough to set his nerves on edge.

"Don't go," she said softly, blinking her eyes several times. "I'm awake now."

"I brought up supper."

"Oh, I guess I napped too long. Has everyone already eaten?"

Kane shook his head. "No, but I thought we'd have the meal in here. Together."

Molly reached for her robe, setting her arms in the sleeves, and swung her legs off the bed. "Don't be silly. I'll get dressed and we'll eat downstairs."

Kane walked over to the bed, sat down next to her and slipped her arms out of the robe. "There's nothing silly about wanting some privacy."

"But where will we eat?"

Kane gestured to the bed. Molly's eyes grew wide as recognition dawned. "We'll eat in bed." Then her face contorted as she questioned him. "Won't that be...difficult?"

Kane shook his head. "Lupe made up a tray with everything we need."

He walked to his side of the bed and sat down, removing his boots and socks. Then he stood to unbutton his shirt and tossed it off. Next came his belt, and all the while Molly watched him. The unabashed look in her eyes made him ache. She followed his movements, her gaze sweeping over him like licking flames.

Kane drew her into his arms, bringing her up on her knees to kiss her lips gently. "Are you hungry?"

Molly glanced at the food and nodded. "It smells delicious."

Kane lifted up and brought the tray to the bed. He sat down again and spread out the small tablecloth Lupe had sent up. Setting down the tray, he sat cross-legged and Molly did the same. They ate from one big dish, facing each other and speaking of the day's events. Molly enjoyed the food, relishing each bite. Kane couldn't help noticing her expression as she chewed and swallowed, the look of sheer delight on her face. Kane had never enjoyed a meal more.

"Kane, I was thinking," she said, her eyes taking on a vibrant glow, "that maybe I could help you with the children."

Kane stopped eating. "What children?"

Molly smiled. "The Cheyenne children, of course."

Skeptical, Kane asked, "What could you do?"

Molly set down her fork and adjusted her position, leaning in slightly, hands in lap, her face animated and full of excitement. "I could teach them. We could set up a little school and I could teach them our language, how to read. There's so much they could learn."

Kane shook his head. "No."

"No?" Molly frowned instantly, the glow in her eyes diminishing. She slumped back. "Why not?"

Kane shook his head again and continued shaking it. "No, Molly. It wouldn't work. You don't know anything about them. They are different from—"

"They're not so different from white children. I saw them today, Kane. I know I could teach them. We could have morning sessions."

"No, Molly."

"But you claim you want to help them."

"I do," Kane said, raising his voice. "But not your way. And you…you fear them. I saw it in your eyes today."

"Yes, I admit I was a little afraid, until I met them. Then I realized that they aren't different from other children I've known. White or Indian, children are children. I've always yearned to teach, Kane. I think I'd be good at it. Perhaps if you trust me, the children would learn to trust me as well."

Kane tightened his lips. "Trust no longer comes easy for the Cheyenne." And Kane thought about the time when Molly would leave the ranch. He thought of her reuniting with her brother. What would happen to her little school then? She would be here only a short while, giving the children hope, a taste of what they might have and then it would be time for Molly to leave.

"Will you think about it?" Molly asked softly. "Please."

Kane relented, softening to her plea. "I'll think about it." But he wouldn't change his mind.

Molly loved Kane, but she didn't love his stubborn nature. How could he not the see the benefits of teaching the children? He'd said himself he wanted to integrate them, maybe not into the outside world, but so that they may work alongside the others on the ranch. What better way to achieve that goal than by education? The more she thought about setting up a school for the children in the village, the more she wanted it.

Molly took a bite of Lupe's cornbread cake, the flavor pungent and sweet as it went down. Kane watched her as she chewed, his eyes no longer harsh from his refusal, but soft like molten silver. That look sent tingles to her toes. "Have some," she said, breaking off a piece and lifting the cake to his mouth. He opened and accepted the cake, licking at her fingers. And when he finished chewing, he held her hand to his mouth and sucked on her fingers, taking one at a time, laving them with his tongue.

Flames erupted inside her belly, the heat traveling lower creating an ache between her thighs. "Oh, Kane," she sighed, and before she knew it, Kane had removed the tray of food and was beside her on the bed. Gently, and with little effort, he pulled down the straps of the chemise that she'd struggled with all evening to keep up. Exposed to him, he looked his fill, his hungry gaze devouring her.

"So beautiful," he whispered in a rough voice.

And while he faced her, both on their knees, he flicked his thumb over one nipple and her whole body reacted, every nerve tightening with desperate need of him.

"I like putting that look on your face, Little Bird."

Molly's breaths grew rapid as he stroked her breasts, and when he brought his mouth down to suckle, heat whipped through her, a piercing arrow aimed straight toward her woman's center. A pleasured moan escaped, "Kane."

He laid her down on the bed and kissed her, his body partway covering hers. He had yet to remove his trousers, but Molly felt his need, the powerful surging of his manhood. He wasted little time, his hand finding her heat. With deft fingers he stroked her, until she moved with his beat, lifting up, meeting him. He brought her body to the edge, where any moment she might slip off.

"We'll try something different tonight," Kane whispered into her mouth. He lifted up, removed his trousers and lay down beside her.

Even through the waning light, Molly saw his powerful erection, the silky fullness that displayed his magnificence. He helped her remove the chemise that had fallen to her hips, then he reached for her, lifting her up and over until she straddled him.

"Take me in, Molly," he beckoned, his voice hoarse. And she did. She took all of him, filling herself full. Kane groaned. "So good."

Molly sighed, the sensation bringing a new series of tingles, more powerful, more absorbing.

"Now move on me, sweetheart. Any way you want."

Grateful for the dimming light, Molly blushed until she was sure she was tomato-red. This new position exposed her, making her more vulnerable, yet more powerful than anything she'd ever experienced in her life. "Oh, Kane."

Kane helped her. He placed both hands on her hips and set a slow grinding pace. She moved on him now, up and down, learning, testing, until she found her rhythm.

Kane released her hips and brought his hands up, each thumb flicking the very tip of her breasts. She moved faster now, harder, pumping up and down, breathless, and it was difficult to tell whose moans grew the loudest, for Molly was deep in a world of her own. She threw her head back, riding the wave, immersed in pleasure almost too painful to bear.

Her release came fast, but endured a long time. And when she finally looked down at her husband, his eyes were on her filled with smoky heat.

She fell onto his chest, exhausted, then rolled to her side. Kane had given her fulfillment. She reached out to him.

She would do the same for him.

And they would not create a child.

Kane woke with Molly cradled in his arms. Morning sun streamed in, the bright light through the curtains making him squint. She stirred and turned in his arms. He held her as she lifted her lids, focusing her eyes only to smile at him.

"Good morning," she said.

"Morning."

"Is it time to get up?"

Kane shook his head. "There's time. Rest some more."

Her curls fell loosely onto her face. Kane reached up to move her hair aside, putting the strands behind her ears. The bouncy curls refused to be tamed, falling forward again.

Molly giggled.

He frowned, not from disobedient hair, but from the dewy look in Molly's eyes, the sexy way she peeked through that thick curtain of curls. He wanted her again. She was like an addiction he couldn't quite control. Kane had given in to his weakness for her once and now it was as though he couldn't stop.

"What's wrong?" she asked, lifting up to a sitting position.

"I have work to do. I must go."

Molly touched his arm and smiled. "Stay in bed a little longer."

He shook his head. "Molly, I can't."

Her lips pursed into a delicate pout. "Can't or won't?"

Kane kissed her deeply then looked straight into her eyes. He spoke slowly trying to get his meaning across. "If I stay, it won't be to rest."

"But why?" she asked, and then it dawned on her. "Oh!"

Kane hated leaving her. He wanted to snuggle in bed and make love again. "Get your rest. I'll see you tonight."

When he swung his legs off the bed, Molly reached for him, speaking from behind. Her soft touch seared through his skin. "I'm not tired, Kane," she whispered. "Not in the least."

Sitting upon the bed, he turned to face her. She smiled with eager eyes. "Stay."

She wiggled her body down on the bed, her head resting on the pillow, and Kane could no sooner leave her there like that than he could cut off his right arm.

He slid in bed beside her and brought her close, slipping her chemise once again from her shoulders. Molly's delicate sigh of pleasure was all he needed to hear.

A short time later, Molly faced Kane in bed, fully sated from a night and early morning of lovemaking. They shared their bodies so intimately, yet Kane refused to share his life. He kept that part of himself locked up and closed off to her. She knew he would rise soon, ready for his day of work on the Bar J and, perhaps, to visit the Cheyenne village. She longed so terribly to go there with him, to meet all the children and to start her school. She needed a purpose on the ranch, and while she loved her time with Bennett, he seemed to need her company less and less, spending more time resting in his room. And for Charlie—the wait seemed endless, the anticipation of reuniting with her brother keeping her on edge.

"Kane, are you going to the village today?"

"Later today, I will spend some time there."

"I might join you," Molly said, realizing that now that she knew where the village was located she didn't really need Kane's permission. "After I go into town to purchase slates and chalk for the children."

Kane grimaced. He rose from the bed and turned to her. She sucked in a breath, seeing his powerful body, naked and slick from their lovemaking. He appeared a fierce warrior in his own right, those gray eyes narrowing on her as she dared to defy him. Even now as she gazed at him, his strength and power came through as well as his anger. "You would disobey me?"

Molly swallowed and stared into his eyes.

"Never mind, of course you would," he said harshly. "When have you ever done as you were told?"

Molly rose then and, mustering her courage, she walked over to him, keeping her eyes trained on him. Exposed and vulnerable in her naked state, she reached out to touch his chest. He flinched as if burned. "Last night, Kane," she said softly. "And this morning, remember?"

Kane's eyes widened. Even Molly couldn't believe she had the audacity to bring up their lovemaking, the way Kane tutored her, the way she willingly gave herself up to his every gentle command. Certainly by Kane's surprised expression, he couldn't believe it, either.

"I have listened and learned," Molly said softly, then smiled. "And enjoyed. But now it's time for you to listen. It's time for you to give me a chance. I'm only asking for a day or two. If the children don't want me there, then you have my promise, I will not force myself on them."

Molly took his hand and squeezed gently, meeting his gaze. "Please."

Kane's eyes softened, his face lost the stubborn set and thankfully, his anger seemed to have evaporated. "You have won your point, Little Bird. You have two days."

Joyous, Molly threw her arms around his neck and jumped into his arms. She kissed him soundly on the mouth. "Thank you. Thank you, Kane. You've made me so happy."

Kane groaned and held her tight, the intimate rub of their bodies not lost on either of them. Molly heated up immediately and Kane, well, she knew that he, too, was affected.

"I have work to do," Kane said, but there was no real effort in his words.

"Yes, and I have to travel into town," Molly agreed.

But when Kane lifted her up and set her down on his bed, both knew their morning plans would have to wait a little bit longer.

Molly's plans to start her school at the Cheyenne village had to be postponed. Kane had had some trouble with the Bar J ranch hands. Two men had quarreled with Kane over the Indians' presence on the ranch, both refusing to work alongside savages. Kane had fired them both and had come up shorthanded with workmen. Now, days later, once Kane had finally hired on two more amiable workmen, Molly set her own plan into action.

Kane had taken her into Bountiful yesterday and now she stood under a cottonwood tree, handing out slates and chalk to a group of children ranging in age from four to fifteen years of age. Molly did a quick tally and counted nine students in all, sitting cross-legged on tall grass and looking more mystified than curious at the moment. Kane had agreed to translate in their native tongue for the first session, but after that Molly was on her own.

"Tell them, I wish to learn all of their names and what it means in my language."

Kane spoke with the children, taking care to make sure even the youngest of the students understood what they were trying to do here. And Molly noticed that she'd also attracted many of the elder Cheyenne as well, most of whom stood back from their little makeshift school in the shade of an old tree, to watch and listen.

Molly recited their names and with Kane's assistance, learned what the names meant in the English language. She knew teaching was a give-and-take endeavor, and for her to be successful she must also be willing to learn about the Cheyenne culture as well. And the one thing she did note almost immediately was that the names given to a child at birth were not always complimentary. Smiling Eyes and Black Raven were pretty enough names, but the Cheyenne named their children according to what was most noticeable about them. Crooked Foot had been born with a foot that curved off to one side and Tall Neck had indeed a long, thin almost birdlike neck.

"My name is Miss Molly." She turned to Kane. "Please have them repeat my name one by one."

And so it went. By the end of three hours, with Molly finishing the lesson by allowing each one to mark on their slate by drawing a favorite scene, she had hoped they were interested enough to wish her back tomorrow.

Kane put forth the question and an overwhelming display of head nods confirmed what Molly had hoped. Perhaps being confined on this little piece of land, the children, too, might have known the same sort of boredom Molly had.

With joy in her heart, Molly smiled at Kane. "Tell them I will see them tomorrow and we will begin to learn the English language."

Kane spoke the next few words as Molly collected the slate boards and chalk. Many of the children glanced with longing at their new learning tool, giving Molly hope. Tomorrow she would make sure they'd have plenty to do with the slate board.

And a short time later, Molly planned her next lesson in her head as she rode beside Kane in the wagon. Her life had new meaning and purpose now, and though she had bullied her way into this, she knew if Kane hadn't really wanted her to teach the children, all her taunts wouldn't have amounted to beans. He'd bought the slate boards and chalk. He had gathered the children up. He'd explained Molly's intentions and agreed to stay for the first session to ease Molly's way.

With gratitude in her heart, Molly leaned over to kiss Kane's cheek. "Thank you."

Kane didn't say a word. He didn't smile. But his hand covered hers on the seat of the wagon and they rode back to Bar J that way, hand in hand. Molly couldn't remember a time when she felt such a keen sense of accomplishment. And having Kane beside her today, having his blessing, albeit somewhat grudgingly, meant a great deal. She'd felt a strong connection to him today, more so than any other time in their brief marriage.

Once they reached the house, Kane helped Molly down and she raced to the front door, eager to tell Bennett of her success today. But just as she reached for the door handle, Bennett appeared, smiling with eyes aglow, looking healthier than she'd ever seen him.

"Molly, we've been waiting on you. Seems there's a young lad who calls himself Roper McCall here to see you."

Chapter Fifteen

"Roper McCall?" Molly's breath caught in her throat as she gazed into Bennett's gleaming eyes. "My brother Charlie is—"

But Molly didn't finish her sentence, because Bennett had taken a sweeping step back.

Charlie appeared in the doorway.

"Hello, sis." He smiled that same impish smile that Molly remembered from their childhood. But Charlie had grown up in the year since she'd seen him. Taller, broader, his dark hair only now highlighted with the auburn tones they'd been born with, Charlie no longer looked like the tintype Molly had been toting around all of west Texas. No, he was a man—well, nearly a man. No wonder he hadn't been recognized. With his grown-up appearance and his name changed to Roper McCall, it all made sense now why she hadn't been able to locate him.

"Charlie," she breathed out, awed and a little bit stunned. She fell into his arms as tears swelled in her eyes. "I can't believe it's you! I can't believe you're here!"

"I know, sis," he said apologetically. "I'm sorry, Molly. Truly sorry."

Molly sobbed now, full out. She cried with both joy and sorrow. She cried for the little boy who'd grown up into such a good-looking man. She cried with relief at having him here, safe and sound in her arms. She cried for the heartache they would both endure when she explained about their mama's death. And she cried deep inside, for one end of Kane's bargain with her was met. He had helped to find her brother. And they were now one step closer to parting.

But Molly wouldn't allow that last thought to mar her joy. Instead, she relished the good news that she was finally reunited with her brother. She broke their tight embrace to look at him, wiping her tears away. "My goodness, Charlie. You've grown."

Charlie raked a hand over his unshaven face. "Some." And then he took a good long look at her. "You're married now. And you look happy. Mr. Jackson has filled me in on what you've been doing. You came here as a mail-order bride?"

Molly smiled, too happy at the moment to admonish Charlie for what he'd put her through. "Yes, I came out west to marry and to search for you. There are things I must tell you, Charlie."

Bennett stepped up then, to intervene. "Why don't you both get comfortable in the parlor? You two can speak in private. Kane and I will see you later on."

Molly agreed and, arm in arm, she guided Charlie to the parlor. She took a seat on the wing chair, while Charlie sat down on the sofa.

Lupe rushed in, bringing a pitcher of lemonade and

a tray of fresh fruit. Molly quickly made introductions, Lupe seeming genuinely happy to meet Charlie. "But he is not a boy," Lupe said easily.

Molly studied Charlie's face. "I know. I'm quite surprised myself."

Lupe nodded. "It is good that you are together again," she said before leaving the room.

"What things, Molly? What did you have to tell me?" Charlie asked.

Molly wanted answers from Charlie, before she would have to deal with all of his questions. "You've been on a cattle drive all this time?"

"Well, most. I traveled a few months before landing a job on the Shannon ranch. Before I knew it, I was herding cattle to Kansas."

"Why did you change your name?"

Heat rose up his cheeks and he shrugged with embarrassment. "It was a stupid thing, I suppose. I was so green when I arrived, that I thought I needed to prove myself and that name seemed to fit out here. But it's over now. I took my real name when I got back."

"So, you're known as Charlie McGuire again?"

He nodded, the green in his eyes, almost an identical match to Molly's, flickered with shame.

"I tried to find you," Molly said, sternly. "I did everything I knew to do until I just ran out of ideas. Bennett and my husband, well, they've been wonderful about helping me."

Again, Charlie appeared repentant. "I shouldn't have run off like that. I meant to make some real money and come back for you. I wrote letter after letter, Molly."

"Mama and I only received one."

Charlie put his head down. "I know about Mama dying. I'm sorry. So sorry I wasn't there."

"How did you find out about her?" Molly asked, finding the pieces of this puzzle a bit too confusing. Her heart ached just speaking of her mama's death. Sharing this news with Charlie brought it all back so vividly.

"I started getting worried while I was out on the trail. Afraid you wouldn't be able to contact me, so I wired home. When I didn't get a response, I sent another wire to Mrs. Wiley. I figured she would know how to contact you."

Mrs. Wiley was their mama's one trusted friend. She lived across town, married to a banker, but she would always find time to visit her childhood friend. Mrs. Wiley had helped Molly with the burial arrangements. She'd also offered Molly a home while she was deciding what to do, but Molly had already made up her mind to come out west to find Charlie. She had no home and no ties any longer in St. Louis. "So Mrs. Wiley told you in a wire?"

Tears stung Charlie's eyes and he nodded. "I found out just one month ago. But Mama had already been gone months before that."

"Oh, Charlie." Molly rushed to his side and put an arm around his shoulder.

He lifted his head to look into her eyes. "You don't know how glad I was to come back from the trail drive to find out you're living here. I almost couldn't believe it. I was going to set out to find you myself."

Molly took his hand. "There's no need for that now. I'm here and we'll never be separated again. Mama would want it that way."

Charlie nodded. "I want it that way, too."

Molly smiled. It's about all she'd asked for when coming west—to reunite with Charlie and be a family once again. But Molly wanted more now. So much more, yet she feared the day when she would lose Bennett, the man she had come to think of as Grandfather, and in turn lose Kane, the husband whom she had come to love.

"There's more to tell, Charlie, but it can wait." Molly debated about telling Charlie the terms of her "marriage vows" to Kane, not wanting to disparage her husband in her brother's eyes. She would wait for the right time to explain to Charlie those circumstances. Right now, Molly just wanted to look her fill at her nearly grown younger brother. "I still can't believe you're here. Tell me that you're home now, for good."

Charlie shook his head and laughed derisively, the familiar sound bringing back memories of their youth in St. Louis when Charlie had gotten in a pickle of some sort. "I wish. I haven't got a home. Or a job anymore. Seems, uh, Parker Shannon fired me the minute I stepped foot on his land. Not because of anything I did on the trail. The trail boss said I did real good for a greenhorn, but uh—"

"It's because of his daughter, isn't it?"

"You know about Lacey?"

Molly nodded, recalling how she learned of Lacey's fascination with Roper McCall at the mercantile that alerted her to Charlie's whereabouts. "It's a good thing that rumors fly faster than a bumblebee in Bountiful, because your name came up along with Miss Lacey Shannon's one day. Or at least, Roper McCall's name came up."

"Shannon is real nice, Molly. But her pa's dead set against me or anybody else seeing her."

"She cares for you, so he fired you?"

"That's about right. What kind of man courts a woman when he's got no home and no job?"

"You have a home and a job now, if you want one," Kane announced.

Molly and Charlie both turned their heads toward the parlor doorway. Kane stood with his shoulder braced casually against the doorjamb, but there was nothing casual in the look in his eyes. He was dead serious, and Molly wanted to grab him around the neck and hug him tight.

"Kane," she breathed out.

Charlie stood.

Kane walked over to Charlie. "I'm Kane Jackson."

"Charlie McGuire." The two men shook hands.

Molly rose from the sofa as well to offer a more proper introduction. "Charlie, I'd like you to meet my husband. And Kane, this is…Charlie, my brother."

Both men's eyes twinkled and they grinned at each other, most likely laughing at Molly's expense, but she didn't care. She was just too thrilled to worry about sounding silly.

"I'm serious about the offer, Charlie," Kane went on. "I'm shorthanded here and I know Molly would like to have you close by since we've spent a good deal of time looking for you."

"I appreciate that. And I'll take you up on your offer. I'm still green, as the boys say, but I learn fast."

Kane nodded. "If you're anything like your sister, I don't doubt it."

A flush rose on Molly's cheeks but the men were too busy shaking hands again to notice.

"I see we have a new employee as well as a new relation. That's what I call a good day," Bennett said, walking into the room. "The boy and I had a bit of time to talk while waiting on you, Molly. I like him."

Molly smiled at Bennett's blunt statement. "Thank you." She beamed with joy thinking that for the time being at least, her life had come full circle.

"Looks like things have come full circle for Molly," Bennett said, lowering himself down into a kitchen chair. He appeared robust but his movements were those of an ailing man. Kane took a seat and the two faced each other.

"What do you mean?" Kane asked.

"Well, Molly's found a home here. She's been reunited with her brother and she seems to have you strung around her finger."

Kane opened his mouth to protest, but his grandfather was quick as a whip.

"Don't get me wrong, I'm happier than a coyote in a henhouse that you two are getting along so well." Bennett lowered his head, and peered at Kane through narrowed eyes. "You are, aren't you? I mean to say, I've seen the bounce in your step when you come downstairs in the morning. And Molly, too, she looks…shall I say, fulfilled."

"Grandfather," Kane warned, realizing his grandfather was taunting him, hoping to gain insight into their marriage. Kane would never tell him the truth about the bargain he'd made with Molly. That bit of information would surely send him to his grave.

"Only thing that's missing," Bennett continued, pretending not to hear Kane's admonishment, "is a child. That would make the circle complete."

Kane held his tongue. His grandfather knew Kane wanted no children. He hadn't changed his mind. And he'd gone to great pains and sacrificed much to ensure that no child would be created in this house. Hell, he ached every night for completion when he bedded his wife, but Kane exercised great willpower. Molly eased his suffering with skillful hands. But Kane often thought about bringing them both to that peak of pleasure at the same time.

Bennett leaned in, refusing to let the subject drop. "Well, have you gotten your wife pregnant yet?"

"Oh!"

The sound of Molly's voice startled them and they turned to find her entering the kitchen, her face rose petal red, her green eyes wide with surprise.

"Come in dear girl," Bennett offered, gesturing for her to take a seat and join them.

"Excuse me for interrupting, but I wanted to speak to Kane about Charlie." Molly looked straight at him, and lately every time she walked into a room his heart pumped a little harder. Today was no different. "If you have a moment?"

Kane nodded and rose from the table, grateful he didn't have to answer his grandfather's probing question. He took her arm and guided her outside. They walked a little bit away from the house finding shade from a small white oak tree.

"I don't know what to say," she began, her eyes misting up. "You've done so much and now, you've given my brother a home and a job."

"It's part of our bargain."

Molly stiffened, her back rearing up like a wary cat.

Kane wished he could bring those words back the moment he'd said them because for the first time today, Molly's joy evaporated and he knew he was to blame.

"Yes, our *bargain*," she repeated, as if the recollection stung her. "I pray Bennett lives a long time…but if he doesn't you'll have both McGuires out of your hair." She turned to leave, holding her head high but not even her valiant pride could conceal a voice filled with pain. Kane reached for her.

"Ah, Little Bird," he said, taking her into his arms. "I didn't mean to bring that up today." In truth, most of the time Kane had forgotten about the bargain. He supposed living as man and wife, making love every night and some nights more than once, did that. Perhaps both had gotten too comfortable in their fake roles. Perhaps his bringing it up was a good thing, but he didn't want to see Molly hurt. And he had hurt her just now.

He cursed under his breath, hating what he'd done.

Molly pulled away from him and the loss shot through him like an arrow. "Sometimes, Kane Jackson, I think you're the most wonderful man in the world. And sometimes," Molly said, lowering her voice to a forced whisper, "I think you have a heart of stone."

Later that evening, Kane walked Charlie to the bunkhouse. "Are you sure you want to stay out here?" he asked. "We have more than enough spare rooms in the house. And you're welcome to any one of them."

Charlie shook his head. "Nah. I'm used to sleeping out on the range. The bunkhouse will seem like a fancy hotel for me. And besides, this is the best way to meet the men."

"It's important for you to fit in, right?"

Charlie nodded. "It ain't always easy when you're green and from the east. I took my share of ribbing on the trail, and I expect I'll get some here, too. But, sooner or later, when they see I'm a hard worker and willing to learn, I'll win them over. I appreciate just having a roof overhead and a job to call my own."

Kane liked his attitude. Under the circumstances Kane would do the same, wanting to earn his keep and work hard, proving himself. He saw a lot of potential in a young man with a whole lot of heart. Just like his sister.

I think you have a heart of stone.

Molly's cutting words came to mind and Kane admitted to himself the truth in them. He had closed himself off, guarding his heart carefully and protecting himself from the kind of hurt that destroys a man. He wasn't being fair to Molly. She deserved more and Kane often thought that when the time came for Molly to leave, she would be free to find the kind of man who would treat her kindly and give her the love she sought. It wouldn't be difficult for someone like Molly to find a man. The thought knifed through his gut, so Kane gave up thinking about the future, keeping his heart of stone intact. He brought his attention back to the present and Charlie.

"Molly wanted you to stay at the house."

Charlie glanced at the main house. "I know, but we talked, and she seemed to understand. I'm a few years younger, but I'm not a little boy anymore. It'll take her a while to get used to that. I can reason with my sister."

Kane laughed. "You can? Tell me how?"

Charlie smiled and shook his head. "Okay, she's headstrong. And once she sets her mind to something, there's usually no stopping her, but she's so happy now that I think she would've agreed to anything."

Kane agreed. Molly had been happy all day long, from the moment she set foot in the Cheyenne village and saw the willingness in the children's eyes, to coming home and finding her brother alive and well. She'd been overjoyed, until Kane spoke harsh words to her—truthful words, but harsh nonetheless, thus destroying her happiness.

Kane sought out Toby and introduced Charlie to his foreman and the other ranch hands. He made sure Charlie had a bunk and the supplies he needed, then bid him swift good-night. Kane had an overwhelming urge to see Molly, to somehow make things right with her.

They'd all eaten dinner together in the dining room and while Charlie did most of the talking, Molly barely spared Kane a glance. She'd taken off with Charlie the moment the meal was over and Kane lost track of them until he'd spotted Molly's brother speaking with one of the hands by the corral.

The night was cool and quiet, except for the whinnies of a few mares settling down for the night. It was a peaceful time, when animals and humans alike sought rest. Kane sought a different kind of peace. He peered up to their bedroom window and noted the lamplight out. Molly had already gone to bed. He entered the house quickly and took two steps at a time up the stairs. With care, he opened their bedroom door and stepped inside.

Moonlight cascaded into the room streaming a ray onto the bed. An uneasy sensation swept through him when he found the bed empty. Molly wasn't there and he hadn't seen her since dinner. Hell, every time his wife turned up missing, she'd gotten into trouble.

"Damn, where'd she go now?" he muttered. He paced the bedroom, marching back and forth contemplating. Occasionally, he glanced out the window. She couldn't be with Bennett. His grandfather had retired early tonight, right after dinner. And the kitchen was quiet. No sign of Lupe. She'd gone to sleep as well.

The only soothing thought Kane had was that Molly wouldn't dream of leaving the Bar J now, not when her beloved brother had returned. Yes, Kane thought, easing his mind some, Molly wouldn't leave the ranch. Of that, he was certain.

Kane headed downstairs. He'd simply wait up for his renegade wife.

Molly tightened the shawl around her shoulders and walked briskly down the path heading toward home. After spending time with her brother tonight she'd taken a long stroll, needing a chance to clear her head. She'd been angry with Kane and injured by his blunt statement. Kane's reminder that the life she enjoyed at the moment was a temporary arrangement had struck her with harsh clarity.

Molly had almost forgotten.

But Kane hadn't lied to her. He'd never portrayed their marriage as anything other than a way to achieve goals, hers to locate her brother, his to ease an old man's last days.

Molly had a home. She had her brother back. She had children to teach. Was she greedy to want more—to want it all? Or was she a fool to fall in love with a man who clearly didn't want the same things in life that she did?

Clouds overhead blocked starlight, and Molly stopped on the path to glance at the surroundings. She'd been distraught earlier, Kane's words echoing in her head, and she'd headed away from the house, her frustration taking her farther than she'd intended. "Don't get lost, Molly," she whispered into the night.

An owl hooted and she jumped.

"Just stay on the right path," she said, convincing herself she was heading in the right direction. There was nothing to fear. She hadn't left Bar J property. No, her fear was buried deep inside and it had nothing to do with not finding her way back home tonight. Her fear stemmed from finding her way when she no longer lived with Kane. When the Bar J would no longer be her home.

She couldn't blame Kane entirely. She'd entered into their bargain knowing the terms and understanding the consequences. And if given the choice again, she wouldn't have changed the time she had with Kane, the way she felt when he held her, the way she felt when their bodies joined. She had decided that she would grasp all she could from their time together.

Molly saw her path clearly now. She would enjoy her time at the Bar J for all its worth. She had so much to be grateful for and she wouldn't fault Kane for what he hadn't been able to give her. Already, he'd given her so much.

A dim light flickered in the distance, and Molly realized she hadn't been far from home at all. She found her way back easily and once she entered the house, she tiptoed quietly, heading for the staircase.

"Has my wife finally decided to come home?" Kane's voice startled her. She turned toward the parlor where he stood, leaning against the opened doorway holding a bottle of liquor.

"K-Kane, I thought you'd be in bed by now."

He smiled ruefully, lifting the bottle to his lips and taking a swallow. "Hoping I was fast asleep?"

"No. Not really."

"Where did you go?"

"For a walk."

Kane took a deep breath then spun around. Molly watched him march into the parlor and sink into the sofa. Slouched, his long legs stretched out. "Kane? Are you drunk?" Molly followed him into the room.

He lifted the half empty bottle of whiskey he held. "Not yet."

Molly sat down next to him on the sofa, eyeing him quietly. She'd never seen Kane like this. He'd always appeared steadfast and strong, but tonight he showed her a different side. As much as she wanted the old Kane back, the one she could rely on, she also wanted to know more of this intriguing man. "Why drink at all?"

Kane ignored her question. Instead he sipped from the bottle. "I haven't been fair to you."

"Wh-what?" she asked in a stunned whisper.

"You deserve better than me, Little Bird."

Molly blinked, but other than that she didn't show Kane her surprise. "No, I don't." If only he knew how much she cared for him, how rich a life they could have together if Kane would tear down his defenses and allow her inside his heart.

Kane's lips curved up but his smile held only regret. "We both know that you do. I have entered into an unholy bargain with you. We have no future together, yet we pretend that we do in front of the ones we care about the most. We're deceiving them and deceiving ourselves. And even now, when I know I've hurt you and brought you pain...I want you. And what's more, I want you to want me."

Kane sat up straight and turned to face her. "I crave you, Molly." He took her hand and set it on his chest, right over his heart. Rapid beats pulsed under her fingertips. "So much."

Molly melted from his honest words. "I crave you, too, Kane."

Kane bent to kiss her, taking her into his arms. He smelled of whiskey and when their lips touched, the warm heady taste stirred her senses. She liked the way Kane tasted, liked the way her body reacted to his scent.

"I want you now, Molly." Kane laid Molly down on the sofa. He came up over her, kissing her lips and working the buttons of her dress.

"Here?" she managed to ask in between kisses.

"Here." He spread open the material of her dress and gazed at her body with hot hungry eyes.

"Now?" A fresh bout of excitement stirred within her. This was highly inappropriate and she'd be mortified if anyone walked in on them, but when Kane claimed her mouth once again then moved lower to suckle her breast, laving the tips with his tongue, Molly's rational thoughts swiftly fled.

"Now," Kane said, unbuttoning his trousers.

Molly reached up to unfasten the buttons on his shirt, and once done, she spread both hands onto his hot skin, her fingers working through the fine hairs to caress the muscles underneath.

Kane didn't bother removing his pants. He didn't bother removing her dress. Instead he hiked her dress up, and kneeling, he entered her with one efficient move. A deep low guttural groan escaped his lips and Molly, too, felt the power and strength of their joining. Like two pieces of a puzzle, they fit. And, oh, the fitting was perfect.

Kane moved inside with slow sweeping strokes, taking Molly higher and higher, her body tuned to his in every way. They climbed to a towering peak, Molly crying out as Kane pushed her to the limit. They went up and over together, their release spontaneous and exquisitely powerful. Kane shuddered, his body taking every last ounce of Molly until both were sated and complete.

It was only later, when her mind and body had calmed, that she realized what had happened. Kane hadn't denied them wonderful fulfillment this time. He hadn't pulled away at the final moment. And it had been beautiful. Molly had never felt closer to another human being in her life.

Buttoning her dress, she sat up and faced Kane. But he wouldn't look at her. Instead, he sat with his head in his hands, looking grim.

Molly touched his arm. "It was wonderful, Kane."

Kane only shook his head. In a self-deprecating tone, he said quietly, "Like I said, you deserve better."

Molly had to disagree. After what they shared, she knew in her heart that there was nothing better.

"Are you sorry?" she asked.

"It was wrong, Molly. And unfair to you."

"Are you sorry?" she asked again, needing to know if what they shared just now had been one-sided.

Kane shook his head. "No, Molly. I'm not sorry, but if you—"

Molly silenced him with her finger to his lips. "I'm not sorry, either. There is a reason for what happens between us."

But Kane looked skeptical. And Molly didn't know how or if she could ever make him understand.

"Let's get some sleep, Little Bird. You have to teach a class tomorrow."

Molly smiled. "Yes, I do, don't I?"

Kane lifted her and carried her up the stairs to their bedroom. He helped her undress and then tucked her in, kissing her one last time. She watched as he headed for the door.

"Where are you going?"

"I'll be sleeping in one of the spare bedrooms from now on, Molly."

Molly bolted straight up. "Don't you dare," she admonished.

Kane found her threat amusing. He smiled briefly, but he spoke with firm resolve. "It's the only way, Little Bird. Don't argue. I'm doing this for you."

"I *don't* want you to go."

"And I don't want to go, but unless I do, what happened tonight will happen again and again."

Molly squeezed her eyes shut. Almost immediately,

she formulated a plan. She wouldn't allow Kane to sleep alone, thinking he was doing right by her or not. Molly cherished her time with Kane. She needed him by her side. And even though he believed he'd failed them both tonight, Molly wholeheartedly disagreed. She and Kane had created a memory that would last her entire lifetime.

"Okay then, don't slam the door on your way out."

Kane narrowed his eyes in puzzlement.

"Good night, Kane." She snuggled into her sheets.

Kane closed the door slowly, shaking his head.

Molly vowed that one way or another, she would make sure Kane returned to their bed once again.

Or her name wasn't Molly McGuire Jackson.

Chapter Sixteen

The next week flew by, as Molly kept busy with her duties at the Cheyenne village. Kane only allowed her to teach on the days he would visit. He would set her down from the wagon, take her hand and deliver her to her makeshift classroom, politely wishing her a good day. But as she taught the students, enmeshed in her task, often she would look out upon the village and their eyes would meet. Kane watched her from a distance even as he taught young Cheyenne men ranching skills, even as he spoke with his mother outside by her lodge.

And on the days she wasn't able to teach, Molly spent time working on her lesson plans, realizing that while the younger of the children seemed more satisfied, the older ones became frustrated easily, impatient to learn and to grasp the knowledge she offered. The sessions went slowly, Molly taking care and time to see that each one understood the lesson before she moved on.

And each night after supper, she would sit outside the house with Bennett and Charlie, enjoying the cool evening air, sharing the events of the day. Bennett seemed to enjoy Charlie's company, but it was Charlie who had completely been taken by Kane.

He spoke of little else but what new skill Kane had taught him that day. How good Kane was with a rope and a gun, and too often he'd expound on one of Kane's adventures while seeking out his late wife's killer. This surprised Molly because she knew Kane didn't often speak of those times, keeping most of that time in his life to himself. But somewhere deep in her heart, Molly believed Kane, had a purpose in sharing with Charlie what his life had been like then. Kane, if Molly was correct in her thinking, wanted to halt any notions that being a gunfighter, even if the cause was a noble one, wasn't all Charlie thought it to be. In truth, Molly believed Kane in the short time he'd known her brother, had changed Charlie's way of thinking.

And Molly loved him all the more for his efforts.

Tonight, after supper, Molly found Kane sitting outside with Bennett and Charlie. She didn't hesitate to take a seat on the bench next to him, brushing her thighs to his. Kane inhaled, a little catch that no one else noticed but Molly. And though she hadn't been able to break down his defenses yet, each night before bed Molly would ask for a good-night kiss before he would enter the room where he slept. And each night, Kane would take her into his arms and kiss her until her knees buckled. Each night their embrace lasted longer and longer, both having more and more difficulty parting.

Molly laid her hand on Kane's thigh and smiled at him. He continued speaking and covered his hand over hers, intertwining their fingers. Molly knew it was an unconscious act, one that he did on instinct.

"Charlie's getting pretty good with a rope," Kane said, and Molly noted admiration in his voice.

"Kane's been teaching me a new way to toss it and, well, I've done better here than I did during the whole time on the trail."

"It takes practice, Charlie," Kane said, "and you're getting your fair share on the ranch. Toby says you're working out just fine."

Charlie beamed from the compliment. "I do all right."

Molly chuckled. "Charlie's roping calves now? Boy, if only Mama could see you."

With that, Charlie's expression fell, and his good mood disappeared in a flash.

Kane broke the awkward silence. "She'd be proud, Charlie. A mother wants her child to succeed in whatever path they choose. There's no reason to think different."

Molly agreed. "Yes, Mama would have been proud of you. She wanted you to be happy, Charlie. We all do."

Charlie's expression lifted and Molly witnessed the subtle change in him—from a little boy with a guilt-ridden face to the young man with hope lighting his eyes.

Bennett coughed and all heads turned toward him. He'd been happier these last few days than Molly had seen him, and his coughing had been to a minimum. But tonight at supper and now, Molly noticed his ashen face. "And how was your day, Grandfather?"

Bennett waved a hand in the air. "The usual. I slept most the day away." He coughed once again, and Molly's stomach clenched, the queasiness she experienced borne of fear in losing such a remarkable man. She'd been preoccupied lately and hadn't spent the time she wanted with him. "Are you ready to turn in?"

Bennett glanced at her. "If you're willing to read me to sleep."

Molly chuckled once again. The Jackson men always seemed to be making deals. "I'd love to." Molly stood and took his hand.

"And make it more interesting than that damn story about those little women."

Charlie jumped up with an offer. "I have dime novels. Don't have much use for them anymore."

Bennett looked at Charlie with affection then slapped him on the back gently. "I'd like that, boy. You go get them and bring them up to my room."

Kane stood to wish his grandfather good-night. "Enjoy the rest of your evening. I'll see you in the morning."

Bennett narrowed his eyes, his gray brows nearly touching. "You take care of Molly now, boy. She's been working too hard and she needs tender loving."

"Grandfather!" Both chorused in unison.

Bennett coughed a few times, his shoulders slumping. Molly waited for this bout to cease, the queasiness in her belly increasing.

But then Bennett didn't stop there. He went on, addressing Kane directly. "And why aren't you sleeping in your room? Did she kick you out? Can't say as I blame her." Bennett winked at Molly, even as she blushed full out. "Don't deny it, boy. I hear you going into the room down from mine every night."

"That's none of your business," Kane said, keeping a steady tone.

"It's because I haven't been feeling well, Grandfather. We didn't want to worry you."

"What's wrong?" he asked with deep concern on his

face. God, Molly hated lying. She hated deceiving this sweet, dying man. So she told him a half truth. "I've been having stomach upsets." Which wasn't much of a lie. Every time she thought about Bennett's worsening condition, she felt poorly.

Molly laid her hand over her stomach and Bennett glanced down, his eyes suddenly a bit more bright. "Now, that's the best news I've heard in months."

Kane was about to correct his assumption, but Molly stopped him with a stern look. "Well then, let's get you upstairs, so we can both rest. Reading always soothes me."

Bennett agreed. "Good night, Kane."

Kane nodded and stared at Molly as she helped Bennett into the house. She'd noticed the concern on his face as well and Molly wondered if Kane feared that Bennett's days were numbered.

But two hours later, after Molly spent the better part of the evening reading to Bennett, she found out the true reason for Kane's sullen expression. She opened her bedroom door to find Kane staring at her stomach. "Are you really feeling poorly?" he asked.

Molly tugged on Kane's arm, gesturing for him to enter the room. She closed the door behind her and placed a hand on her stomach. Though she didn't want Kane's sympathy, she was glad he'd come to their bedroom tonight. His noble effort to keep his distance had put her on edge and every look and accidental touch reminded her of how much she wanted her husband. And his passionate good-night kisses told her that Kane wanted the same. "Yes, at times my stomach aches. Nerves, I think. And worry over your grandfather. He didn't look well tonight."

Kane drew a breath that sounded like relief. "He's sleeping?"

"Yes, I guess my reading does that. Puts a man to sleep."

Kane smiled at her little joke and her breath caught in her throat seeing that genuine expression. She missed her husband and wanted things back to the way they'd been before Kane had decided his need for her had been unfair. Perhaps he'd been right, but Molly no longer cared. She only knew what her heart told her.

"Actually, I'm glad you've come to see me tonight."

Kane's eyes narrowed. "I come every night, to say good night."

"Yes, but," she began and turned around, pointing to her back. "I've been struggling with this dress. I can't quite undo the buttons."

Kane hesitated, the silence deafening. "Where's Lupe?"

"Asleep. Wouldn't you know she'd help me put on the dress this morning, but she probably figured it was your job to take it off me."

Kane cleared his throat.

"Please?" She swiveled her head to see why he hesitated.

He stood with hands on hips with an apparent battle going on in his head.

Molly turned to face him and in a velvety tone she'd practiced earlier, she said, "You're so good at taking off my clothes, Kane. Or have you forgotten?"

Kane pinched the bridge of his nose, a gesture she noticed him do, more and more lately. "No, I haven't forgotten."

And when he finally relented and approached her, Molly's heart pounded against her chest. She held her breath when he touched her, his hands brushing the curls off her shoulder. His fingers worked quickly, unbuttoning the tiny buttons until she felt cool air caressing her back. She turned to him slowly and let the dress fall from her shoulders then she shimmied the rest of the way out of the garment, keeping her gaze trained on him.

"What are you doing?" he asked in a raspy whisper.

Molly crossed her arms over her chest to slip her fingers under the straps of her satiny chemise. She pulled the straps down and stood before Kane, nearly naked but for the tug of one flimsy garment. "Seducing my husband, I think."

Kane groaned and came forward, his eyes hungry, his mouth hungrier. He kissed her hard, crushing his lips to hers, his hands flattening her breasts and his manhood pressing firmly against her belly. Molly moaned, throwing back her head allowing him access to her body. Kane moved her toward the wall and once he secured her against it, his hand came between her thighs. She cried out when his fingers parted the warm flesh and stroked her back and forth, creating sharp tingling jolts that seared through her entire body. "Kane, Kane," she cried out, between kisses. "I miss you."

"I miss you, too, Little Bird," Kane admitted, his voice rough, "and now, fly."

Kane stroked her faster, harder and her release came swiftly and with such power that she shuddered, her body rocking against the wall.

Kane undid the fasteners on his trousers and entered her, her body ready to take all of him in. His thrusts hard, lifting her up slightly so that she had to grab his neck for support. But she knew, even through his passion, Kane would not stay with her, if he lost control again.

"Careful, Gray Wolf," she said softly, speaking his Cheyenne name for the first time.

And Kane understood. He slowed his pace and they began a steady rhythm of thrusts until Kane had nearly come to completion.

He kissed her one last time and left her body, holding her in a tight embrace, his own body still raw with need.

Molly took hold of his hand and smiled with love in her heart. "Come to bed, Kane."

And a short time later, as Kane slept cradling her in his arms, Molly knew they'd come to terms with silent understanding. Kane was back where he belonged, in his bed with Molly right beside him.

"Tall Neck spelled out his name today on the slate." Molly beamed, unable to hold back her excitement. She sat next to Kane on the wagon seat as they headed back to the Bar J. "And Smiling Eyes can recite the first ten letters of the alphabet."

Molly knew she was bending Kane's ear with talk of her students' accomplishments, but she couldn't remember a time in her life when she'd been happier. After just several weeks of instruction, her pupils had surprised her not only with their willingness to learn, but also with the rapid rate at which they did learn. Difficult as it was to hold each student's attention due to the vast differences in their ages, Molly tried doubly hard to give each one individual instruction and she'd been greatly rewarded. The students were learning.

"They have a good teacher," Kane said in earnest. "The children like your school, mainly because they like you. I confess I was wrong about you, Molly."

Molly grinned. "I know, but it's nice to hear you admit it."

Kane grinned back, shaking his head. "Sometimes, Mrs. Jackson, you're too clever for your britches."

Molly liked the sound of her married name, especially coming from Kane's lips. She placed her hand on his thigh. "And sometimes, Mr. Jackson, you're too handsome for yours."

Kane slanted her a quick look, his gaze hot and hungry and filled with promise for the night ahead. Molly took a deep breath in anticipation.

But her thoughts were interrupted as soon as Kane reined the horses to a stop in front of the barn. Lupe came running out of the house, yelling out in broken English and Spanish phrases, making no sense at all.

"Senor Kane, Senor Kane, something *es* wrong!"

She rattled the next sentences off in Spanish, speaking more rapidly than Molly had ever heard anyone speak in her life. Molly's heart pounded like a hammer, thinking that something was indeed terribly wrong. Lupe was excitable, but she'd never been this upset before.

Kane bounded from the wagon and met Lupe in the middle of the yard. He took hold of her shoulders, trying to calm her.

"What is it, Lupe?

"*Es* Senor Bennett. He *es* gone!"

Knots formed in Molly's stomach and they worsened when she witnessed Kane's troubled expression. "Gone? Did we lose him?"

"Sí, sí. He es lost."

Kane glanced at the house, his gaze traveling to the second story where Bennett must be lying in his bed. Oh, God. Tears stung Molly's eyes. They'd just spent the evening with Bennett last night, Charlie entertaining the older man with his tales from the trail. And Bennett had laughed until he nearly cried from her brother's anecdotes.

Molly jumped down from the wagon and stood by Kane's side, taking hold of his hand. She had dreaded this day from the moment she realized her fondness for the older man. "Poor Bennett."

Kane hugged her and the power of his embrace told her how much he ached for the loss himself. Then he turned to Lupe. "Were you with him when he died?"

Puzzled, Lupe's brown eyes opened wide. "Died?" She began shaking her head. "*No es muerto.* No dead. Senor Bennett *es* gone. Lupe bring him his meal, but Senor Bennett no answer. Lupe tried to open door, but bedroom door locked. Lupe get Charlie and he open door. Senor Bennett no in his room."

Kane glanced at Molly then he took her hand. "Let's check this out." They did a quick search of the house, finding no trace of Bennett, but what they did find was a very suspicious opened window in his bedroom. Curtains billowed and a refreshing breeze blew in. Kane stuck his head out the window and spotted Toby in the yard. He called out to his foreman, "Hey Toby. Wait right there."

They met Toby in front of the house and Kane questioned the foreman. "Bennett is missing. What do you know about it?"

Toby found the dirt on his boots real interesting. He shuffled around a bit, running a hand down his face.

"Toby? You do know something, don't you? If my grandfather's in trouble, I need to know."

Toby took his hat off and scratched his head. "He ain't in no trouble. That's for darn sure. Except maybe with you all."

Kane pursed his lips and stood rooted to the spot, his sharp gaze focused on the Bar J's most trusted employee. "And why is that?"

Toby explained. "I've worked for Bennett Jackson for twenty years. He and I go way back. He's the best damn cattleman in Texas. When Bennett asks me to do something, I do it and keep my mouth shut about it."

"I'm sure my grandfather appreciates your loyalty, but there's a lot more at stake here than you think. Now, where is he?"

Toby replied quickly. "Don't know. I never asked."

Molly saw Kane fist his hands, his patience ebbing quickly. She spoke up. "Toby, please tell us what you do know? Lupe and I are frantic." She glanced at Kane. "We all are."

Toby nodded, apparently taken by Molly's sincere plea. "Okay, all I know is, some days Mr. Jackson asks me to put the ladder up by his window at a certain time of day. I get his mare ready and tie her reins out back a ways, behind a tree. I figure it's his own business where he goes. But he always comes back a few hours later."

Kane looked at Molly. "I'm going to find him. I'll pick up his trail from that tree."

Molly nodded and grabbed Kane's arm before he got away. "Wait. I'm going with you."

Before Kane could protest, Molly gave her reasons.

"I have just as much at stake in this as you do. I want to know what Bennett is up to."

Kane inhaled, taking a quick moment to think, then he agreed. "Have Charlie saddle up our horses. Make sure you take Sweet Pea, Molly. I'm going to check out that tree. Toby?"

Toby walked off with Kane to show him where Bennett made his escape. And a short time later, Molly and Kane were on the path, heading off the Bar J following the trail left by Bennett's horse.

Kane rode in silence, his suspicions keeping him on edge. His grandfather was up to something and Kane feared he knew what it was, but he kept his thoughts to himself. No sense alerting Molly. They'd find out the truth soon enough.

Molly rode beside him, she, too, keeping quiet. But her silence was filled with worry and concern over a man who perhaps didn't deserve it. Whereas Kane, well, he'd had his suspicions for a long time now. He just didn't believe his grandfather capable of such deception. But then Bennett Jackson was nothing if not clever. He'd outsmarted his rivals from the day he stepped foot in Bountiful, building a herd and ranch bigger and better than any other in the territory.

Unfortunately, knowing his history for obtaining his goals meant that he very well could be guilty of the greatest deception of all.

"Do you know where we're heading?" Molly asked in a whisper.

Kane nodded. "I have an idea. There's only one thing up ahead. A lake. It's small and secluded. I came upon it when I first arrived looking for a good place to settle the Cheyenne. But it was half the distance to Bountiful and off Bar J land where too many others might stumble upon it, so I chose the other area for the village."

"What do you suppose we'll find there?"

Kane chuckled, but in his heart he found nothing amusing about this. "My grandfather. And Lord only knows what else."

Ten minutes later, Kane had them dismount. He tied the horses to a nearby shrub and took Molly's hand. "It's just up ahead. Keep quiet and move quickly."

Molly followed him the short distance to the lake. And once there, both froze in place. Molly put a hand to her mouth, but that didn't stifle her gasp of surprise. Kane, too, looked on, but with no such surprise. He'd had his suspicions.

There, sitting on a quilt at the bank of the lake and having themselves a fine time were his grandfather and Mrs. Penelope Rose.

"I don't believe it," Molly whispered. "I can't believe what I'm seeing."

Bennett took Penelope's hand then and they walked to the lake. With his pants rolled up, Bennett entered the water, splashing and laughing, hardly the antics of a dying man.

Even from this distance, Kane heard his booming voice, the laughter, devoid of any violent coughing, and noted his grandfather's fine physical form. "Dying, huh?"

"What are you saying?" Molly asked.

Kane shook his head. "Let's find out for sure." He took Molly's hand once again.

"Wait, we can't just interrupt them."

Kane grinned a devil's smile. He found himself relishing the idea of catching his grandfather in the act. "You bet we can. You coming, Little Bird?"

"Yes, yes. But this is so…so awkward."

"All the better."

They were nearly at the bank of the lake when Bennett and Penelope noticed them. Penelope nearly fainted. Bennett grabbed her by the waist to keep her from falling into the water, but his gaze was focused on Kane. "You should know better than to sneak up on a body, boy."

"Oh, dear," Penelope sighed, her face flushed with embarrassment and guilt.

Bennett walked her up the bank and out of the sun. "Are you all right?"

Penelope nodded, but her eyes were directed at Kane. "I'm better."

Bennett faced Kane head on. "You followed me?"

Kane quelled his anger for the moment. "After you gave Lupe and Molly a scare, damn right I followed you."

Bennett appeared repentant, giving Molly a sincere look. "Sorry for the worry, dear girl."

"That's…okay," Molly said. "As long as you're all right."

"He's fine, Molly," Kane said harshly. "Better than fine. My grandfather is healthier than all of us. Isn't that right, Bennett?"

Bennett guided Penelope back to their quilt. "Have a seat, Penny." He helped her sit down and once certain she was comfortable, he turned to face Kane squarely. "Yes, that's right. I'm fit as a fiddle. And I make no apology about it."

"You lied to us both."

"Yes, and I'd do it again. Hell, boy, you've got your-self a beautiful wife and a fine home and someday you'll own the Bar J entirely. You got nothing to complain about. I did it for you. A man's got to have a family, Kane."

"So you pretended you were dying? That's just plain cruel, Grandfather."

"I don't see it that way. You need a wife and child, Kane. Whether you know it or not and you're halfway there. Hell, boy, I thought you'd have Molly with child by now, so I could stop the deception. What's wrong with you, anyway?"

Molly blushed full out and Kane took Bennett's com-ment to heart. "I told you over and over, I didn't want a wife and I certainly don't want a child."

"You're a married man, Kane. You've got a home and land so abundant, that it'd be a sin of God not to pass down the legacy to your child."

"There is no child, Grandfather. And I'm thinking you're the one sinning in front of God, not me. You de-liberately deceived Molly into coming here as a mail-order bride. And you worried us all for weeks, thinking you're on your last days."

"I've got me at least twenty more years, boy. And I plan to make the most of it." He glanced at Penelope and this time—the talkative woman blushed pink and kept her mouth quiet. "And what's more, I've asked Penel-ope to marry me and she's agreed."

Kane glanced at Penelope Rose and saw her in a new light. The woman appeared happy and much younger. When she rose to stand beside Bennett, Kane noted that the two made a fine-looking couple. But Kane was too angry with his grandfather to offer congratulations. He was surprised though that Molly hadn't chimed in to offer her own congratulations. If Molly was anything, she was sentimental.

But he noticed that Molly had left his side. He turned around, searching for his wife. He found her mounting Sweet Pea, her face downcast and sullen. She reined her horse around and without waiting for Kane she spurred the mare on, heading for home.

Bennett didn't miss her departure. "You've said some real unkind things, Kane. Maybe it's time you gave some serious thought to what you really want in life. Go after your wife. Make things right. You'd be a fool to lose such a wonderful gal."

Kane watched Molly ride away until she was long out of sight. He knew that there was no way to make things right by Molly. Bennett's deception had hurt them both in ways his grandfather would never understand.

The bargain Kane made with Molly was now null and void. His grandfather wasn't dying, a fact Kane didn't relish at the moment. He'd wanted to strangle the man himself for his meddling and lies. And now that Charlie was home, there was no reason to keep up their ruse of marriage.

Kane's gut clenched. He felt a stabbing in his heart.

It was time to let Molly go.

Chapter Seventeen

Molly waited for Charlie at the bunkhouse, her heart heavy with despair. She'd always known this day would come, but she hadn't anticipated the *way* in which her bargain with Kane would finally be met.

No, how could one possibly guess that a man would fake an illness and pretend to be dying? Molly understood Bennett's motives, but when he applied this ruse he had no way of knowing how much destruction it would cause.

He had no way of knowing that while Kane had agreed to marry a woman brought here by deception, he never had any intention to remain married, much less create a child.

But if Molly's suspicions were right, then she and Kane had indeed created a child. She'd been having stomach upsets for weeks now and her monthlies were late. The only way she'd know for sure would be to see a doctor, which was exactly what Molly planned on doing. She had to leave the Bar J and make a new life for herself. Her bargain with Kane was over.

I told you over and over, I didn't want a wife and I certainly don't want a child.

Kane's words drummed in her head, pounding away until she couldn't think anymore. All she could do was feel. And Molly did feel. She felt cold inside. She felt betrayed by circumstances. And she felt sad for the loss of the life she and Kane might have shared. She hated the deception. Both Bennett's and the ruse she and Kane had entered into. As far as she was concerned, all of them were at fault. And one tiny little infant would suffer the most. For that, Molly was truly sorry. If she was with child, Molly thought, placing a hand over her belly, then she had to do what's best for them all and that included explaining things to Charlie. He had a right to know the truth about Molly's marriage to Kane.

And she prayed that Charlie wouldn't blame himself.

"Hey, sis." Charlie rounded the corner of the bunkhouse, surprising her. She hadn't seen him coming, but she also couldn't get over the change in him. He was tall and lean, wearing leather chaps and a black Stetson, and his once youthful face was marked by a day-old beard, which said he'd grown up, through and through. Sometimes the transition from boy to man stunned her. Sometimes, like today, she realized how far both of them had come from their days of poverty in St. Louis.

Tears she couldn't control trickled down her cheeks.

"Hey, what's wrong, Molly?" Charlie's face contorted with confusion—that look a man gets when he doesn't understand, and more so, when he doesn't *want* to understand what's in a woman's head. Molly was only sorry that she had to put him through this, but he deserved to know the whole truth. And she couldn't put it off another day.

"I'm leaving the Bar J."

Charlie's eyebrows lifted nearly to the brim of his hat. "What?"

Molly sat down on a bench against the back wall of the bunkhouse, hoping she'd be out of view from everyone else on the ranch. "Sit down, Charlie. I have a long story to tell you."

Charlie sat and listened and sometimes he questioned her, but for the most part, he gave her his support. And when the whole complicated tale was out, Charlie took her hand. "None of this would have happened if I hadn't run away. You wouldn't have had to find a way to chase me to Texas. You wouldn't have had to marry Kane and—"

"I'm not sorry I came to Texas. I like it here, Charlie. I can't imagine being in the city anymore. Here, there are opportunities and wide open spaces and well, where else can you rise in the morning and bed down at night smelling the wonderful scent of cow dung?"

That put a smile on Charlie's lips. "You're always trying to make me feel better."

"I mean it, Charlie. As for Kane, I love him. And I wouldn't trade my time being married to him for anything under the sun. But he doesn't feel the same way. He never bargained for a wife. And Charlie, there's more. I—" Molly began, not knowing just how to tell her brother that he might be an uncle soon. "I think I'm going to have a baby."

"A baby?" Charlie swallowed and stared at her belly.

"Yes, but Kane never wanted a child. He's made that abundantly clear."

"You're not going to tell him?" Charlie asked.

"No. I know how he feels. I don't want him saddled

with me out of some sense of obligation. If Bennett finds out, he'll needle Kane into staying married to me. But I don't want Kane that way." She shook her head. "So you see, I have to leave the ranch. I can get a job in town. I'm going to see if there's a position open for a schoolteacher. And if not in Bountiful then somewhere else. But first I have to see Dr. Beckman."

Charlie nodded. "Sis, I'm not running away again. We're going to do this together. You and me and if there is a little one, I'm going to help you. We're family and we're sticking together from now on."

"Oh, Charlie," Molly cried, hugging her brother tight. "Thank you. I'm so glad you're here."

"I like working on the Bar J, sis. But not without you here. Besides, I wouldn't be able to keep your secret if I stayed on. It's better if we both left."

"Listen, Charlie, please don't quit your job yet. Stay on for a while. I want to see the doctor first and then I'll send word to you. I need some time to myself."

"Are you sure?" he asked.

"I'm very sure," she said sending him a reassuring smile. "I'm going up to pack. I'll leave first thing in the morning. I suppose I'll have to say goodbye to Kane. And Bennett." Molly braced herself, wishing she could just disappear instead of facing Kane. The farewell wouldn't come easy, her heart already aching at the notion. She loved Kane and she might be carrying his child—a child who would never know the love of a father. Both Molly and Charlie had been deprived of a father's love, her own father choosing to abandon his family when the children were too young to remember him. Molly would see to it that her child would be surrounded by love despite not having Kane in its life. But she felt terrible to put her brother in the middle of all this. He'd been happy at the ranch, enjoying the work and finally being accepted by men he greatly admired.

She rose and hugged her brother one last time. "Don't worry. We'll be fine."

Charlie grinned. "I was just gonna say the same thing. We will be fine, sis."

Molly guarded her heart the best she could and faced the fact that soon she would have to say farewell to two men in her life she had come to love.

Molly entered the house ready to take the stairs when she noticed Bennett slumped down on the parlor chair, his face ashen. This time she doubted his pretense. Bennett appeared truly shaken. Molly walked into the room quietly and took a seat next to him on the sofa.

"Bennett," she began softly. "I know your reasons for doing what you did and I don't blame you entirely. But now I must say goodbye. I'm leaving in the morning. My marriage to Kane…was a mistake."

"Molly, dear girl," he said, taking her hand. "I never meant any harm. I only wanted what was best for my grandson."

"You lied to him and deceived us both," she said quietly. "But I'm glad you're not dying. I have grown fond of you and wish you well. You and Mrs. Rose will have a good life together."

He waved that notion off. "Penny isn't speaking to me."

"She's angry?"

"Chewed my ear off when Kane explained everything. How was I to know your marriage was temporary? He spoke of the bargain he made with you, and I guess I underestimated my grandson's stupidity."

Molly smiled. "What?"

"Even though I deceived you into coming to Bountiful, once you married Kane, I believed you had fallen in love with each other. I was feeling mighty proud of myself for the union."

Molly squeezed his hand. "You were half right. I love Kane, but today he made his wishes clear, didn't he? He doesn't want the marriage or a future with me. He never did."

"Stupid, I say."

Molly agreed, but Kane had never deceived her in that regard. She always knew that he wouldn't abide the marriage. "Maybe, but I can't change his wishes. I'm leaving the Bar J. There's no reason to stay any longer. I'm sure Kane will—" Molly began but had trouble even saying the words "—I'm sure he'll find a way to dissolve our marriage."

Bennett leaned forward and put his face in his hands, shaking his head. "I wish you would stay."

"I…can't."

"I'm sorry, Molly. If I could undo any of this, I would. I'm so sorry."

Molly believed Bennett's remorse and regret, but that didn't change anything. "I will always be grateful for your assistance in helping me locate my brother. And for making me feel welcome in your home." Her eyes burned with unshed tears. "Goodbye, Grandfather." She kissed his cheek then dashed out of the room.

* * *

Kane stood outside his bedroom door, hesitant, wondering what to say to Molly. He thought to turn away and leave her be for a while, to let her settle down. He figured she'd give him a good piece of her mind and Kane didn't fear the confrontation, he just didn't know how to make her understand.

Tell her the truth.

The voice in Kane's head plagued him. Kane had valid reasons to let Molly go. She deserved more from a man than he could give. But he had held back the one reason that would surely make Molly see his position differently.

Kane didn't know if he was ready to admit his deepest failure to her. It had tortured him for years, the darkness inside leading him to a life of revenge.

When he heard Molly's sob from the other side of the door, he didn't bother knocking. He opened the door wide and entered. She stood over the bed, folding clothes into her valise, tears dripping down her face.

Kane shouldn't have been shocked to see her packing, yet the fact remained, the sight left him numb. "Ah, Little Bird."

Molly lifted her eyes to him, her face stained with tears. She wiped them away and held her head high. "Please, don't call me that."

Sharp memories entered his mind of all the times he had used that affectionate name—when they made love, when their bodies joined so perfectly, when she helped ease his desire with tutored hands. It pained him to abide Molly's wishes, but he realized that he no longer had the right to speak to her in that way. "You don't have to leave."

Molly shook her head and continued with her task. "I do, Kane. I have to leave. First thing in the morning, I'll be gone."

"You can stay, you know. You can live here."

But as Kane said the words, he knew what he proposed wouldn't work. He knew that with Molly around, he wouldn't be able to think, much less get his life back to the way it was before she arrived.

She cast him a sad smile. "You know that isn't possible."

A deep anguished sigh escaped at the notion of letting Molly go. "You don't have to leave so soon."

Molly snapped her valise closed. "There's no reason to stay any longer. We both have what we want."

The bitterness in her voice stung. He'd never heard Molly use that tone. "Where will you go?"

"Bountiful. I'm going to look for a teaching position."

"What of the Cheyenne?" Kane asked unfairly.

Tears flowed down Molly's cheeks, but she quickly wiped them away. "I've written a letter to the children." Molly walked over to the dresser and lifted a piece of paper. She hugged the parchment to her chest before approaching Kane. "I would hope you could read this to them. It's somewhat of an explanation they might understand."

Kane brushed his hand over Molly's to receive the paper, the contact perhaps the last he would have with her. On instinct, he reached out and took her hand. "Molly," he breathed out, a hot, raw pain searing his heart.

"I'll be fine, Kane." She stared into his eyes for a moment then slipped her hand from his.

Kane dropped his arms to his side. "I'll take you into town."

"No need. Charlie's offered to drive me."

Kane closed his eyes briefly, realizing that he might never see this woman again, realizing that Molly would leave, perhaps to find fulfillment and happiness in the arms of another man.

Kane snapped his eyes open, gazing at her one last time. He took in her tawny red curls, the way the hair flowed over her shoulders and touched the very tips of her breasts. Her face, soft and sweet and stained with tears, looked beautiful as ever. He gazed one last time at her petite form, slight enough that a strong breeze might blow her over, yet she stood firm, all bravado and courage, perusing him in the same way.

"I would guess that you would seek legal counsel for the…" Molly said, taking a swallow.

"There's time for that, Molly."

"No, I would prefer you do that immediately."

Stung again, Kane got the impression Molly couldn't wait to dissolve their marriage. She wanted to get on with her life. Determined and intelligent, Molly would make her way in this life. He had no doubt. But he hadn't bargained for the way letting her go made him feel. Empty. Lost. Desolate.

He asked himself once again if this was for the best.

And Kane had come to the same conclusion.

He would free his little bird and watch her fly away.

"I want to thank you for helping me find Charlie. You did everything in your power to hold up your end of the bargain," she said softly, "and I will never forget how you saved me, over and over. I will never forget…you."

Molly reached up and kissed his lips, taking him clearly by surprise. Her soft, sweet scent invaded his senses. He kissed her back fully, sweeping his tongue in her mouth, mating with her this way for the very last time. He held her tight, his arms reaching out and wrapping around her tiny waist, pulling her up to his body, relishing the way she fit him, so perfectly. He held her a long time, keeping her tight against him, but it was Molly who broke away first, shaking her head, tears streaming down her face. "Goodbye, Kane."

"Molly," was all he could say as he stared at her once more, before turning and walking out the door.

Molly stood on Mrs. Rose's boardinghouse steps, much as she had the first day, when Kane had escorted her here. Little did she know then that her life would take such a drastic turn. Little did she know that she would come to love living in Bountiful, the town and its surroundings feeling more welcoming than her home in St. Louis. Little did she know she would fall in love with an obstinate rancher, a wily landowner and a small tribe of Cheyenne children. But she had and now all she could do was to try to put the shattered pieces of her life together and start fresh.

She knocked on Mrs. Rose's door.

When she opened the door, the older woman gasped in surprise and hurriedly ushered Molly inside. "Oh, you poor dear girl. I told you that those Jacksons couldn't be trusted. And now, here you are, with your valise in hand? Heavens, you're not planning on leaving town, are you? Why, I'd never forgive myself for not catching on. Why, if you leave, I'll never marry that old coot,

Bennett Jackson. He and his grandson have caused you more than enough grief."

Even Penelope's ranting didn't bother her. In truth, Molly welcomed the familiarity. She welcomed the talkative woman with the kind heart and wished to call her a friend.

"I'm not leaving Bountiful, but I have left the Bar J. And Kane. I left my husband," Molly admitted, her head downcast.

Mrs. Rose sighed, shaking her head. "Come, dear girl. Sit down in the kitchen. I'll make you a pot of tea. Calms the nerves, you know." And Molly followed her into the kitchen.

She watched Penelope Rose shuffle around her kitchen, preparing hot water for the tea. Even though Bennett claimed Penelope wasn't speaking to him, Molly had no doubt that the two belonged together. They'd been sweethearts years prior and she thought it endearing that after all these years, they'd found each other again.

Penelope looked twenty years younger these days, wearing more stylish clothes and fixing her hair differently, but Molly noted the twinkle in her eyes, and the shining glow on her face.

That, more than her new clothes, spoke of the love she had for Bennett.

Mrs. Rose sat down to face her, the tea forgotten for now. "Now, tell me, was it all Bennett's doing? Did he cause your heartache?"

"Well, yes and no," Molly began. "You see, I was desperate to find Charlie. And, well, Bennett had the same kind of desperation. He wanted his grandson married and producing heirs for the Bar J. I don't fault Bennett too much. He had valid reasons, but he did deceive me."

"And me, too," Penelope said, reaching out to grasp Molly's hand. "Heavens, Bennett lied to us all. I, uh, I hope you know I had no part in this. When I first came to visit him at the Bar J, well, there were sparks, lots of them between us. But we all knew he'd been sick and there was little hope of his recovery. I thought I might ease his last days. And then, one day, he showed up on my doorstep. And he began courting me," Mrs. Rose went on, a little chuckle escaping. "Like we were your age, Molly. He brought me flowers and confessed some things to me. He said he'd been very ill and he wasn't sure if he'd made a complete recovery, but just in case, he didn't want to give you or Kane false hope. So we kept our visits secret. We would picnic, and take long afternoon strolls. I swear, on my late husband's grave, I had no idea that he was sneaking out of his room, while all of you thought he was taking his last breath."

"I believe you. Bennett is quite clever when he wants something. And I guess he wanted for Kane and I to believe he was dying, but he wanted you, as well. And he found a way to get both. Until he got caught."

Mrs. Rose made an unladylike sound. "Hmmmph!"

"But Kane and I were deceiving him as well. I know you've heard about our bargain. Kane was to help me find Charlie, if I stayed married to him until Bennett passed on. Kane never wanted a wife or a marriage." Molly held back tears, but her voice shook anyway. "I, uh, I probably should have never married him."

"Nonsense, child. You did the right thing."

Molly snapped her head up. "But you never liked

Kane. And you surely didn't trust him. You warned me about him."

"Yes, but I'd never seen the way you looked at him, especially after you were married. Kane made you happy, Molly."

"Yes." And then Molly added, "It's that way for you, too, Penelope. Bennett makes you happy."

She waved her hand as if shooing the thought away. "I'm not sure what I'll do about him."

"You're going to marry him. You love him."

Mrs. Rose stood to pour the hot tea. She brought over two lovely hand-painted china cups, decorated with red roses. She set one down in front of Molly then brought over a dish of fresh biscuits with honey. "Maybe, but I'm going to let him stew a bit, first. He's got to learn not to meddle in others' lives."

Molly thought that sounded extremely funny coming from Mrs. Rose, the master of all gossip, but she remained silent.

Molly sipped her tea and actually felt up to eating a biscuit. Speaking with another woman really did help. Molly had been alone, without much female companionship for so very long. She sat and enjoyed a moment of peace, nibbling on the wonderful fare and listening to Mrs. Rose.

"I want you to know I'm glad you came here, Molly. You have a home here, for as long as you like. But tell me, what are your plans?"

Molly finished her biscuit, sipped the tea, then leaned back in her chair. "I hope to find employment as a schoolteacher. If not here in Bountiful then somewhere nearby. There's bound to be a town in need, or even a landowner who might want private instruction for their children. I'll do just about anything."

Mrs. Rose pouted, her face becoming tight. "Did Kane throw you out?"

"No! Nothing like that. In fact, he said I could stay." Molly shook her head. "But I can't live with him in that house and not *live* with him." Molly blushed full out, heat climbing up her neck. "If you know what I mean."

"Lord, dear girl, it's been ages. But I do know what you mean. You love that man, don't you?"

Molly nodded, her heart shredding into small pieces. "With all my heart."

"Bennett called him a fool and now I know why."

"Kane never lied to me, Penelope. He had said from the start he didn't want a marriage or a wife. We'd only planned on staying married until Bennett passed away, but looks like that man's going to live a long time."

Penelope twisted her lips. "Only the good die young."

"You don't mean that!"

Then the older woman smiled. "No, I'm angry with him, but I'm glad he's healthy."

"Even after all he's put us through, I'm glad, too. He's a wonderful man in many regards, Penelope."

Mrs. Rose acquiesced and Molly felt a bit better about this situation. No sense any more people getting hurt because of all the lies and deception. "As far as you're concerned if you don't find a teaching position, then I'd like you to consider becoming my partner, here at the boardinghouse. Bennett wants me to sell it, but I just can't right now. It's been my life for so long. I would love to turn it over to you."

Molly bounded up from the chair and hugged Mrs. Rose around the neck, surprising the woman…and herself. "Thank you. That's the kindest offer I've ever received. And after I see…" Molly stopped herself from divulging too much about her appointment with Dr. Beckman. She had hoped to get an appointment immediately, but his assistant said he was visiting family and would return the day after tomorrow. "After I see about a teaching position, I'll let you know."

Molly wanted to stay in Bountiful to be close to her brother, but she had Kane to worry about. She'd pressed him to dissolve the marriage quickly, because if she did indeed carry his child, she wanted no ties to him. She had accepted the fact that she would raise her child alone, with the help of Charlie and perhaps her friend, Penelope.

Either way, Molly had no intention of telling Kane about the child. But Bennett on the other hand, might have something to say about it, and she wondered how on earth she could keep the truth from him. She wouldn't ask Penelope Rose to lie for her.

Molly placed her hand on her belly and prayed for guidance. Deep down, she believed that staying on in Bountiful wouldn't be the wisest of decisions. But she wondered if it came right down to it would she have the heart to leave?

Chapter Eighteen

Kane entered the Cheyenne village with Molly's note tucked safely inside his buckskin shirt. As he approached the lodges mounted on his mare, he noted curious young eyes questioning him. This was the first time he'd arrived here without Molly since she'd started the school. Apparently, most of the children, as well as the adults seemed to notice.

He bypassed those curious eyes, not quite ready to read her note, not quite ready to disappoint the children who had treated Molly like one of their own. He shouldn't have been too surprised. Many here were the same people who had taken him in when he was just a frightened little boy as well, making him feel welcome and part of the tribe without qualm.

Molly's note found a warm place against his skin. And he wondered if his reluctance to read it aloud had more to do with him than the children. The finality of her decision felt like a limb being severed, the wound deep and lasting. Would the final dissolution of their marriage feel like death itself?

Kane dismounted, leaving his horse to a young brave who would secure the animal in a corral for the time being and greeted his mother outside her lodge. She met his somber look with one of her own. "May we speak, Mother?"

She nodded and entered the lodge. Kane found his place and sat down, eager to speak to Singing Bird—the only mother he had truly known.

"I have news," he began. "My marriage has ended. Molly will no longer teach here. She will no longer be a wife. She has moved to town."

Singing Bird remained silent a long time and finally when she spoke it was to ask a question. "Are these your wishes, Gray Wolf?"

"My wishes?" Kane exhaled deeply. "This is the way it must be. Our bargain is no longer. My grandfather is not dying but rather played a role of deception. There is no need for the marriage now."

"No need? So, you do not *need* this woman you have married?"

Kane had always disliked his mother's pointed questions, but none more so than now. She'd taken him back to his childhood when she would ask her purposeful questions.

So, you have decided to run with the young braves instead of finishing your chores?

So, you have more than enough pemmican, but you chose not to share with your friend?

Kane had asked himself a dozen times the same question. Did he need Molly? But the better question had always been, did she need him? Kane didn't think so. His wife, for however long she would be considered his wife, was a smart, determined, brave woman who would find what she truly wanted in life.

Kane closed his eyes briefly, unable to picture Molly in any other role than his wife, teacher to the Cheyenne and granddaughter to the most cunning man this side of the Mississippi.

"She and I have no future. Destiny has intervened."

Singing Bird leaned forward to take both of his hands in hers. "*She* is your destiny, Kane."

Kane blinked, hearing his mother use his white name for the very first time in his life.

"You are my son, but you are also a man of honor. I know you have sacrificed much for us, but it is time for you to think of what you want. It is time for you to think about what this woman means to you."

"I didn't want to marry."

"She wanted a man who would not turn her away. And neither of you is happy now. It is not too late. Search your heart, my son. See what I see. You love this woman. She is in your heart."

"What if I can't?"

Singing Bird turned away, folding her arms. Gone were the softly spoken wise words. Kane had angered her. "Then you are not the son I raised. You must learn to forgive. And the forgiving begins inside yourself."

Kane stared at his mother's profile, so proud, so strong. She had always been the one he'd turned to when he needed help. And she had always given him sound advice.

Then there was Bennett. His grandfather wouldn't let him walk out the door today, without calling him ten kinds of fool.

"She loves you, Kane. She told me so."

Kane had trouble believing anything his grandfather said lately, but for some reason, his words resonated deep in his soul.

She loves you.

Kane believed it to be true. Aside from Bennett's pronouncement, he had witnessed the glow of love in Molly's eyes. He had felt it in her touch. And he had heard it in the tone of her voice. Kane had denied this truth for a long time, not wanting it to be so.

His mother faced him once again. "Little Swan is gone. She will not return. You were not to blame for her death. But there is another woman, one who loves you. Are you so certain this woman will not need you? Are you so certain she will not face dangers alone? Are you so ready to throw away your happiness?"

Kane lifted Molly's letter out of his shirt. He read it silently, hearing her say the words in his head, her voice soft and sweet. Kane read the anguish in her words, the heartfelt sincerity. He'd taken so much from her. He'd hurt her deeply time and again.

"Do you love your wife, my son?"

Kane nodded, without hesitation. He loved Molly. He had tried not to, but she was too strong a match for him. He had fallen in love with his renegade bride.

Kane ripped up her note, throwing the little pieces into the fire, the low burning embers swallowing them up. He rose and looked down at his mother. "I hope I'm not too late."

"Go," Singing Bird said. "A woman will wait if the man is worthy."

Kane didn't know if he was worthy of Molly's love.

But he had little time to waste. He had to find her. She'd already been gone two days and they'd been the loneliest two days of his life.

Molly faced Dr. Beckman as he confirmed what she'd already known. Molly was with child. Dr. Beckman beamed with the news, probably thinking Molly would also be joyous. And as she faced the truth of her pregnancy, she realized in that very moment she did feel truly happy. Not with the circumstances, but with the thought of having a child. Kane's child.

Molly smiled, although perhaps a bit sadly.

"Not the news you had hoped for?" Dr. Beckman asked with genuine concern. Molly decided she liked the new young doctor who had arrived in town just a few months before she had. He had performed his examination gently and spoken with compassion, explaining to Molly that he believed her to be just barely pregnant, no more than a month or six weeks. Molly thought back to the night of the thunderstorm when she and Kane had made love for the first time under the wagon.

"I'm happy to be with child, Doctor, but…" And as Molly contemplated how to bring her situation to light, she paid close attention to her words. "But I'm afraid the news will not be taken well by my husband. You see," she explained, deciding she had had enough of deception and untruths, "I am living at Mrs. Rose's boardinghouse. My marriage is all but over."

Dr. Beckman appeared shocked, though he tried overly hard to contain his expression. "I see."

"It's not common knowledge." She peered up at him from her place on his examining table. .

"You have my word that I will keep this to myself."

"And I do not wish my husband to know of this child. At least, not yet. I will tell him only when the time is right."

"Again, this examination is a private matter. No one will know the outcome."

Then Dr. Beckman sighed, running a hand into his sandy blond hair. A handsome man with fair skin and light eyes, he seemed so different than Kane, in appearance and manner. But no man could compare to Kane Jackson in her mind or in her heart.

"I only hope I have no call to see any of the Jacksons again, but that might not be the case, since I seem to be the only physician in the territory."

Molly thought that an odd statement. "And why is that?"

"Bennett Jackson nearly ruined my reputation. He assured me that my services were no longer needed, after I had expressly told him his pneumonia could kill him."

"So, you mean to say he really was very sick?"

"Yes, when I examined him, he certainly was. But he dismissed my services shortly after that. I had no choice but to honor his wishes. Apparently he made a full recovery."

"Yes, yes, he did," Molly confirmed.

"But Mrs. Rose came in here this morning giving me quite an earful. She accused me of being an accomplice in his deception. 'What deception?' I asked. She explained how Bennett pretended to be dying, for whatever gain I don't know. She didn't elaborate. I swear to you, I had no knowledge of his ruse."

"I believe you. Bennett duped many of us. He did

have a reason, but he didn't stop to realize how much pain he would cause the people who love him." Molly put her head down, overwhelmed at all that had occurred these past few days.

"I'm sorry. I shouldn't have brought that up. You have so much to deal with right now."

He helped Molly down from the examining table and faced her with a respectful smile. "I'm closing up for the evening, heading for a lonely supper. Would you care to join me for a meal at the café?"

Molly began to shake her head no but he continued on. "You need to keep your strength up, for one. And you need to get your mind on something else. We're both new to this town. I wouldn't mind making a new friend, would you?"

Molly smiled, her mood lifting a bit. And she welcomed the thought of a peaceful meal. "I could use a new friend. Yes, thank you. I would like to join you."

"Wonderful. It'll just take me a minute to lock up. Would you care to wait for me in the front room?"

Molly agreed and took a few moments to sit down to gather her thoughts. She had so much to consider, so much to think about, and Dr. Beckman's gracious invitation to dinner would be the distraction she needed.

Just minutes later, Dr. Beckman walked in, wearing a suitcoat rather than his white doctor's apron, making him appear much more youthful.

"Shall we go?" he asked. When she stood he offered her his arm.

They walked down the sidewalk, Dr. Beckman making light and pleasant conversation, helping to keep Molly from thinking of her very uncertain future.

* * *

Bennett and Kane Jackson stood outside Mrs. Rose's boardinghouse, the woman refusing to allow them entrance inside.

"Ah, come on, Penny. We need to talk," Bennett said.

She stood on the porch, her lips pursed, her stance unyielding. With arms folded around her middle, she shook her head. "I'm not ready to speak with you, Bennett. You have done damage again with your unthinking maneuvering. You have lied to me and deceived people who have come to care for you. You did this with no thought to the outcome to others. You're ruthless and I'm not sure I want that kind of man."

Kane stepped up. He'd heard enough. As far as he was concerned, his grandfather was on his own. He had his own fences to mend. "Is Molly here?"

Mrs. Rose turned her glaring gaze on him. "Maybe she is and maybe she isn't."

Kane gritted his teeth. He supposed he deserved her ire as well, but he had to find Molly. "Please, Penelope. I need to speak with her."

Mrs. Rose flinched. Kane had never spoken to her as a friend. He'd never used her first name when addressing her. "Why, so you can deliver more bad news to her?"

"No. Because I love her. I want to bring her back home."

She gasped and staggered back a step, her expression softening. "How can I believe you?"

"Believe him, Penny," Bennett said. "He's come to his senses. Finally." Bennett put his arm around Kane's shoulder. "My grandson realizes what he almost lost— a good woman who loves him. Tell him where she is, so that someone around here can find happiness."

Mrs. Rose stood silent a moment, studying Kane, making up her mind. "If you hurt her again—"

"I won't."

"He won't," Bennett said at the same time.

Mrs. Rose came down the steps and looked Kane squarely in the eyes. "She's not here. She went into town, but I'm not at liberty to say where. Be quick. She's contemplating leaving Bountiful."

Kane grabbed Penelope, hugging her tight. "Thank you," he said. He kissed her cheek. "You won't be sorry."

Mrs. Rose smiled and for the first time, Kane noticed the warmth and goodness in her, qualities that would make her a good match for his cantankerous grandfather.

She looked deeply into his eyes. "I know."

Kane glanced quickly at his grandfather. "My grandfather loves you, Penelope. I can see why. I think he realizes what he almost lost as well. He's come to his senses. Give him a second chance."

Bennett stepped up to take Penelope's hands. "Yes, I've come to my senses. But you see, I wasn't wrong about Molly and Kane, they—"

Kane grabbed his arm. "Stop while you're ahead, Grandfather."

Bennett smiled at Penelope Rose and nodded.

Kane left them holding hands and climbing up the steps of the boardinghouse.

He dashed down the street, not certain where Molly had gone. He passed the schoolhouse, peering inside but at this hour the students and teacher had already gone. And as he walked farther down into the center of town, Kane spotted something that halted him right in place. His search over, he'd found his wife.

Walking arm in arm with young Dr. Beckman.

Emotions seared into his gut, cutting him like a knife. Seeing Molly with another man as she strolled leisurely down the street tore down all his defenses. He couldn't possibly doubt his love for her now, not when he witnessed firsthand what life would be like without her. Jealousy played a part and Kane couldn't recall a time when he'd ever been jealous.

Except now.

He had more than one quarrel with Dr. Beckman. And he'd be damned to stand here and watch the man court his woman.

"Molly!" he called out from the center of the street, much like a man would call out a gunslinger.

Both heads turned in his direction. Molly appeared shocked and Dr. Beckman steadied her with an arm around her shoulder.

Kane took long strides to meet up with her. He glared at the doctor. "Get your hands off my wife."

Dr. Beckman immediately complied, removing his arm from Molly's shoulder.

"Kane, what is it?"

"What are you doing with him?" Kane asked, his anger strong. Though he knew he should be repentant, he needed to know why the two of them were together.

Molly stood silent.

Dr. Beckman glanced at her as if they had some secret between them. Kane didn't like any of it.

"Well?"

"Molly agreed to have dinner with me, that's all."

Kane stared at Molly, guilt written all over her face.

"He's a friend, Kane."

Kane glared once again at the doctor. "A *friend?*
Does a *friend* lie about a man's health? Does a *friend,*
who has taken an oath to heal the sick, deceive instead?
What manner of *friend* are you? You told me my grandfather was dying."

"He *was* dying. When I attended to your grandfather,
he had a severe case of pneumonia. Most men his age
don't come through. When I spoke with you, I believed
with all my heart that Bennett Jackson wasn't long for
this earth. But he fooled us all, didn't he?"

Kane narrowed his eyes at the doctor.

Dr. Beckman went on, "He dismissed me from service shortly after the diagnosis—against my wishes, I
might add. I had no choice in the matter."

"It's true, Kane," Molly said, adding, "Dr. Beckman
wasn't a part of your grandfather's plan."

It irked Kane that Molly would take the doctor's side,
but Kane had a more important issue to discuss with his
wife. He faced Molly, looking directly into her wide
green eyes. "I need to speak with you."

"Now?"

He nodded. "It can't wait."

She glanced at Dr. Beckman. "Will you excuse me?"

He took a long look at Kane then nodded to Molly.
"Are you sure?"

"Yes, I'm sure."

Kane wanted to bloody the man's nose. It was a damn
good thing he bid Molly a quick—and if Kane had anything to do about it, final—farewell, or he might just
have indulged in that small bit of violence.

"What did you want to speak with me about?"

"I want you to come home."

Stunned, Molly blinked.

He took hold of her hands and his blood rushed immediately from the soft familiar contact. "I need to speak with you privately."

"No, Kane. We've said everything there is to say."

"There's more I have to say."

"I…don't…know," she said in a tone that gave him hope. "It was very hard for me to leave the Bar J. I don't think I can go back."

"Then will you hear me out here?"

Molly glanced around. They stood on the sidewalk, ten yards from the Bounty Café as patrons passed them by. Strong scents flavored the air of dishes seasoned with onions and garlic and herbs. "Here?"

"Not here, exactly." And then he thought of the perfect place. "Walk with me to the church grounds. We can talk there privately."

Molly agreed and Kane led her to the edge of town where a chapel stood, its tall steeple lifting up to the setting sun. He found a bench on the south side of the building. Kane waited until Molly found a seat, then he sat down beside her, their legs brushing.

Kane sat quietly for a time, trying to find a way to tell Molly what was in heart. He'd never spoken of these things before. Opening up to his wife shouldn't be so difficult, but the outcome of her decision weighed heavily on his mind.

He hadn't wanted a wife, much less one as feisty as Molly McGuire. He hadn't wanted a marriage, either. He'd had it all once before and never thought he'd want it again. But he did. He wanted a life with Molly beside him. And the only way he knew to persuade her would be to speak honestly, trusting in Molly to understand.

Kane braced himself. He spoke quietly, staring out onto the church grounds. "Little Swan was with child when she was murdered," he began, speaking a truth that he had held inside his injured heart for years. "I never knew pain like that before. I never knew a man could hurt so damn bad. It was like a knife had sliced into my chest, the blade gutting out my heart. But the hollowness soon filled with bitter rage for what was done—for the injustice. My wife and child were dead. I went after their killer and I avenged their deaths. I vowed to never love again. To never have another child. I held myself responsible and didn't think I could take another loss. I didn't think I could stand that pain again."

"Oh, Kane. I'm so sorry," Molly said, as twin tears trickled down her cheeks. She put her head down and nodded with anguished understanding. "How horrible for you to lose a wife and child at the same time."

Kane turned fully toward her, lifting her face with both hands and tilting her head to stare deeply into her eyes. "But there's a worse kind of pain, Molly. There's the pain that goes along with foolishly losing someone you love."

Molly blinked, her sad eyes growing wide and alert.

"I love you, Molly."

He smiled.

And Molly cast him a tentative smile. "You do?"

"Yes, I do. Very much. It's taken my grandfather's dying ploy, my mother's wise words and a search deep in my heart to figure it out. I'm stubborn, but not stupid. I realize now how much you mean to me. I can only hope I haven't hurt you too badly. I can only hope you can forgive me."

Kane kissed her gently on the lips, her soft perfect mouth giving back warmth and tenderness. "I want you to come home. Come back to the Bar J. Be my wife. Have my children."

"You want children?" Molly asked, surprised.

Kane had given her no reason to believe other-wise. He'd gone to great lengths not to create a child with her. But now, it's what he wanted more than anything.

"Yes, with you. I want us to fill the ranch with chil-dren. It kills me to think how happy this will make my grandfather after what he's done, but I don't care. All I know is that I don't want to live at the Bar J without you."

Kane realized how much he loved this woman. And the thought of having Molly's little red-haired children made him smile. If nothing else, a houseful of children would settle his renegade bride down. Maybe she wouldn't get herself into too much trouble that way. Maybe she wouldn't run off on a whim anymore. Kane, too, would know a world of peace.

"When?" Molly asked, her voice squeaky soft. "When do you want children?"

Kane's lips turned upward, realizing he was finally able to put the past behind him, finally able to look for-ward to a future with Molly. "The sooner the better, Lit-tle Bird."

"Oh, Kane!" A sweet joyous expression stole over Molly's face. She jumped into his arms with happy tears flowing. "I love you too, Kane Jackson. Are you sure you want children right away?"

"Yes, I'm sure," Kane answered, with no doubt in his mind.

"That's good, because you're going to be a father next spring."

Stunned, Kane hadn't thought it possible. He blinked, his mind working fast recalling the times he had not been overly careful with Molly. Back then, he had prayed that they would be spared the conception of a child, but now, well, he thanked God for the precious gift. He grinned, full out, leaving no room for doubt. "I am?"

"Yes. Our baby will be born during the Moon When the Horses Get Fat."

Kane chuckled. Molly was a wonderful teacher, but apparently she'd learned something of the Cheyenne as well. Kane laid a hand on Molly's stomach. "The horses won't be the only ones getting fat."

Molly laughed, a cheerful sound that brought him great joy. "It's a good thing I'm so happy now, or I'd make you pay dearly for that comment."

Kane kissed her again. "You'll grow fat with our child, but I have no doubt you'll be even more beautiful than you are right now."

Kane took her hand and squeezed gently. "I miss you, Molly. Will you move back to the Bar J?"

Molly nodded, her green eyes bright with love. "Yes, the Bar J is my home. It's where I'll teach the children, both ours and the Cheyenne. It's where I'll keep Bennett in line and Charlie out of trouble."

"And what of me, your husband?"

Molly grinned. "It's where I'll make baby after baby with you, Kane."

Kane stood and reached for Molly. But instead of allowing her to rise on her own, he lifted her up, kissing her gently and declaring his love for her once again. He carried her away from the church grounds.

Molly didn't protest. Instead she wrapped her arms around his neck, telling him with unspoken words she would go anywhere with him. "Where are we going?"

Kane grinned. "You and I deserve a 'real' honeymoon, sweetheart. We're taking a room at the hotel. We'll have all the privacy we need to get reacquainted. I'm sending word to Bennett not to expect us home anytime soon."

"Oh, Kane, I missed you so," Molly said on a deep sigh.

Kane tightened his hold on his pregnant wife. "I have one last bargain for you, Little Bird."

"And what would that be?" Molly asked, her gaze holding his.

"That we'll never be apart again."

"Hmm, I think I like the sound of that." Molly's face lit with love and adoration.

Kane couldn't believe how lucky he was to be given this second chance in life. He loved Molly with his whole heart. He didn't want to face another day without her.

"Shall we shake on it?" Molly put out her hand.

Kane took her hand and brought it to his lips. He kissed the back of her hand then laced his fingers with hers. "I have a better way to seal our fate."

"And how is that, my love?"

"Three days up in that hotel room might just settle the matter."

Molly snuggled closer into his arms. "Sounds like a bargain made in heaven."

Kane could only smile at his new, young wife. He would keep his promise to her. They would never part again.

Once and for all, his renegade wife was coming home.

* * * * *

HARLEQUIN®

Super Romance

OPEN SECRET

by Janice Kay Johnson

HSR #1332

Three siblings, separated after their parents'
death, grow up in very different homes,
lacking the sense of belonging that family
brings. The oldest, Suzanne, makes up her
mind to search for her brother and sister,
never guessing how dramatically her
decision will change their lives.

Also available:
LOST CAUSE (June 2006)

On sale March 2006
Available wherever Harlequin books are sold!

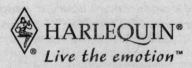

HARLEQUIN®
Live the emotion™

If you enjoyed what you just read,
then we've got an offer you can't resist!

Take 2 bestselling
love stories FREE!
Plus get a FREE surprise gift!

Clip this page and mail it to Harlequin Reader Service®

IN U.S.A.	IN CANADA
3010 Walden Ave.	P.O. Box 609
P.O. Box 1867	Fort Erie, Ontario
Buffalo, N.Y. 14240-1867	L2A 5X3

YES! Please send me 2 free Harlequin Historicals® novels and my free surprise gift. After receiving them, if I don't wish to receive anymore, I can return the shipping statement marked cancel. If I don't cancel, I will receive 6 brand-new novels every month, before they're available in stores! In the U.S.A., bill me at the bargain price of $4.69 plus 25¢ shipping and handling per book and applicable sales tax, if any*. In Canada, bill me at the bargain price of $5.24 plus 25¢ shipping and handling per book and applicable taxes**. That's the complete price and a savings of over 10% off the cover prices—what a great deal! I understand that accepting the 2 free books and gift places me under no obligation ever to buy any books. I can always return a shipment and cancel at any time. Even if I never buy another book from Harlequin, the 2 free books and gift are mine to keep forever.

246 HDN DZ7Q
349 HDN DZ7R

Name	(PLEASE PRINT)	
Address	Apt.#	
City	State/Prov.	Zip/Postal Code

Not valid to current Harlequin Historicals® subscribers.

Want to try two free books from another series?
Call 1-800-873-8635 or visit www.morefreebooks.com.

* Terms and prices subject to change without notice. Sales tax applicable in N.Y.
** Canadian residents will be charged applicable provincial taxes and GST.
All orders subject to approval. Offer limited to one per household.
® are registered trademarks owned and used by the trademark owner or its licensee.

HIST04R   ©2004 Harlequin Enterprises Limited

THE
ELLIOTTS
Mixing business with pleasure

The series continues with

Cause for Scandal

by
ANNA DePALO

(Silhouette Desire #1711)

She posed as her identical twin to meet a sexy rock star—but Summer Elliott certainly didn't expect to end up in bed with him. Now the scandal is about to hit the news and she has some explaining to do...to her prominent family and her lover.

On sale March 2006!

HARLEQUIN®

Super Romance®

*A compelling and emotional story
from a critically acclaimed writer.*

How To
Get Married

by *Margot Early*

SR #1333

When Sophie Creed comes home to
Colorado, one person she doesn't want to
see is William Ludlow, her almost-husband
of fifteen years ago—or his daughter, Amy.
Especially since Sophie's got a secret that
could change Amy's life.

On sale March 2006
Available wherever Harlequin books are sold!

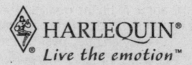

HARLEQUIN®
Live the emotion™